THE SAPPHIRE DEATH: THE ADVENTURES
OF PETER THE BRAZEN, VOLUME 7

BOOKS IN THE ARGOSY LIBRARY:

THE SAPPHIRE DEATH

THE ADVENTURES OF PETER THE BRAZEN, VOLUME 7

LORING BRENT

ILLUSTRATED BY
SAMUEL CAHAN

COVER BY
PAUL STAHR

POPULAR PUBLICATIONS · 2024

TABLE OF CONTENTS

THE SAPPHIRE DEATH

Peter the Brazen took the most dangerous road—one he must follow till he smashed the Blue Scorpion's evil power over Asia

1

FORGOTTEN WHITE MAN

THE TALL YOUNG American ran swiftly down the hall to Room 318. He unlocked the door and let himself in. Closing the door quickly, he locked it with the key and shot the bolt. He tossed a newspaper-wrapped bundle onto the bed.

He was breathless from the exertion of running up three flights of stairs; breathless, too, from nervous tension. The question was: Had the three elderly Chinese seen him? If they had, his time was very short indeed.

He placed an ear against the door, but he heard nothing but the thumping of his own heart. The ear away from the door was busier, for a variety of sounds came swarming in at the open bedroom window. These were the sounds of a Chinese city at night: the *click-clack* of high wooden sandals; the *plip-plop* and sing-song-sing of unshod coolies dragging rickshaws through the moist and mud-streaked alleys; the mournful, far-away mooing of a tramp freighter, creeping into the harbor. Above all these, like an insect chorus, the sustained humming of the native quarter—the voice, as it were, of China as she went about her mysterious affairs.

The man in Room 318, in the obscure little hotel on Ice House Lane, heard these outer noises, yet heard nothing.

Saying that he heard nothing meant that he heard, with either ear, nothing that seemed to be menacing his life.

A loaded automatic pistol lay on the dresser, ready for any enemy who might break in upon him before his work was done. Every nerve of his lean, hard body was alert to an emergency, a gathering of dark and sinister forces. The most vital, most dangerous task to which he had ever set

The Chinese killer hurtled from his precarious perch.

himself was getting under way this night. Never, in the course of his reckless life, had he been in such jeopardy. It was as if two bright threads, one of adventure, one of danger, met here and joined—in this room, on this night, at this precise hour.

Having satisfied himself that for the moment, at least, he was safe from interruption, he proceeded with his affairs— the first steps in a plan which, if it succeeded, would shock the whole continent of Asia. His actions were swift and sure—those of a man accustomed to thinking efficiently under the most terrific pressure.

He stripped off all his clothing to the bare skin, including shoes and socks. From the paper bundle he removed shabby garments: a dirty threadbare blue workshirt; ancient blue trousers, frayed at the cuffs and spotted with grease or oil; a nondescript coat, likewise a shapeless thing, frayed and spotted with oil or grease; a brown slouch hat, dirty and shapeless; a pair of battered brown oxfords, so badly in need of repair that they were almost comic. Frayed strings served for laces. The uppers were scuffed, cracked and filthy. The soles were, as the French say, "gaping at the mouth."

The man in Room 318 swiftly arrayed himself in these strange habiliments. With the shabby coat collar turned up about his neck, he went to the rippling, cracked mirror above the dresser and studied his face as if he were measuring that of a dangerous antagonist. Under the deep sunbrown, that face had the pallor of nervous excitement. The thin, hard jaws, the chin and the upper lip, were darkly covered with a five-day growth of stubble. The man's blond hair, under the slouch hat, was thick, tousled, unkempt, badly in need of the shears. Below it, his eyes, bright blue, were sharp with determination.

He looked tough. He looked a little too tough, in fact. He created the wrong impression. And somehow, a veneer of civilization still clung to him.

A SMALL FLAT can beside the automatic pistol on the dresser contained dust which he had scraped off shelves in the hotel cellar. He applied this in dabs and streaks to his face and neck, working it in with his fingertips until he was satisfied that he had the look of a man who has not bathed in weeks. He shook some of the dust onto his coat collar, and lapels, working it in, too, to give the garment an even more disreputable air.

Again he looked at himself. The dust had rubbed away the veneer and the toughness. In his tatterdemalion outfit, with his dirty, unshaved face, his tangled hair, he now resembled any beachcomber who might be found cadging meals or whining for dimes on the waterfront of any busy port in the world.

He now attended to his eyes. Telltale eyes these were— too bright, too light in color. He remedied that with a lemon. With a pocketknife which he had whetted to a razor edge for another and more painful purpose, he sliced the lemon into halves. Then, tilting his head back, he squeezed a few drops of the stinging juice into each eye.

For a few seconds the pain was almost unbearable. He gripped the edge of the dresser. Tears streamed from under his clenched lids. Presently he opened them and swabbed out the moisture with a handkerchief. Again he looked at the mirror. His eyes were no longer bright blue. The lemon juice had changed them, had made them feverishly blood-shot and given them a dull leaden color.

These details attended to, he went efficiently and silently about the next task. He kicked up the rug. He pulled the bed from the wall at a crazy angle. He carefully upset a chair. With a swift blow of the pistol butt he smashed the mirror. Next he pulled out drawers and strewed their contents over the floor. Documents and garments of various kinds he kicked about and stamped on.

In less than sixty seconds he gave the room an appearance which the shrewdest observer would say without hesitation had been caused by a fight to the death.

He now wiped the knife blade clean on the handkerchief. He set his teeth hard against his lower lip, and holding the knife securely in his right hand, he slashed the other hand along the outer edge of the palm. Blood welled out of the gash and flowed freely, and he walked about the room deliberately letting blood spill here, spatter there.

Beside the washstand was a clear space of floor. The young man knelt down and traced roughly, in blood, the words "Lin Cho."

He now climbed onto the washstand and scooped his fingerprint into a corner of the ceiling. A cobweb which had hung there now clung to one finger. This filament of gray web he spun between his fingers into a slender cylinder. He packed the cylinder down into the slash in his hand, then bound the hand with his handkerchief.

Quickly moving over toward the bed, he wrapped up in the newspaper the white drill clothing which he had changed for the shabby outfit he now wore. He included shoes, socks, underwear, shirt, necktie—even a fine gold wristwatch. This package he placed on the window sill.

TIPTOEING TO THE door, he listened again. He had proved, by experiment, that it was impossible for any one to proceed along that hall without making certain boards squeak, no matter how carefully he moved. He knew that a spy—a bullet-headed coolie with a shaved poll— was reporting his goings and coming to the three elderly Chinese. That man—or the three—might come along the hall at any moment. The man in Room 318 must be out of the hotel before that happened. If they surprised him, the success of his whole audacious plan was endangered.

On the floor near the window was a coil of rope. It was just long enough to reach from a leg of the heavy iron bed to the cobblestones in the alley, three stories below. The problem of a getaway had been the most puzzling of all. How could he possibly escape from the hotel, even disguised as he was, without being seen and detected? His plan depended upon his being recognized by no one.

A rope had suggested itself as the most logical solution. But how could a man make his escape down a rope without leaving the rope dangling there? Damning evidence! He had solved this problem ingeniously. On one end of the rope was a stout iron hook to which a trigger was attached. The hook was fastened to a leg of the bed, and to the trigger a coil of heavy fishline was attached.

The rest was simple. When the man had slid down the rope he had merely to give the fishline a jerk, and hook, rope, fishline—the whole contraption—would come tumbling down, to be tossed into the sewer manhole fifty feet down the alley!

There was only one risk. In descending the rope, he must be careful not to become entangled in the fishline, for a jerk on the fishline would send him hurtling to the cobblestones!

He attached the hook to the leg of the bed, and paid out rope and fishline into the darkness. He took a final look about the room. In plunging into this adventure, he must leave behind him every one of his prized possessions, quite as if he were, in truth, dead. All of his clothing except that in the bundle, his personal articles, his letters—everything must be left behind.

Most of all, he hated to part with the camera snapshot which leaned against the fractured mirror. It showed a slim, dark-eyed young woman of about twenty-one. Even in this somewhat blurred snapshot, she was beautiful. She was smiling jauntily, and one of her hands was flung up as if she were about to wave to some one. Just under her small, high-heeled slippers, the young man had written in ink, "The Trouble Hunter."

He gave the snapshot a brief, grim smile, a mocking salute with his fingertips. Then he glanced at the pistol. That admirable weapon had stood by him in a number of scrapes; but it too must be left behind. The task to which he had dedicated himself required, not force of arms, but the quickest of wits.

He strode to the window and looked down. Nothing below but blackness. Rain was drizzling outside, and there was a chill wind. The air coming in at the window felt damp and raw. Light from Des Voeux Road was a pallid glow in the slanting streaks of rain.

The young man picked up the bundle of clothes, leaned

out and dropped it into the alley. He waited to head the sound of its thud, then went to the door, slid back the bolt and turned the key. With the key in his hand, he opened the door and peered out. Empty!

He stepped out, shut the door and locked it, retaining the key. He backed across the hall, put his shoulder down and charged the door. His shoulder struck it with battering-ram force. It flew open with a splintering crash.

He tossed the key on the floor as he ran to the window. He grasped the rope and swung over the sill. Hand over hand, he went down the rope.

AN UPSET TO his elaborate plans took place when he was about two-thirds of the way down the side of the building. Looking upward at the window he had vacated, he saw the silhouette of a bullet-shaped, shaven head.

The young man gripped the rope, stopped his descent, and stared up. Fine drops of rain spattered into his eyes. He was conscious of a sudden upboiling of fury. At the last moment his plan was to be ruined!

As he hesitated, he saw shoulders follow the bullet head. Then a short, thick leg swung out over the sill; and for a brief moment, the American saw the glitter of a revolver in his pursuer's hand.

Cobblestones came up and met his heels as he slid the rest of the way. The man above him had stopped about eight feet below the window ledge, with his legs wrapped about the rope, so that his hands were free. A ray of cold white light beaconed from his hand, and fell dazzlingly into the eyes of the American. The American knew that the bullet-headed coolie was training the pistol on him in the light of the pocket torch; that he would shoot down at him as mercilessly as a man might shoot a rat in a well.

He reached for the fishline. He found it, gave it a sharp jerk, and leaped back against the brick wall across the alley. He had not dreamed that this ingenious little device might be instrumental in saving his life.

There was a momentary illusion of a falling meteor, as the electric torch came slicing through the drizzle. It struck the cobbles with a sound of shattering glass. Then occurred the sharper clatter of the pistol striking.

The bullet-headed assassin came next, plunging to swift doom in a tangle of rope and fishline. He struck the cobbles at the American's feet with a loud, sickening thump.

The young man knelt down and ran his hands over the crumpled Chinese. The bullet head was smashed. All evidences of this episode must be promptly and thoroughly erased, and so the young man acted swiftly. Fifty feet down the alley, was the manhole of a sewer, into which he had planned to throw the rope. He dragged the dead man there, lifted the manhole, and pushed him in. Then he returned for the rope, the pistol, the crumpled flash light and the package containing his discarded clothing. These he carried to the manhole and dropped in, replacing the perforated iron lid. He turned up his collar and pulled the shabby hat more tightly about his ears. At a shambling gait, he started toward the mouth of the alley.

To all intents and purposes, Peter Moore, better known to the Orient as Peter the Brazen, had ceased to exist. In his place was a forlorn, threadbare human derelict—one of the host of forgotten white men who eke out a mysterious and miserable existence in the ports of the Far East.

2

"PETER MOORE IS DEAD!"

THE AMERICAN HAD not been gone five minutes when a trio of solemn, elderly Chinese men came softly down the corridor and hesitated at the half-opened door of Room 318. In the black Manchu hats, the black and purple satin robes, and the ornate, felt-soled slippers of an older day, they resembled mandarins. They were not and never had been mandarins, however. They belonged to the oldest of all guilds—the Guild of the Killers. These three dignified and somewhat pompous Chinese gentlemen were murderers—hatchetmen—and their visit tonight was professional.

With their hands in their sleeves, they entered the room. And in the generous illumination provided by the single bright mazda bulb burning over the washstand, they looked about them. In the course of their careers they had doubtless gazed upon countless scenes similar to this one, for there were evident here many of the signatures of their own calling.

But they were shrewd men, too—three men not easily fooled. With the efficiency and patience for which their land has been famous for centuries, they examined the scene. They went through the clothes closet. They examined the snapshot of the beautiful girl. They looked at but did not touch the automatic pistol. But their greatest interest was in the bloody scrawl on the floor near the washstand. They looked at it and pondered it again and again. They reëxamined garments and papers. They studied the bed. They studied with inexhaustible patience every square inch of floor and walls. Not one item escaped their scrutiny.

As each new discovery presented itself, they whisperingly discussed it and ascribed to it a proper meaning. They were like a jury deliberating.

The three members of that ancient guild came at length to a verdict, and it was that the man they had come to kill had already been killed.

Thereupon, as silently as they had come, the three hatchetmen departed, and each went his separate way. One of them, a man with a silver-white scar like the blade of a dagger across his forehead, took a devious route to the waterfront. Hands tucked into sleeves, he walked rapidly along Queen's Road to Tong Kai Alley, then down Cleverly Street to Connaught Road. Crossing this embarcadero, he walked out to the end of Pasig Wharf.

The drizzle had perceptibly increased. Rain was now falling heavily. It hissed into the water of the harbor and drummed on the roofs of sampans.

Light from a streetlamp glinted on the oiled hood which protected the head of a tall harbor *fokie* slowly moving the heavy sweep of a sampan. Forty or fifty feet offshore, his craft was a dark ghost; he himself a specter. He might have been the keeper of a ferry on the River of the Dead.

The man on Pasig Wharf watched him a moment, then made a clicking sound with his tongue. Water astern of the sampan went frothy as the *fokie* worked the sweep. The sampan lurched in toward the wharf and vanished under the shadow it cast upon the water. A bony yellow hand reached up like a claw into the feeble light. The man with the silver scar placed in the *fokie's* hand a small pyramid of blue chalk, on one face of which was scratched the chinese symbol for the word *"death!"*

The hatchetman's job was done, and the *fokie's* was just begun. He would drive his craft at its fastest speed to a bleak, deserted island beyond Lyeemoon Pass, in Tathong Channel, and there, he would pass the mystic pyramid on to another man. Swiftly thus, passing from hand to hand, that symbol of death would travel westward through the hinterland of southern China until it reached the region of the Purple Mountains of the Moon, in western Sze-Chwan. It would, in the course of days and nights, traverse rivers, deserts, mountains and forests, to reach a hideously malformed human creature—part man, part fiend, part deathless genius—who lived in a fantastic marble palace built under the waters of a lake cupped in by iron and cobalt hills.

The tiny blue chalk pyramid, delivered with such superhuman effort, would be but the verification of a known fact. For within ten minutes after the departure of the three hatchetmen from the hotel bedroom in Hong Kong, the human monster who lived under the Lake of the Flying Dragon knew that the young American known the length and breadth of China as Peter the Brazen had violently met his death.

FIFTEEN HUNDRED MILES to the south of Hong Kong, in the ballroom of a Singapore hotel, the girl of Peter Moore's snapshot was dancing in the arms of an Australian aviator.

She was slim and beautiful in a gown of pale green. She was laughing up into Bill Jameson's face, and Bill Jameson, as they danced about the ballroom, was asking her to marry him.

He was a tall, handsome young man—decidedly eligible. The trouble with him—the trouble with all the men who had asked the girl to marry them since her arrival in the Far East—was that they had to stand comparison with Peter Moore.

Listening to Bill Jameson's soft and persuasive love talk, she wished that she had never met Peter the Brazen. Since the night of their meeting on the Transpacific crossing a little more than a year ago, she had been in love with Peter. Because she was modern and accustomed to having what she wanted, she had told him repeatedly that she would marry him if he would have her.

The trouble was, he didn't want her. She was, he declared, much too rich. And he was, she retaliated, stupid to take that attitude. It was false pride—vanity!

He had said, furthermore, that she had too large an appetite for dangerous excitement. She had plunged them into many adventures. More than once, she had imperiled his life as well as her own.

Her answer to that was: what is life for, if not for the sake of dangerous excitement? Why settle down into a conventional groove? Life, to her way of thinking, must be thrilling; otherwise she didn't want life. Moore's argument was that he had lived dangerously most of his life and was tired of being known as a trouble-hunting vagabond.

Their latest quarrel had taken place in Hong Kong a

few weeks previously, and she had angrily left Hong Kong, vowing that she would never see him again.

"We're all washed up," she had said. "Gosh! How I hate you!"

Now, even as she laughed up into the aviator's dark, handsome, intense face, she was thinking of Peter Moore. She was missing him, and she was planning to return to Hong Kong by the first ship. It was simply a crime that no other man appealed to her as he did!

A young Chinese in European clothing was watching her from a doorway. His yellow face, with its lashless, browless eyes, looked sleepy. But there was a queer glint in those strange eyes.

Susan O'Gilvie slowly became aware that he was attempting to capture her attention. His arms were folded on his chest, and the forefinger of one hand was gently beckoning her toward a wide veranda. Susan watched the wriggling finger.

The Chinese moved across the corner of the ballroom to another doorway. That one gave upon the veranda. It was a dark veranda.

Susan considered the situation. She didn't care for dark verandas in the company of strange men—especially, strange Chinamen. She was learning that the Far East contains countless traps into which a rich and beautiful American girl can fall and be instantly helpless.

Already she had learned that Singapore is a treacherous city.

What did he want? Was it safe to join him on that dark veranda? Caution was not one of Susan's outstanding traits.

She was curious. What did that elegant young Chinese want of her?

It did not occur to her to invite Bill Jameson to accompany her.

She said, "Bill, I want to think something over. Meet me in the bar."

WHEN SHE REACHED the veranda, the young Chinese was standing with his back to the rail, smoking a scented cigarette. Except for him, the veranda was deserted.

A humid breath from the steaming Malayan jungles crept over the city. The heat was like a throbbing in the night.

Alert, suspicious, Susan looked all about her before she left the doorway. She saw no other lurking figures, and just across the street she saw a British colonial soldier strolling in an alert way that was reassuring.

She went quickly across the veranda and looked up in the darkness at the pale oval face of the oriental.

He said quietly, "Are you Miss Susan O'Gilvie?"

"Yes."

"I have a message for you.—I am sorry. It is very tragic news. Peter Moore is dead."

Momentarily stunned, the girl looked up into that inscrutable face without moving. Then she recovered her poise. She was sure that this was but a clever preliminary to some new trick, some dangerous new trap.

Quietly she asked, "When did it happen?"

"Tonight. It was discovered about a half-hour ago."

"Who—who did it?"

"I didn't learn. The body was destroyed."

"Who sent you here?"

"I am an old friend of Mr. Moore's.—I repeat: I am very sorry."

Bowing, he left her.

Susan turned slowly on one high, diamond-studded heel as the man walked away. She was suspicious, but uncertain.

She did not see how this could possibly be the preliminary to any sinister plan against her wealth or her safety.

In spite of the vibrant jungle heat of the night, she shivered. Staring at the doorway through which the unknown Chinese had passed, she was suddenly frightened; her heart began to thump. She put out an unsteady hand to the rail and gripped it. All of a sudden the world was spinning. It couldn't be true! It must not be true!

Without realizing that she was moving, she ran to the ballroom door. She did not see the eyes staring at her white face, her violet eyes, large and dark with terror. She entirely forgot her obligation to Bill Jameson.

SHE RAN DOWN a hall and into the crowded lobby, elbowing past people who blocked her way. The Sikh doorman salaamed. She pushed him aside and cried huskily, "Rickshaw!—Rickshaw!"

Half-a-dozen yellow men leaped to their feet and came pounding toward her, their vehicles colliding, wheels locking.

She selected the coolie who seemed to be the most powerful, and scrambled into his rickshaw.

She cried, "Hing Sing Joy's—Brah Basah Road! Chop—chop!"

Hing Sing Joy was the proprietor of a jade shop which lay at the end of an old trail. An urge to satisfy a tremendous curiosity had brought her to Hing Sing Joy's shortly after her arrival in Singapore.

It was a twenty-minute rickshaw ride through crowded streets. Arriving in front of the dark, shuttered, low building, she flung some coins to the coolie as she scrambled down. Running to the iron door, she began beating upon it with her fists.

A crowd collected. Chinese, Japs, Malays, thin Tamils, an Arab or two, a Hindu in his red turban—all pressing about to grin at the beautiful mad American woman in her outlandish pale-green evening gown.

A bolt clanked. A tall, thin, elderly Chinese in black satin pushed open the iron door.

Susan O'Gilvie panted, "I've just heard a rumor that Peter Moore has been murdered."

Hing Sing Joy slowly nodded, nodded. "Yes," he said.

"It isn't true!" the girl cried.

"Yes, Miss O'Gilvie, it's true. I am very sorry. Come in."

His eyes had caught the twinkle of her diamond-studded heels. He licked his lips.

"The news," he said, "just reached me."

"Who did it?"

"Lin Cho—the opium king of Hong Kong. The body of your lover was destroyed. That is Lin Cho's method."

The girl cried hysterically, "No! It was the Blue Scorpion!"

3

PLACE OF GLORIOUS REPOSE

ONE OF THE army of living ghosts who slink by night through the alleys of "The Pearl of the Orient," the man who was supposed to be dead, was making his way down Lascar Row toward Tung Street.

Rain, falling in torrents, had driven from the streets of Hong Kong all but those who had urgent business. Yet there were numbers of these. A beggar whom Moore recognized as a stool pigeon of the Hong Kong police peered into his face at the corner of Upper Lascar Row and Ladder Street. But the beggar glanced away without interest. Likewise, a Sikh watchman, a Chinese policeman, a Butterfield and Swire coolie, these and perhaps others, going about their businesses, stared at Peter Moore, whom they knew, without recognition. To all of these, and to others he passed who may or may not have known him, he was now one with the human flotsam washed into this particular port by the tides of ill fortune—a creature to be shunned.

Not until later would he know for sure, however, whether or not he had made that important and dangerous journey without being recognized. He could only hope that his disguise had not been penetrated.

His objective was a low, forbidding, unlighted building near the native cemetery; a ginger factory. Here, the spicy fruit which grows so abundantly in southern China was boiled in sugar syrup or dried on trays and packed for shipment in earthen grass-bound jugs or flat tins.

Peter Moore tapped with his fingernail four times on a darkened pane, then three times, and waited. A heavy teakwood door was opened by a specter, and Moore slipped into the warm, sickly sweet atmosphere.

The man who had opened the door to his signal now closed it again and shot the heavy iron bolts. In silence, he then conducted the American through black rooms, a half-dozen of them, to a sliding door. Once again, he was in the rain. Diffused light from the streets disclosed a muddy compound about ten feet square. Across the little compound was a door painted green. This was the entrance to the Place of Glorious Repose and Divine Contentment.

His guide left him as Moore approached it. Once again, the American gave the signal, but more boldly—with his knuckles, this time.

A voice from an invisble source said clearly, in the dialect of South China, "The stupid man ventures over an unknown threshold with his heart poised on the point of a dagger."

"But a wise man," Moore responded in kind, "crosses a familiar threshold, sure of his welcome."

The voice, acid with Oriental humor, "Who is this night-crawling creature who speaks of wisdom?"

And Moore gave answer, "You address so flippantly the man-god, blessed alike by the earth and the stars and the lightning bolt—Ren Beh Tung!" This was the name by which he was known to the Chinese; literally, Man of Bronze.

MORE BOLTS CLANKED. The green door swung ajar, and the American stepped into the stinging, smoldering atmosphere of opium smoke. A grizzled old Chinese with popping eyes like a crab's was the guardian of this gate. He closed the door with a ceremonious clank.

"You are expected, son of the earth and the stars and the lightning bolt. Honesty is inscribed on your brow in letters like liquid fire."

"But from yours," Moore said amiably, "it was long ago washed by the liquids of dissipation."

Cerberus bared toothless gums at him in an unholy grin of appreciation, and Moore walked down the corridor, slouch hat over eyes, shoulders hunched up, hands thrust into trousers pockets—playing his part.

Opium smoke floated rankly in the air, a gray fog, seeping from alcoves in which bunks were built. Somewhere a man sang Li Po's "Ode to the Lute" in an opium dream. Beyond a sandalwood panel, another voice screamed in nightmare. And through an open door, the slouching white man met the dream-enlarged eyes of a Eurasian girl—as slim, as beautiful, as rankly poisonous as a flower of the densest jungle. But her eyes, shining in her trance, saw no shambling human derelict.

Moore shuffled along. There were three doors to select from at the end of the long corridor. He jerked open the middle one, and a new odor swept into his nostrils—good sandalwood incense. It writhed up in agonized blue plumes from pot-bellied braziers set one on either side of a carved teakwood dais piled with cushions.

Here was such a room as any opium addict, in his happiest abandon, might have dreamed about. The walls were panelled with vermilion silk on which coiled blue and green dragons with silver tongues and golden fangs. A ceiling of sapphire-blue satin studded with realistic golden stars sagged in the middle like the top of an Arab chieftain's tent. Dragon rugs of ultramarine and cobalt blue on a field of emerald green overlapped luxuriantly on the floor. And all about the floor, against the walls, were brilliant satin cushions, each large enough to conceal a man. Light was supplied by oil wicks burning in brass dongs set about on little taborets.

This room might have been the very heart of the fabulous, magic Orient.

On the teakwood dais, lounging amidst huge satin cushions of orange and purple and blue and cadmium yellow, was possibly the fattest man in China. His face was a mango moon, round and yellow and oily, in which his little black eyes were like the raisins set in the head of a gingerbread man. The furrows of his face might have been furrows drawn in a lump of soft tallow by a gouging finger. His hands were wads of yellow flesh from which stubby fingers protruded. These were crusted with diamonds and emeralds. His enormously fat body was clothed in folds of purple satin embroidered with gold and cardinal red. He had seven chins.

He was grotesque. He was monstrous. He might have been a Chinese comedian. But he was not; he was Lin Cho, the opium king of Hong Kong, a man proud of his reputation as the most slippery, most dangerous rascal in southern China.

AS MOORE ENTERED this fantastic satin chamber and shut the door, Lin Cho thrust his head forward.

The American said, "Hi, Lin Cho! Gaze upon a man who has leaped the dragon gate!"

Lin Cho's whispery voice answered, "Yes—I have heard you are dead."

He reached up with one pudgy hand and began toying with the long string of carved emeralds about his neck. His eyes, set deep in folds of yellow fat, were snapping with anger. His mouth, with its coarse, thick lips, was open a little, as it always was. You could watch him by the hour and never see him breathe. It was as if life went on in that great carcass by some magic of its own. Only his piglike black eyes and his pudgy hands betrayed the energy that animated him. His hands were never still. The tiny, angry eyes were scrutinizing the American inch by inch, from the disreputable hat to the gaping shoes.

In flowery Cantonese, he said, "A fool on a dangerous mission digs his grave with his undone deeds."

Moore was gliding about the room, poking at the huge satin pillows with his feet, searching mysterious black shadows where trouble might lurk.

He answered over his shoulder, with a grin:

"But the superior man overlooks neither the whisker of a rat nor the glitter of a dewdrop."

"Heaven," quoted the opium king, "smiles on the considerate man who refrains from tossing his dead cats on others' doorsteps!"

From the end of the room, Moore turned and surveyed him with a grin of derision. When he had scrawled Lin Cho's name in blood on the bedroom floor, he had realized that the opium king would dislike the publicity. He had known that Lin Cho would be wrathful. Yet some signature to that make-believe murder had been required!

"The bravery of the superior man," Moore said maliciously, "is a mountain behind which dead cats can neither be seen nor smelled. By the teeth of Buddha, Lin Cho, you should be proud to be the man who murdered me!"

Lin Cho's eyes, in their resentment, took on the look of rubies, burning red. He was furious.

"By Buddha and Buddha!" he puffed. "I am shaken with doubts. For a long time you have declared that you are finished with all adventure. You have been a business man. When you have been approached with suggestions to embark on dangerous missions, or to take part in exciting exploits, you have cried 'No!' Your eyes have been upon the star of probity, and your feet have been set down in the path of prudence. Yet now, on the very spur of some mad impulse, you cast all this aside, as if it had been a mask.— You become a man of singing steel, thirsting for blood!"

"Perhaps," the American answered, "I was realizing all this time that a horse, no matter how fast he travels, is always closely followed by his tail." He grinned.

Lin Cho shook his head gloomily. "Can a falcon become a snail?" he asked. "Can a fox become a fish?"

"A man born to trouble," Moore answered, "must pursue trouble or be pursued by trouble. That was why I stopped being a businessman. That was why I put aside the mask. Adventure is in my blood. Can the salt be removed from the ocean?"

Lin Cho regarded him with sharp little eyes. He looked doubtful, uneasy and resentful.

"I know," he said. "Once you start trouble, you involve every one. How am I paid in return for my kindly offer to help?"

"You forget—I *commanded* you to help."

"Yes! And wrote my name in blood as your murderer! I was willing to help, but what am I to think?"

Kicking a great purple cushion, Moore answered, "You are not to think, pig."

LIN CHO SWALLOWED a great gulp of air and gurgled with wrath; but before he could deliver any of his immense store of Chinese profanity, the American barked, in English.

"Hey! What's this?"

He had pulled aside a suspicious-looking vermilion wallpiece. A man was crouching against the stone wall behind it; a half-naked yellow man. His torso to the waist glistened with undried rain. His ragged blue denim pants were dark with rain.

Peter Moore, no longer amiable, ran his eyes from naked wet feet up and up to the shaggy blue-black hair of a Mongolian who must have measured, when he stood erect, a full six feet seven inches. Malignant, close-set black eyes glared at Moore from under an ape-like brow.

The fellow crouched lower, preparing to spring out at him. Moore's right hand shot out. His fingers fastened upon the matted blue-black hair. With a savage jerk, he impelled the tall stranger into the middle of the room.

In English, he snapped, "Who the hell is this?"

"Me no savvy!" Lin Cho wheezed, in pidgin.

"What the hell's he doing here?"

"Catchee bhobbery! Look see!" Lin Cho answered, and sharply clapped his fat hands.

The Mongolian giant struck out at Peter with arms as long and powerful as a gorilla's. Moore sidestepped and slugged him once in the jaw. The tall one gasped and fell on the dragon rug with bedazzled eyes.

Doors opened. Coolies—Lin Cho's watchdogs—came swarming in.

Lin Cho wrathfully asked them the question: "Who is this Mongolian rat, and what is he doing here?"

The watchdogs did not know. They had never seen the fellow before. So help them Buddha, they hadn't the slightest idea of how he had stolen in here!

"Search this room," Moore said. "Lin Cho, you are careless. If this fellow had escaped, everything would have been ruined."

He thrust his hand into the single pocket which the Mongolian's pants contained; brought it,out again. On the palm there reposed a small blue chalk pyramid!

"Lock this man up," Moore said. "Keep him prisoner until you hear from me. If you hear nothing, let him go at the end of one year."

"Slit his throat!" Lin Cho amended.

"No!" Moore snapped. "I may have a use for him later."

Lin Cho's little black eyes were again snapping with anger.

"As the heaven-born desires," he growled. He was perspiring a little. The spy who had slipped in and hidden here would have made a bad story in high quarters.

He yelped at the watchdogs, "Have you ears of stone? Have you legs and arms of mud? Did you hear the heaven-born give you commands? Addle-brained offspring of ducks—act!"

WHEN THE ROOM had been searched and the spy removed, Lin Cho reached with trembling hands to a black lacquer tray on a taboret beside him. It contained a jade pot of the treacly *chandoo,* the *yen-hok,* the *yen-shi-gow,* and a golden rack of pipes. He chose one—of satinwood, with a brown tortoise-shell tip and an apple green silk tassel—plied needle, puffed on flame, kneaded amber-colored opium cube, and inhaled the gray smoke deeply.

The biting fumes were a sedative to his resentment and burning envy of this audacious American, who dared the unthinkable, whose lean, hard youth, whose scornful courage, whose reputation for brazen daring made an opium king's possessions so much chaff!

He wheezed, puffed, inhaled and regained his poise. He declared: "May the son of heaven find all details, as I have attended to them in my miserable clumsy way, to his liking. I am but a worm to be spurned by the heel of a steel god who strides the earth. A boat is waiting for you off the Star Ferry Pier. The password to the very end of your journey is 'Tiger of the Night.'"

Moore said crisply, "Give me the amulet."

The green of kingfisher jade glittered in the opium king's pudgy yellow hand. It was a delicate little slab of the semi-precious stuff, green as green, about two inches long, an inch wide, an eighth of an inch thick—smooth as if by contact with countless hands. It looked like a small, worn cake of green soap. In his other hand, Lin Cho extended a short dagger, carved ebony handle foremost.

Lin Cho wheezed, "It has carved its way through nine kinds of trouble. It will bring luck."

Moore accepted the amulet; dropped it into a hip pocket.

The knife he disposed of in a side pocket of his coat, and went to the door.

The opium king said rapidly, "If a man is a man, the mills of heaven and earth grind him to perfection; if not—to destruction! Go with Buddha!"

The American brought up one finger to the brim of his shabby hat in a jaunty salute. The amulet was a one-way ticket to the most amazing, most perilous adventure he had ever undertaken. There was no turning back now.

4

THROUGH THE EARTH

IN THE CORRIDOR, Peter Moore paused with his back to the door, sniffing the biting reek of opium smoke, making sure that the corridor was empty, that he was not being watched. He quickly opened a door on his left, which gave upon another corridor. For perhaps ten minutes he followed a labyrinth of short and long corridors, emerging at length into a small, square room, unfurnished except for a cheap yellow-and-blue Peking rug which covered the floor.

He rolled up the rug until he exposed a trap door set into the floor. He lifted this. A bamboo ladder extended down into darkness. From the square aperture a steady cold breath of raw, wet earth flowed up into his face.

Holding the trap door up with his shoulders, he slowly went down the ladder, giving the rug a push at the last moment so that it would roll back into place.

He descended perhaps thirty-five feet into the earth. When his feet touched the hard-packed dirt at the bottom, he stopped and listened for fully a minute. At first, there was no sound but the roaring of utter silence in a confined place. Then he heard the faint, measured dripping of water, and as he started forward, the scurrying of a river rat.

Moore followed the tunnel for approximately a quarter of a mile, making his way over terrain every inch of which was familiar to him. The tunnel twisted this way and that. At intervals it forked. Now and then it was crossed by other tunnels. It was part of the elaborate system of tunnels with which the earth under Hong Kong's native section is honeycombed. The very odor of danger was in his nostrils here.

He could have gone another way, but he preferred this because it was in the nature of a test. If he had been betrayed, if his plans were now known to his enemies, or if he had been recognized and reported on his way to Lin Cho's, he would certainly learn about it here, perhaps at the cost of his life. But he was willing to take that chance. If he encountered no one in this underground passageway, then he would know for certain that his plan of vanishing, of being reported dead, had succeeded.

He carried his hand about the haft of the knife Lin Cho had given him—and reached the mouth of the tunnel without adventure. It was one of many mouths. This particular one permitted a man to issue from the tunnel system by means of an exit beneath a disused, rotting wharf. Planks had been lashed to bamboo piling to serve as a footbridge. Waves softly gurgled and sucked against the soft mud of the bank. The tide was out, and the mud flats gave off a stench which is peculiar to all Oriental harbors, from Vladivostok to Bombay.

Rain was streaming down. It crackled on the surface of the harbor, sending up a gray fog which drifted down the wind, and drummed on the rotting planks overhead.

Moore made his way along the footbridge until he

could reach up and grasp the edge of the wharf. He hauled himself up, swung a knee over a jutting beam, and made his way inshore. He turned up his coat collar against the pelting rain and jerked down the brim of his hat. Hunching his shoulders, he slouched off down the bund in the direction of the Star Ferry Pier.

He was a caricature of human desolation. Yet he was strangely happy. A fierce feeling of exaltation ran through his veins. He had closed the door on his dull, respectable past; and ahead of him stretched the high road to great adventure. The wet clammy air of the rainswept night was zestful with romance and exciting possibilities.

He drew in deep lungfuls of it and exulted. He was free! No more office desks! No more dealings with dull, stodgy businessmen! He felt more alive than in many months. He had died and had been reborn! A feeling of magical strength rippled along his muscles. The feeling of freedom was as intoxicating as wine.

Let the rain pour! Let the wind howl!

SO OCCUPIED WAS Peter Moore with these new, exhilarating thoughts that he did not see, approaching him, a tall, wide-shouldered figure. There was a sudden head-on collision.

A big voice brayed, "Look where ya're goin', yuh lousy punk!"

A big red hand came flat against Moore's chest and gave him a hearty shove. Moore, caught unprepared, went stumbling back, nearly falling into a deep mud puddle.

Yesterday—only this morning—he might have stood aside. He might have made some apology. Not now, however, for he was no longer the polite business man.

Recapturing his balance, he walked with quick decision toward the big fellow who had shoved him. There was a narrow lane of pavement between puddles. One or the other would have to stand aside; and Moore was determined that it would not be he.

He sized his man up as he approached: a sailor—probably a deckhand off an American tramp—the bullying kind of sailor who runs a fo'c's'le with a pair of iron fists.

"Out of my way!" Moore said.

"Oh, yeah?" the big man said.

"Yeah," the reborn adventurer growled.

The big stranger sent a fist with a savage intent in the direction of Moore's face. Moore lightly stepped aside, and as the fist shot past his nose, clamped down with steel fingers on the man's wrist. He gave it a jerk, a sudden twist—and stepped back as the big man went plunging, belly down, into the deepest puddle. Mingled with the splash was a roar of rage.

"Come and get some more!" Moore invited him, laughing.

The big fellow scrambled up and accepted the invitation. But the situation was suddenly made serious by the introduction of steel. A dirk was clutched in the big fellow's ham-like fist as he came rushing.

Moore had been in knife-fights before. He knew the technique, and he knew some of the tricks. It occurred to him again that yesterday—even this morning—he might have run from naked steel; he might have remembered his reputation as a courteous young businessman. Not tonight. He snatched from his pocket the ebony-handled knife, and steel clashed on steel. The big fellow disengaged his blade, brought it up and down at a sharp angle. Steel clashed again. Knives locked at the guards.

Moore gave a sharp twist, a quick downward lunge; he instantly sidestepped.

The big fellow was panting curses and tremendous threats. "I'm gonna carve your lousy heart out! S'help me—!"

Moore made a sudden flescending spiral motion with his knife hand. It was the climax to the neatest knife trick he had ever learned. An old Malay had taught him that trick. As if by magic, the knife leaped out of his antagonist's hand. It went soaring up into the rain, and the thin glint of a distant streetlight indicated that the dirk was describing a parabola on its way into Hong Kong harbor.

The enemy had sprung back, almost sobbing in his profane fury.

"I'll take yuh apart!" he gritted.

"Shove off!" Moore said.

All at once the big fellow uttered an amazed "Huh!" and broke into a run. He left the scene of the misunderstanding, splashing through puddles, lifting his big feet and putting them down with the rhythm of a locomotive's driving rods. He seemed fairly to fly down the bund.

He paused a block away, looked back, ran on.

MOORE RESUMED HIS progress. He hadn't had a fight in months. He hadn't had a knife fight in years. Freedom was wonderful! His muscles felt better now; and his head felt clearer. There was a snap to his step now. He had to force himself to shamble along like a waterfront bum. He mustn't forget himself. The fight had tuned him up like a tonic. Careful!

He must play his part daringly but cleverly, for he was embarking on the most dangerous adventure he had ever undertaken. The Blue Scorpion—that misshapen human monster who dwelled in his incredible palace beneath the waters of the Lake of the Flying Dragon—must continue to believe that Peter Moore was dead.

Always in the past, the young American had run away from Mr. Lu. Now he was going to attack. And the man with sufficient temerity to plot against the power of the Blue Scorpion must measure his steps with the greatest care. For Lu was certainly the most powerful, the most mysterious figure in all of Asia. He was a genius, a fabulous Chinese who saw in himself an Oriental Cæsar who would some day rule the world. He had tried to enlist Peter Moore's scientific knowledge in this ambitious scheme, and when Moore had refused to be used, had ordered Moore's death. Tracked and hunted by Lu's men for the past few weeks—almost trapped at the last moment—the American had now eluded them, he hoped, with his daring self-murder. The way was now clear for his attempt at destroying the power wielded by the Blue Scorpion over all of Asia.

Moore's objective was the notorious Temple of the Coiled Serpent, in the steaming jungles of Tong-King. This temple was a monument to the Blue Scorpion—to Lu, genius of Asia! There, each year, an elaborate ceremony took place. By means of bloody contests, a new high priest of the Temple of the Coiled Serpent was selected. Each year, tens of thousands of pilgrims made the journey from all parts of the Far East to watch these contests and the other ceremonies.

Not only was this jungle temple a monument to the Blue Scorpion—it was an amazing specimen, a material manifestation of his shrewd understanding of the Oriental. He had founded this cult of the Coiled Serpent for the sole purpose of enlisting the loyalty of great masses of Orientals to his causes—actually, a great army to be called upon when he needed it. And in enlisting this great army of fanatical worshipers, he had betrayed his cleverness, his master showmanship. For the yearly ceremonies at the Temple of the Coiled Serpent were well worth attending.

Keyed to the Oriental mind and to Oriental tastes, these ceremonies were horrible almost beyond belief. The climax was the sacrifice of a maiden chosen for her beauty. Lu himself slit the throat of the lovely girl selected from among a host of beauties, all fanatically anxious for the privilege!

The selected maiden, Moore had been told, climbed a flight of marble stairs into a dazzling blue glare in which Lu was concealed. And within that dazzling blue nimbus, the girl's throat was cut.

This hideous religion, founded by the Blue Scorpion, was actually the source of his incalculable power over Asia. Peter Moore, with his newfound spirit of adventure, was going to attempt to smash that power!

But he must walk warily. He must play his part to perfection. There must be no misstep, no mistakes. The plan was reckless enough; its execution must be the soul of caution. **HE SHUFFLED ALONG** to Star Ferry Pier, deserted and dismal in the rain. He saw no sampans about, except those huddled along the embankment beyond Queen's Statue Wharf. But he didn't want a sampan.

At the end of the pier he looked out into the misty blackness. Like a ghost, a hundred yards offshore, was the low-lying form of a long yellow launch. It rode at anchor, almost invisible; it carried no lights, except for a dim riding light; and its ports were all dark.

For perhaps fifteen minutes, Moore squatted down at the end of the pier and intently studied the launch and the water in its vicinity. Except for the spatter of the falling rain, nothing moved. Evidently satisfied, he finally got up and looked behind him. No one in sight.

He peeled off coat and shirt. In them he rolled up shoes and hat. This bundle he dropped into the water, and when it had sunk, he took a deep breath and dived in.

He swam out to the yellow power boat with long, easy strokes, sharply watching the sampans and junks anchored farther out as he progressed.

A dimly lit lantern appeared at the rail, and a round yellow face rose up from the deck of the launch as he came within reach of the steel hull. The face said, in Cantonese, "Who comes?"

Moore whispered, "A friend."

"With what word?"

"Tiger of the Night."

Promptly, there was other activity aboard the yellow steel launch. Figures like phantoms arose and moved stealthily about. Hands reached down and pulled the swimmer aboard, A dozen men gathered about him in the rainswept darkness, and a voice said, *"Aie!* Ren Beh Tung!" A light glittered in his eyes, and by the gleam of it Moore saw a familiar face, that of a thickset, one-eyed old Chinaman,

Jim Fong, a man who had once escaped execution in Canton as a river pirate.

Moore produced the amulet—his passport. The old river wolf rubbed it between thumb and forefinger, returned it, and whispered, "Master, I am a poor worm who crawls humbly at your feet. What are your commands?"

"Get under way at once."

The human circle about Moore magically dissolved, leaving only a young man on whose naked wet shoulders the shore lights laid golden gleams. He had the fine shoulders, the lean hips, the dark skin of Tong-King.

"I am Ling. I am your slave."

Moore heard the soft rumble of the anchor chain as Ling conducted him aft to the stateroom he would occupy. It was a spacious room of satinwood panelling. This launch, the *Luchow,* had once been a mandarin's yacht; and this and the adjoining room and the bathroom comprised the royal suite. There was native clothing laid out on the wide bunk, and on a table were jugs and pots of hair dye and skin stain.

The new alteration in his appearance was begun at once. Ling dyed his hair blue-black to the roots, and worked golden oils into his skin. He shaved the white man's eyebrows so that they acquired an upward, Oriental slant, then dyed these and the lashes.

It took a couple of hours, during which time the two men talked in the tongue of Ling's country—the one with swift ease, the other falteringly. Peter Moore had once spoken Tonkinese with a fair degree of glibness, but his tongue had gone rusty. He must perfect his command of that tongue. Too busy with plans, too excited to sleep, he spent the night in the stateroom with Ling, talking and drinking rice wine.

Greasy gray dawn at last fought its way through billowing rain clouds. When Moore looked through a porthole, the *Luchow* was swimming through a litter of junks and sampans, with the flat, gray, rain-soaked banks of the Pearl River on either side.

Shortly after dawn, the vessel slid behind an island and lay in hiding there until night. With nightfall, its powerful twin engines hummed to life again, and its sharp prow pointed upriver.

THAT EVENING, PETER Moore had an upsetting experience. He had spent the day in his cabin with Ling, talking Tonkinese; and he had just slipped out on deck for a breath of fresh air.

Off the starboard bow, a mass of twinkling lights was approaching. It was, he realized, the night boat just pulling out of Canton for Hong Kong. It would pass close to the *Luchow,* in this narrow stretch of channel.

As the river steamer passed, the adventurer saw a cluster of men and women in evening dress on the wide promenade deck, evidently preparing to go down to dinner. Then the steamer, ablaze with lights, swept past; and as it did so, Moore thought he caught a whiff of a familiar rare Parisian perfume. He was suddenly and forcibly reminded of Susan O'Gilvie. The final scene of their last quarrel had taken place on the Hong Kong bund, not far from the pier where that steamer would tie up. Slim and beautiful in a white silk evening gown, radiantly lovely in her furious mood, she had told him to go to the devil. His last recollection of her, as she stormed away on her ridiculous little high heels, was that alluring French perfume, lingering in the air like the very scent of her personality.

The thought of her temper made him sigh now. He had missed that beautiful and reckless young woman more than he cared to admit. Her loveliness, her generosity, the romance of her personality were endearing. But she was out of his life forever. That was tragic, in a way, but sensible. He had not notified Susan of his present plans, partly because of the possibility that his message, however cleverly worded, might fall into the wrong hands; partly because of Susan's inability to keep a secret. Her weakness, when angry, of saying what was on her mind had once all but cost both of them their lives, when she had blurted out a secret of the Blue Scorpion—within hearing of the Blue Scorpion's spy.

The news of his death would be a shock to her, but it was better that she believed him dead. There was certainly no place for her, in the career on which he had embarked. His life would be in constant peril; and he wanted neither to expose her to such peril nor expose himself to her faculty for getting into dangerous mischief.

Susan, he argued to himself, would now do what she should have done long ago—marry some worthwhile young man and settle down. She would stop being a thrill hunter. She would forget Peter Moore; and Peter Moore would, he hoped, forget her. But with that perfume lingering like a sharp memory in the air, it was hard to drive her out of his thoughts. In imagination he could see her face very clearly now, slim and eager, with soft red lips, pert little nose, eyes which were large and dark violet, fringed with long, thick, black lashes.

He told himself, sensibly, that Susan O'Gilvie was too rich. She was too spoiled. She was a constant source of trouble. She was, in short, the kind of girl that men cannot forget no matter how hard they try. He was sorry for Susan. She was so young, so eager, so innocent and unfortunately, so much in love with him. But it was a comfort to know that once she heard the rumor of his death Susan would soon forget him.

5

THE PRICE OF VENGEANCE

THERE IS A Chinese saying: "Harder to predict than the course of a lightning bolt is the mind of a woman." At the moment when Peter Moore caught that whiff of Parisian perfume from the river steamer, the beautiful young woman whom it called so sharply to mind was counting bags of gold in her hotel room, in Singapore.

The night was hot and humid and still. At the least exertion, tiny pearls of perspiration appeared on the girl's forehead. Counting bags of gold is hard work when there are so many bags to count—and when one is so rich that a roomful of gold, more or less, doesn't matter.

The fair trouble hunter wore white silk pyjamas which clung to her slender body. She was small but most energetic. As she bent down to recount the bags of gold, her dark curly hair would tumble down over her eyes and she would impatiently brush it back with a small, nervous hand. The trouble hunter was also terribly nervous. Her deep violet eyes were sparkling with excitement. Her cheeks were flushed. From time to time she darted a wary look about the room. Shades and shutters were closely drawn over both windows. Both doors—the one into the hall and the one into the hotel compound—were locked and bolted.

It was nearing ten o'clock when she counted her bags of gold for the last time. It had come out right again—eighty bags. Each bag contained $2,500 in American gold, in eagles and double eagles. A tidy fortune of $200,000 in good American gold!

With these eighty bags of precious yellow metal, the girl with violet eyes was purchasing a sizable lump of trouble. She had not suspected that $200,000 in gold would represent so much in bulk. Her fortune, to be sure, was hardly scratched by the subtraction of this sum; yet she had never seen so much money in her life as was now stacked along the wall of this room. And she was preparing to exchange these eighty bags of gold for the certainty of losing her life.

But the thrill hunter did not put it into those terms. She was paying $200,000 for an opportunity to avenge the death of a brave young man—a man whom she had loved more than life itself. There was still some question that the rumor she had heard last night was unfounded—still a chance that Peter Moore was not really dead. These past twenty-four hours of suspense had taught her the meaning of the word hell. Hell on earth—not knowing, not being able to think of another thing. Regretting her fury at their last meeting—their last parting. Regretting the thousand and one little thoughtless, cruel things she had said since she had known him.

Hing Sing Joy, the exile who ran the jade shop on Brah Basah Road, had taken charge of the investigation. He had cabled and wirelessed friends in high and low quarters in Hong Kong. He had instructed them to spare no expense, to leave no stone unturned, in ascertaining whether or not Peter Moore had really been murdered.

Susan had paid Hing Sing Joy handsomely for his services; and she was now prepared to pay that mysterious, greedy old Chinaman these eighty bags of gold for the possession of certain very dangerous intelligence in the event that the rumors of Peter Moore's death were confirmed.

IT LACKED A minute or two of ten o'clock when soft knuckles rapped at the door that gave upon the compound. Two raps—a pause—four raps—a pause—one rap. The signal had been prearranged, but the trouble-hunter was taking no chances. She removed from a pocket in her pyjama trousers a small black pistol. She had learned that Singapore is not only the most cosmopolitan city in the Far East, but also the most treacherous. She was quite aware that in this city tonight any one of countless thousands of men, yellow and brown and white, would have been delighted to slit her throat to possess these eighty bags of gold.

With the pistol ready, she went to the door. "Who is there?"—a whisper.

The answer came, softer than her own, hardly more than a shadow of sound, "It is Hing Sing Joy."

The richest girl in all the East turned the key and shot back the bolt. She opened the door an inch, holding the pistol in readiness, still prepared for an unpleasant surprise.

A tall thin man whose face was in shadow stood on the flagging. Behind him, the compound was in velvety blackness, except for the radiance diffused by palm fronds which caught the silver brilliance of the full moon. A scent of spices crept in through the crack.

The girl whispered, "Give me the word."

The man answered, "Blue night."

This was the prearranged password. Making sure that the man was alone, the girl opened the door and let him in. Then she closed the door, locked and bolted it.

Turning, she stared with tremulous anticipation at her visitor. Hing Sing Joy was about forty-five years old, with a complexion burned by tropical suns and winds to the color and texture of dried orange rind. He wore silver-rimmed spectacles.

His beady eyes darted to the rows of canvas bags stacked against the wall. Greed glittered in his looks. Hing Sing Joy licked his thin, cracked lips.

The girl took these evidences of greed, so to speak, in her stride. She was accustomed to greed. She knew that Hing Sing Joy's only interest in her was money—good American gold. She felt horribly alone, horribly afraid. When the greed left the man's eyes, sadness remained.

She gasped, "Well?"

"I regret very much, Miss O'Gilvie, that last night's report was true. More than a dozen men have investigated the rumor. No doubt can possibly remain.—Your lover was killed last night."

Susan O'Gilvie was standing near a chair. She suddenly sat down. The color had left her face, and the luster had left her large violet eyes. She moistened her lips. Her throat gave a little convulsion as if she found difficulty in swallowing.

She said faintly, "Is—is there any question who—who did it?"

Hing Sing Joy nodded. "Lin Cho, the opium king, is suspected. But that may mean nothing."

The girl's eyes seemed to grow enormous. In her white face, they were startling, shocking. All her life seemed concentrated in her eyes.

Hing Sing Joy looked uneasy, for Miss O'Gilvie had the appearance of a girl who might, at any moment, burst into screams. But when her voice came again it was hardly audible.

"The Blue Scorpion!" she said. Then, "How was it done?"

"He was presumably killed with a knife. There was much blood. The body was not found. It was presumably thrown into a sewer."

SUSAN O'GILVIE SANK teeth into lower lip and weakly got up. She moved uncertainly to the dressing table on which her golden toilet articles were arranged. She touched a gold-backed brush. She ran her little fingers over the golden tops of a long row of cosmetic jars much as a woman, deep in thought, might run her fingers along the keys of a piano. She was like a girl in a trance—or a girl suddenly bereft of the desire to continue living.

The Chinese watched her with an air of shrewd understanding. Perhaps he appreciated the valiant fight she was making for self control. Perhaps he marveled at her courage. Or perhaps, in the depths of his Oriental brain, he marveled at the stunning effect of his news.

Her fists were clenched at her sides. As if by sheer will power, she was forcing color back into her cheeks. "It was the Blue Scorpion," she repeated quietly.

"Quite possibly," Hing Sing Joy agreed.

She made an impatient gesture toward the eighty bags of gold. "There is the two hundred thousand dollars in gold exactly. Twenty-five hundred to a bag. Eighty bags. Do you wish to count them?"

He smiled sadly. "Naturally, I take your word."

He tiptoed to the hall door, quickly unlocked and unbolted it, threw it open.

With a half smile for the emptiness of the hall, he closed, locked, and bolted the door once more. He proceeded to the windows and peered behind the curtains. In an excess of caution, he even peered into the clothes closet and under the bed.

"A man who imparts dangerous secrets," he said, "lives in the shadow of a sword. First of all, you must promise me that if you should be captured—if you should be put to torture—you will not admit where you secured this information."

The girl said coldly, "You have my promise."

"IF YOU WILL proceed," Hing Sing Joy continued, in a whisper, "to the province of Tong-King, in northern Indo-China, there, in the heart of the jungle, you will find the Temple of the Coiled Serpent. Once each year, Mr. Lu— or the Blue Scorpion, as you and many others prefer to call him—visits the Temple of the Coiled Serpent. For just one day!

"Pilgrimages are made yearly from all parts of Asia to that temple. The object of the pilgrimages I will tell you later. The main point, as it concerns you, is this. On that day a beautiful girl is selected from among the pilgrims. Her life is sacrificed. She is the one person in the world who, on that day or any day, is for even one brief moment alone with Mr. Lu.

"This girl, unattended, proceeds up a long flight of steps to where Mr. Lu sits waiting, invisible in a zone of blinding blue light. When she reaches him, he rises and—cuts her throat. The Sapphire Death! It is the climax of the ceremony which binds his followers to the worship of Mr. Lu.

"That girl might possibly have an opportunity—for a fleeting instant of time—to strike a dagger, if she so wished, into the heart of Mr. Lu. It is the one vulnerable moment in Mr. Lu's life from one year's end to the next—that one moment in the one day.

"At this year's ceremony, the possibility becomes a probability. Previously, when the girl reached the top of the stairs, she disappeared from sight in that blinding sapphire light—so blinding that neither she nor the worshipers saw Mr. Lu. No one knew for a certainty that he was there, that it was he who cut her throat. This year, Mr. Lu has announced that at the moment of the Sapphire Death he will show himself for the first time to his people!"

Hing Sing Joy paused and gave the girl beside him a thin smile. "Is this information—this opportunity—worth two hundred thousand dollars?"

"Yes," she said quietly.

Hing Sing Joy sent another greedy glance at the eighty bags of gold.

"I think I should warn you once more," he said, "that this mission you are undertaking is certain to cost you your life. If your disguise is penetrated, if your motive is even suspected, you will be brutally murdered. You understand?"

"I do."

"So that, whether you succeed or fail," he continued, "you cannot escape death. Once you have stabbed Lu—if you succeed in making the most of that single brief moment— you will be killed."

"I am prepared for death. All I want is the chance to kill the Blue Scorpion before I die."

6

HOPELESS!

HIDING IN BAYOUS or behind deserted islands by day, and steaming at top speed during the hours of darkness, the yacht Luchow dropped anchor off the village of Chu-Kiang shortly after dark on the fifth night out of Hong Kong.

In parting with Jim Fong, Peter Moore said to the old river pirate: "Do not let your greed be tempted by the thoughts of quick, big profits. Put down the temptation to slit throats for gold."

The old river wolf grinned. "Master, I have but one thought in mind to keep a rendezvous six months, three days and eleven hours from this. I will be prudent. My clumsy feet shall follow the paths of virtue. By the whiskers of Buddha, I will not fail!"

A few minutes later, Moore, sitting in the stern of the small boat that took him and Ling ashore, watched the jungle take form in the pale light of the scimitar moon. The rank, overripe scent of flowers and vegetation came to his nostrils. And once again he thrilled to the breath of danger and adventure. Beyond that rising black wall of jungle lay a challenge to the sharpest wits, the highest courage.

The small boat avoided the spidery wharves along the village front; put in a half mile above it. The oarsmen maneuvered it alongside a small pier. Ling and Moore climbed out and waited in the shadow of a mahogany tree until the boat vanished. Then Ling led the way into the jungle along a footpath.

An hour of fast walking brought them into a small clearing. Here, a dozen men with rifles were gathered about a picket-line of horses. A tall, dark fellow with a shock of unruly black hair advanced to meet the newcomers.

He softly called, in Tonkinese, "Who comes?"

Moore answered, "Ren Beh Tung."

The tall man, with rifle ready, looked at him in the moonlight "Lies fall from the lips of men more fluently than water from a dam in the rainy season. What is the word?"

"Tiger of the Night."

Moore held out the amulet, like a large green lozenge. The tall man rubbed it between thumb and forefinger. Returning it, he bowed low and said, "I am Cheng-Lat. I am the heaven-born's slave. What is his pleasure?"

And Moore said, "We start immediately."

Horses were brought for Moore and Ling, and the cavalcade started south. They climbed up and up until the jungle was left behind. By midnight they had reached a still higher country, of black ravines, many waterfalls and vegetation of a less tropical nature. Cold winds blew gustily in this region. Actually, they were in the foothills of the Himalayas.

THE CAVALCADE HALTED presently under a large banyan tree. Ling reined in his horse beside Moore's and said:

"Master, we part here. Cheng-Lat and I return to join Jim Fong. I will proceed immediately to Hai-Phong to give Lak-Yan, the cobbler, his instructions. You have only five *li* more to go, and that you must go afoot. Follow this trail down the ravine. Watch for the cleft in the hill on the southeast. There, you will see the red star rise. It rises tonight at the hour of the crow. Wait by the great black rock that shines. By the ten thousand and ten epochs of Buddha, may you succeed!"

The young American dismounted. He flipped an airy salute to Ling, and to Cheng-Lat, and waited under the tree until the horsemen had vanished, until the drumming of hoofs had diminished to a faint and faraway tattoo. He waited until this sound had dwindled, and until silence, broken only by the distant murmur of waterfalls, descended.

All about him were black and tortured hills, the result, in some past age, of a titanic upheaval of the earth's crust. Here was utter desolation.

He waited until he was quite sure of his surroundings, until he had the "feel" of the place. He was quite certain that his escape from Hong Kong had been attended by no suspicious circumstance, that his enemies had been completely outwitted. Alone upon this plateau in northern Tongking, he grinned. He saluted the moon. So far, safe! The first step of his new adventure had been boldly planned and executed. Once again he felt rising within him that tide of excitement and anticipation. He was as free as these winds! Once again, he was on the trail of danger, excitement, adventure!

He started at a fast walk along the twisting narrow trail in the ravine, drinking in deep lungfuls of the crisp mountain air. His heart sang a song older than the world,

The panther whirled on him like a flash.

younger than the newest dawn. It was as if the meaning and purpose of life had suddenly become clear to him. He saw the ravine as a giant's playground—full of great rocks and boulders. The wind shouted.

As he strode down the ravine, he watched the southeastern rim of the mountains for the V-shaped cleft. It revealed itself at the end of about an hour—a V as clean-cut as if it had been hewn with a cleaver. He turned down a dim, tortuous trail toward it, and presently approached a little round lake as smooth as a mirror, as black as India ink. At the end of the lake a grove of pepper trees tossed about like plumes in the wind and spilled their spicy fragrance.

Just beyond these, at the very edge of the lake, was the grandfather of all rocks—a mass as large as a ten-story office building, as black and glossy as a lump of coal.

The adventurer waited impatiently in the shadow of the rock and fixed his eyes on the V-shaped cleft. His nerves were tingling with anticipation. His heart was thumping.

He waited for perhaps twenty minutes. Then, suddenly, in the very point of the cleft, a spark of orange-red materialized. The red star, Mars.

Quite as suddenly, however, a great cold hand clasped the back of his neck. Another hand clasped his thigh. Effortless strength lifted him high into the air. A sudden cessation of this strength let him fall with a crash that all but knocked the wind out of him. A yellow giant was on him, twisting his arm, forcing his shoulders to the sharp little stones beside the grandfather of all rocks.

PETER THE BRAZEN writhed, twisted; forced every ounce of his strength into an attempt to free his shoulders from the relentless pressure which was forcing them to the earth. He was helpless. He might have been, with all his strength, at the mercy of some gigantic machine of steel and bronze.

Down went his shoulders, little by little, until the sharp, small stones cut into his flesh.

The mysterious giant who had leaped upon him in the shadow of the black rock then climbed off Moore's inert body and growled, in English, "Terrible! Simply terrible! Come here."

He walked to a shelf of rock which overhung the lake. Panting, Moore followed him. The other man, of about his age, was perhaps three inches taller. He had the magnificent shoulder and the lean hips of a gladiator. His stride was that of the panther.

He paused at the edge of the rock ledge, with the still, black water below him.

"This lake is twenty feet deep," he said. "Deep enough. Here! Grab a rock to hold you under. When I count three, jump. Stay down longer than I do. Jump!"

They jumped simultaneously. The water was icy cold—so cold that once again Peter Moore's breath was all but knocked out of him. He sank down—down—down into liquid cold blackness, hugging the chunk of rock to his chest.

He began to count seconds. At the count of twenty, his lungs were begging for air. At the count of forty, his lungs were demanding air in no uncertain terms. His heart was pounding. Uneasiness filled him as he recalled how far it was to the surface. He wanted to breathe. He had to breathe. Fifty, fifty-one, fifty-two. He must breathe. He couldn't stay down any longer. It wis impossible for any man to stay down any longer. He had been under almost a full minute.

With his lungs frantically demanding air, he let go the rock. He jumped and swam. His head broke the surface.

The yellow giant was not to be seen. Gasping, Moore feebly paddled to shore and pulled himself out, shivering in the crisp night wind. He watched the little lake. He waited. His gaspings ceased. His heart returned to the even tenor of its ways. Still the yellow giant did not appear.

Moore grew worried. Surely this was impossible. No man could stay under water this long and live.

He began to count again. He had been under about a minute. He had been up about a minute when he began to count again. He estimated that altogether five minutes had passed. Still no sign of the yellow giant. Another minute passed.

Then the yellow giant appeared. His head came to the surface. Moonlight gleamed in his black eyes, glittered on his large white teeth. He was laughing. He wasn't gasping with any particular effort.

With strong, slow, easy strokes, he reached the bank and effortlessly pulled himself up.

"How long were you down?" he asked.

"About a minute."

"Quitter!" the giant cried. "You're hopeless! You're terrible!"

Moore said nothing. He watched the drops of water slide off the great, snake-like muscles, the fatless flesh of the other man.

"Rested?" asked the giant.

"Yep," Moore said grimly.

"Come on. Let's see. Let's see how lousy you really are."

With feelings of anger Moore followed him up the bank to the side of the mountain. Here, in a sharp black shadow, was the entrance to a cave. He hadn't noticed it before because of the shadow. The yellow giant went inside. He came out immediately with a pair of gleaming scimitars held in the crook of a mighty elbow. He extended both handles to Peter Moore.

"Both the same, but take your choice."

Moore chose one and gripped the handle. He was not an expert swordsman, but he was not a novice. He placed his left hand behind his back. The yellow giant took the same attitude, facing him.

"Ready?" the giant asked.

"Ready."

The two curved, wicked blades met with a clash. Moore

thrust, parried, sidestepped. And suddenly it was as if a powerful hand had snatched his blade. He had played a similar trick on a waterfront bully in Hong Kong, with daggers. That had been skill and strength; this was superhuman skill and superhuman strength.

The scimitar was snatched from his hand as if by an irresistible machine. It went up into the air, and it clattered to the ground.

The yellow giant tossed his own scimitar to the ground, placed his back to the mountain wall, and began to laugh. He punctuated his bursts of laughter with insults. Peter Moore learned then that he was a weakling, that he was utterly and incurably hopeless.

The young giant reached a crescendo of mirth and mockery.

"And you," he roared, "expect to become the high priest of the Temple of the Coiled Serpent!"

"Yes," Moore said grimly.

7

AN OLD ACQUAINTANCE

PETER MOORE HAD first met Dekka Lan Shan, the yellow giant, in Hong Kong one night about six weeks previously, under circumstances which were not only dramatic but amazing. On the night following Susan O'Gilvie's abrupt exit from his life, Moore had left his hotel to walk until he decided just what was to be done with himself.

His aimless steps took him in the direction of Causeway Bay. In a stinking black alley he had stumbled upon one of those night-time adventures which, in the Far East, may be the beginning or the end of an exciting personal history—a glimpse of mystery seen for an instant—gone forever!

As he walked down the alley, picking his way, he saw, with the aid of some dim effulgence which penetrated the gloom, a thing that appeared to his startled glance to be an octopus on land. There it was writhing and squirming in the mud of the alley just ahead of him, a thing with a great body and countless legs which kicked and writhed.

It had been his experience that Nature, in her most whimsical moment, had never designed a land-going octopus. A further consideration of the many-legged creature presently informed him that what he beheld was a mass of many men attached like leeches to one central figure. A still closer inspection disclosed that one man, down, was being attacked in utter silence by many.

Unlike most street brawls, nothing was being said. There were neither appeals for help nor curses of anguish or fury.

Peter Moore, a participant in many brawls, did not pause to inquire into the causes which had precipitated this one. Automatically, he took sides with the underdog. Fortunately, he had gone for his walk equipped with a strong ironwood walking stick.

With this excellent weapon, he promptly began to crack skulls. So swift and efficient was his work that the seven or eight members of the attacking party were lying unconscious before any of them had had time to realize that there was an intruder.

Moore grasped the tough flannel jacket worn by the intended victim, and half-carrying him, hastened down the alley to the nearest brightly lighted thoroughfare. There, to his astonishment, he found that he had rescued a member of the crew of the U.S. Cruiser California, then on the China station, and at the moment anchored in Hong Kong Harbor.

His astonishment increased when he discovered that the man whom he had rescued was not white, but yellow—a veritable yellow giant, bleeding from a knife wound in his arm, partly unconscious from the blows of fists and feet that had been rained upon him.

The yellow giant, Moore quickly saw, was neither Japanese, Chinese, nor Indo-Chinese. Despite his wide knowledge of Asians, Moore could not quite place his nationality.

He propped him against a convenient lamp post and knotted his handkerchief about the gashed forearm. His beneficiary, panting for breath, presently recovered it and said, with a deep grunt, "Neat work, guy."

"I'll take you back to your ship," Moore said.

"Nix!" said the big young man. "I'm through with the Navy."

THEN HE STEADIED himself on his two large feet and looked closely at his rescuer. Having completed his inspection, he brushed his big hand across his eyes, as if he were removing cobwebs, and said:

"You're the guy they call Peter the Brazen. This is my lucky night. The same human scorpion who is after you just sent that gang to do me in."

At this use of the word "scorpion," Moore stiffened. Incredible as it was, he understood that the man he had rescued from supposed waterfront thugs was referring to Lu, otherwise the Blue Scorpion, Moore's mortal enemy.

"He got wise I was a gob on the California," the big stranger said, "so I quit the ship. I was on my way to lose myself when this gang jumped me. I'm through with the Navy.—I'm through with everything unless something is done about it right now. I don't know Hong Kong."

"I do," Moore said.

"There's no time to waste, then. I've got to get out of this town."

"Yes," Moore agreed. "What did you do to Lu?"

"It's a long story.—But come on. Those guys are going to take notice pretty quick. Where do we go?"

"A sampan," Moore said. And he led the ex-gob down dark, angling alleys to the waterfront. He knew an old sampan *fokie* who was under a lifelong obligation to him, and who could be depended upon to keep his mouth shut in the very face of death.

The sampan man was asleep. Moore woke him up and instructed him to take them to the middle of the harbor. Here, in comparative safety, the ex-gob told his story. To Moore, it was neither amazing nor incredible, for he had spent his life among men who led amazing and incredible careers—men, like himself, who followed the dangerous and exciting road of adventure.

Dekka Lan Shan was twenty-six years old. He had been born in San Francisco's Chinatown, of Tibetan parents. At the age of fifteen he was shipped to Bombay, and there was met by a number of uncles who escorted him, virtually a prisoner, northward over India and into Tibet.

At Dekka Lan Shan's birth, it had been decreed by grandparents and countless uncles that he was to devote his life to the priesthood. He was taken to the grand lamasery in Lhassa, and there—a boy of fifteen—his training was begun. Very much against his wishes, he took the blood-oath of the lamas. He was initiated into occult mysteries, was given the priceless, age-old secrets of the lamas— yogism. He was trained to perform feats of superhuman strength, and he was trained to acquire powers of mental concentration unknown to others.

Dekka Lan Shan hated it. Born an American, brought up with American ideas and ideals, he hated Tibet; the Tibetans, with their narrow, fanatical views; and most of all, the lamas who crowded into his young brain their priceless secrets.

After five years of it, Dekka made his escape. In themselves his wanderings comprised a fabulous tale. He had made his way afoot from the snow-clad peaks and wind-swept plateaus of Tibet into India. He had joined an elephant caravan into Farther India. He had become a mahout. He had lived always with the threat of recapture hanging over his head, and that would mean death.

Driven by this knife-edged necessity, he visited all parts of the Far East, from Korea to Turkestan. He was a camel boy in the Goblyn Gobi. He was a snake-charmer in Bang-kok. He told fortunes and took money from gullible tourists in Singapore.

AND ONE DAY he heard of the competition by which the head priest of the most fantastic of all Oriental temples is selected once each year—the Temple of the Coiled Serpent—the temple owned and controlled by Lu, the Blue Scorpion.

Now nothing on earth draws two adventurous young men closer than a common enemy. Many times the cohorts of Mr. Lu had made attempts on Peter Moore's life. Many times they had made similar attempts on the life of Dekka Lan Shan.

Mr. Lu, the mythological monster! The Blue Scorpion, so-called, who lived in a castle built under the waters of a lake cupped in by cobalt hills in the Purple Mountains of the Moon, in northern China!

No man had yet succeeded in disproving the fantastic legends which were told about Lu. He was said to be three hundred years old. At the age of nineteen, he had fallen from a cliff, wiped off his face, smashed his skull and broken most of his bones. A witch-doctor, so the legend ran, had pieced him together, patched him up, set his bones, given him a brain of purest kingfisher jade in place of the injured brain, and endowed him at the same time with everlasting life or eternal youth—or both!

"Believe it or not," Dekka Lan Shan said that night in the sampan to Peter Moore, "millions of Asiatics believe it. Now let me tell you something about the Temple of the Coiled Serpent, fellow. Of course, you've heard about it. But let me tell you the facts. I fought my way to become the high priest of that temple for a year, and I know 'em all. In an inner shrine in that temple there is a skull made of sapphires.

"That skull is supposed to contain the real brain of Lu— the brain which the surgeon took out of him two hundred-odd years ago, when Lu fell over the cliff. According to the stories, that sapphire skull has magical powers. You can bank on it that Lu spread that story around. Just when the Temple of the Coiled Serpent was built I don't know. Never could find out. But it's been up there in the jungles of Tongking for a good many years.

"Lu saw to it that the fame of the sapphire skull spread. As you know, it's now famous all over Asia. Every year, pilgrims from all over Asia go to the Temple of the Coiled Serpent to see the new head priest selected, and to watch the excitement.

"No matter how phony the legend is, one point is certain: Lu is a wonderful showman. He understands the Oriental imagination. He gives those pilgrims something worth watching! Each year, the new head priest is selected by contests which are supposed to bring out the strength and cleverness of the contestants. The head priest who is selected has only one job: to guard the sapphire skull.

"It sounded hot, so I decided to try for it. I entered the

contests. I won through to the high priesthood and became
the guardian of the sapphire skull. That was fine. It kept
me out of my uncle's reach for a solid year—and maybe I'd
learn some new tricks! But the joke was on me. At the end
of the year, a new priest was selected. Then I found that my
fate wasn't so funny. I was to go back with Lu to the Lake
of the Flying Dragon—and vanish!"

"*What!*" Peter Moore interrupted.

"That's all. Vanish.—I didn't cotton to the idea. When
I vanish, I like to have full charge of the whole act. So I
watched my chance and made my getaway. Down came
Mr. Lu's wrath! I skipped out of China. I stowed away on
a German tramp steamer bound for New York, in ballast.
When I reached New York I skipped ship. In New York,
Lu's agents tracked me down again. Fellow, I was busier
than a flea on a hot griddle! The safest place for me, says
I, was to join up with Uncle Sam's Navy. So up I joined.
I got my birth certificate, proving my citizenship, from
California.

"Right off the bat, my ship was sent out to the China
station. What a break! We got here a month ago. And Lu's
agents found out about it. I got shore leave tonight, intend-
ing to make my getaway, and this gang jumped me. If it
hadn't been for you, they'd have nailed me.—Now what?"

PETER MOORE HAD listened to this narrative, on that
night on the waterfront, without excitement, without
comment. Not only was he familiar with narratives of that
type; in some ways, Dekka Lan Shan's experiences paral-
leled his own. One jump ahead of trouble or death all the
way!

It wasn't astonishment that made him thoughtful. Dekka Lan Shan had given him an idea.

Peter said, "There's no time to talk now. I'm being watched. Even now, we may be in danger. You've given me a hunch. I'm going to act on it—and kill two birds with one stone. If you'll help me!"

Dekka Lan Shan grinned in the gloom of the sampan's cabin. "According to my code of conduct, fellow," he said, "what you say, I do. My life wouldn't bring much in the open market, but—what can I do for you?"

"So far as I know," Moore had answered, "there's only one route of escape. Up this river. This old *fokie* will take you up there. Does it suggest anything?"

Dekka Lan Shan laughed. "Certainly! Tongking! I know where there's a fine hiding place not a day's walk from the Temple of the Coiled Serpent. Am I a Yogi? Is my guess close?"

"Yes. How do I find that cave?"

"I'll send a man named Ling to guide you. How will we contact?"

"Through Lin Cho, the opium king. He will arrange everything for me. It's an old debt."

Dekka Lan Shan fell to laughing again. "You're what I expected," he said. "You think fast. You jump right down opportunity's throat. So you're going to become—with my assistance—the new head priest of the Temple of the Coiled Serpent?"

Moore said dryly, "You think pretty rapidly yourself."

"Wrong! I am a Yogi. I read men's minds. I am a master of men and of magic. Tonight I become your slave!"

8

MAN OF CHROMIUM

APPROXIMATELY SIX WEEKS later, squatting on the ground in the moonlight outside Dekka Lan Shan's mountain cave in northern Tongking, Dekka gazed obliquely at the blond young American who now passed for a black-haired Chinese. Mirthfully he shook his head.

"Maybe you can, and maybe you can't. All you have is possibilities. To become the high priest of the Temple of the Coiled Serpent, you must become more than a man. What's your plan?"

"To steal the sapphire skull and destroy it!"

"That's a mighty big order." Dekka, looking at him, frowned and gloomily shook his head. "Better men than you have tried that. Most of them died by the death-of-a-thousand-cuts. I'd call it, without hesitation, the riskiest job in the whole of Asia. Sure! By stealing that skull, you could destroy Lu's power over millions of people. The trouble is, it's a super-man-sized idea. Say! Just what is your grievance against Lu?"

"First," Peter answered, "he's been out for me. Now I'm going out for him."

"Sweet revenge, eh?"

"In more senses than one. A few months ago, he ordered

one of my friends killed—a man who had done him absolutely no harm. Killed him to throw the fear of God into me."

"Revenge, again. Any more reasons?"

"Plenty! I've been bottled up too long—trying to be a sensible business man. I've decided to cut loose. I've picked the biggest adventure I could find."

"You certainly have."

Peter was staring at the stars. "And," he said, "it's time someone nipped a few of Lu's schemes in the bud. I'm not talking about the Lu legend. Let that ride. I'm talking about his schemes. He's a menace to civilization."

"I've heard that legend, too."

"It's no legend! I know some of his schemes. He sees himself as the Napoleon, or Cæsar, of China. He wants to conquer the world—subdue and smash modern civilization. Rule the universe!"

"Madness!" Dekka snorted.

"Not all of it. He's a genius. I've talked to him when I was his prisoner. He's an inventive genius. I've seen the results of some of his work with a queer kind of remote control radio system, or machine. That's how I met him. He wanted me to work on it. My first job, after perfecting it, was to wreck all the big American cities."

"And you want to give his plans a set-back by destroying his power over Asia."

"It would smash his grip on his followers if I could steal that skull!"

"Yeah. I understand that, fellow. But you've got a worse case of over-ambition than the guy who charged windmills with a wooden spear. It can be done—but you can't do it."

"I'm going to do it."

"Sure! So am I going to jump over the moon! You've got the right spirit, fellow. But here's the hitch. Tough and willing as you are, you're softer than candle-wax. Great grief, Pete! Just look at you! It took me seven seconds to pin you on your back. I out-stayed you six to one under water. And it took me five seconds to snap the scimitar out of your hand. Don't you realize that it takes a better man than you to win through the contests and become the high priest of that temple?"

"How did you do it?"

"Hah!—Yogism!"

"Horsefeathers! If you did it, I can do it."

"YEAH? LISTEN, LAD. In these contests, you will be up against at least a hundred of the toughest, smartest lads in the whole Far East—human gorillas who have been train-ing for this, some of them, for years—since they were kids. And you expect, with six months' training, to fight your way through a gang like that?"

"Yep."

"Boy, I hand it to you! You are the world's champion optimist. Lu puts on these yearly contests that he may select the smartest, bravest, toughest, strongest men in entire Asia. And the worst of it is, no one knows in advance what these contests are to be. Every year they're different. There's always a fire test and a water test, and there's sure to be an elimination by the sword. On top of that, there is always some new test, personally devised by Lu—some-thing horrible. Different every year.

"The Chinese call you Man of Bronze, but to win through those tests, you've got to change your name to chromium! I can teach you plenty. I can build you up for the elimination tests. I can teach you to walk on coals of fire. All I learned in the lamasery will be helpful. But will it help enough? Nix!

"Look at this with a clear eye, fellow. Lu knows you. If he recognizes you—curtains!"

"Yes. I've been worried about my eyes. But, first—you've actually seen Lu. I never have. What does he look like?"

"I've never seen him. No high priest has ever seen him. He remains hidden in a blinding glare of blue light."

"Well, how about my eyes? How can I make them tilt up at the corners to give me an oriental look?"

"That's easy. I simply nick a little muscle with a sharp knife—don't cut it, just nick it. It's a Yogi trick. Your eyes will twirk up at the outer corners for a week or two, then those muscles will heal and you'll get back your normal appearance. Such details don't worry me. It's the contests! There's a big chance that you'll be killed off at the very start of the tests. Those contests are doped out so that they will result in the deaths of great numbers of men. Every year dozens of these lads are killed off like cattle. And suppose you do win? How're you going to get away with the sapphire skull?

"I was high priest for a year. I don't know how it can be done."

"I'm not worrying about that now," Peter answered. "The question is, will you help to whip me into condition?"

Dekka Lan Shan looked glumly at the lake. "Sure, I will. And 'whip' is the word. You'll hate the sight of me before we're through. Because it's going to be tougher than any course of physical training you ever heard about. We've got just six months to prepare you for those contests. Every minute, every second has to count. You'll have to do what I tell you, without question and without reservation.—It's time now we got some sleep. Take your clothes off."

"Where do I sleep?"

"Right out here in the open—without any clothes—without any bedclothes—without anything under you. Right here on these stones! These sharp ones. You're going to live like a wild animal—and get tough. We'll kill our own food, and we'll eat it raw. Good-night! Sweet dreams!"

THUS BEGAN PETER Moore's training for the contests by which he hoped to become, six months from now, the high priest of Mr. Lu's Temple of the Coiled Serpent. He had always kept himself in excellent physical condition, but he had quickly learned that according to Dekka Lan Shan's standard he was little more than a weakling.

He could not have undertaken a more rigorous period of training had he been planning to compete for the world's heavyweight boxing or wrestling championship. Dekka was thorough, and Dekka was heartless. The time would come when Peter would be able to sleep comfortably naked, and with no mattress or covering on the sharp stones; but for the first few nights he suffered agonies from the cold, and other agonies from the little pointed stones.

On the morning following his arrival, his training systematically began. Having finally slept, he did not wake up until the sun was high in the heavens. Dekka was seated beside him, devouring raw the meat of a deer he had killed with a rock sling.

"Pile in!" Dekka invited him. "Tear off a hunk of the neck meat. It's bloodier, and it has more what you need."

With distaste, Peter tried it. He ate little of that first raw meal. Later, hunger would drive him to it. But not this morning.

Stiff and sore from those hours on the rocks, he went through the day's routine as Dekka dictated it. A swim; further attempts at staying under water longer than a minute; a run, barefoot, along the stony trails; mountain climbing; wrestling; ju-jitsu; scimitar practice; rope-jumping; *parang* practice. A *parang* is a Malayan dagger about ten inches in length, with a tapering curved blade—one of the most dangerous edged weapons in existence. In addition to these exertions, Dekka taught him the Yogi breathing exercises—exhaling through one nostril, inhaling through the other while he concentrated on the "flame in his heart." This was a mysterious ritual, but Peter soon found that it was tremendously effective. It cleared his brain and refreshed his heart and his tired muscles.

Night found him exhausted—another night in the chill, gusty wind, with nothing over him but the stars. But as the days passed, he lost his stiffness and soreness, and he set himself in every way to attain physical perfection.

He walked and ran miles each day, barefoot over the sharp stones. The soles of his feet soon became calloused, and so tough that he could leap from a height of twelve or fifteen feet onto sharp stones without pain or discomfort. With this and his barefoot crosscountry runs, Dekka began to prepare him for fire walking.

"I will not be satisfied," said Dekka, "until you can walk without pain over an acre of burning coals."

"No matter how calloused they were, one's feet could never stand that," Peter protested.

"Do what I tell you and you will not be burned."

"Black magic," Peter said.

"Yogism," Dekka corrected him.

While Peter was busy with other activities which did not require Dekka's presence, the young Tibetan roamed far afield in search of herbs. When he had secured the necessary herbs, he made a stew of them, then strained off the leaves and roots, leaving a thick, dark green liquor. With this he massaged Peter's feet and hands morning and night. It was a secret formula, known only to the Yogis, for toughening the skin.

WHEN DEKKA CONSIDERED that Peter's feet were toug3h enough, the preliminaries to fire walking were begun. Peter walked over sharp stones, later over heated pebbles, next over areas of burning twigs, and finally over hot coals.

To be sure, from beginning to end, all of this stretched over almost the entire period of six months, as his feet grew tougher and tougher.

Walking over white hot coals was one of the most amazing sensations he had ever known. He did not feel the heat in his feet at all. The hairs of his calves were singed and scorched off, but his feet felt no pain.

"Yogism!" Dekka declared triumphantly. But by that time Peter had ceased questioning or doubting Dekka's magic.

Another of Dekka's magical formulas was a thin, aromatic, purple liquid. Peter believed that it was derived chiefly from a reddish-purple flower which grew in cracks high up on the mountainsides, and from a resinous gum secured in the jungles. With this liquid Dekka massaged him every morning. The results were almost incredible. A few seconds after the stuff had been rubbed in, Peter's skin began to itch and burn. This itching and burning presently communicated itself to his muscles and, it seemed, to all of his veins. The sensation produced in his brain was one of intense irritability, verging almost on anger—a kind of chemical indignation. The treatment made him restless, and at any stint, it made him difficult to overcome. In wrestling, ju-jitsu and swordsmanship, it made him somehow more determined; and it was building up a feeling of fierceness in him which Dekka was counting on.

At least two hours of every evening were spent in perfecting Peter's command of Tonkinese. He must be able to use the language with the fluency of a native Tongking, because he must present himself to the priest in charge of the contests as a native of Asia, from some particular town or city, and he must be prepared to answer questions relating to family, occupation, and the like.

Arrangements for Peter's family background were now being made by the faithful Ling. A humble cobbler, in Hai-Phong, under an old debt to Peter, would be mentioned as Peter's father; and Peter had spent enough time in Hai-Phong to answer all questions concerning that busy Oriental port with fluency.

He was not worried on that score. It was solely the difficulty of whipping himself into suitable shape physically which gave him his pessimistic moments.

Yet at the end of his first month of training, it is doubtful if any pugilist had ever been in better fighting trim than was Peter Moore. His muscles had grown massive and tough. There was a new clearness in his eyes, a new alertness in his brain. The time came, even by the end of the second month, when he was no longer an easy match for Dekka. He made Dekka work harder to pin his shoulders to the ground.

His swordsmanship was improving. And he could now remain submerged in the lake upwards of two and a half minutes.

In spite of that, he was not progressing rapidly enough to please Dekka. Dekka never complimented him. Dekka was never satisfied. He constantly said that he did not believe Peter could make the grade.

EACH MORNING WHEN Peter awoke on his bed of sharp stones, Dekka had some fresh surprise for him. Once it was a panther. Another time it was a pair of king cobras. Peter was to learn to fight, not only men, but all manner of jungle beasts.

Peter never did learn how Dekka captured these animals. Dekka, with a wise look in his wide-set, high black eyes, would always say:

"Yogism."

"Hypnotism?"

"Call it whatever you want."

"You don't catch them with your bare hands!"

"It's a gift, lad."

Whatever it was, it was effective. The panther, for example, was roped to one of the pepper trees—a leaping, bawling, snarling yellow monster. But its nails had been clipped to the quick!

"How did you do it?" Peter asked.

With that mocking look in his eyes, Dekka answered merely, "Yogism!"

The panther, he explained, was for a friendly little bout.

"I clipped his claws so he couldn't hook your entrails out. His teeth are up to you. Look at those fangs, fellow!"

Peter was looking. That panther might have been a saber-toothed tiger.

"Do I fight him with bare hands?"

"Not quite. You use a ten-inch ebony club."

Dekka fearlessly approached the panther and untied the rope at the tree. The panther snarled and bawled, but it made no attempt to tackle Dekka. It did not seem afraid of Dekka, yet it made no attempt to hurt him.

It was a cold morning, but Peter was already perspiring. Dekka led the panther up a mountain trail. At the top was a small plateau, and in the center of this was a cup-shaped depression, a geological freak. The pit thus formed was about fifteen feet in diameter and nine feet deep, with sheer sides.

Peter stared down into it with misgivings.

"The stunt," Dekka explained cheerfully, "is this. I push old hellfire in from one side, and the minute he jumps in, you jump in from the other side with your club. May the best animal win!"

Peter looked at the little ebony club which Dekka had given him. He gripped his lower lip in his teeth. He had any normal man's respect for a dangerous cat animal. He did not see how he could possibly escape from that pit without losing at least a limb. But he did not back down. One glimpse of Dekka's malicious grin sent the blood pounding angrily into his brain; more blood, as if at command, went racing into his chest and arm muscles until he could feel them swell and harden.

"Ready!" Dekka cried.

"Ready!" Peter snarled, and gripped the club.

His memories of that encounter in the pit with the fresh-caught panther were always a little hazy. Dekka gave the animal a hearty shove. As the panther leaped into the pit, Peter jumped down.

9

THE SUPERMAN

FACE TO FACE with horrible yellow eyes, Peter struck out with the club. The panther roared and leaped back. Its back crashed against the pit wall. It rebounded, sweeping its long, powerful forearms like great hooks, the purpose of this being to sweep the man into an embrace, to claw him to shreds with the powerful hind feet, and to tear the rest of him to ribbons with those enormous yellow fangs.

What Peter remembered perhaps most vividly was the strong stench of the cat animal.

Before the beast could sweep him into that deadly embrace, Peter was delivering nicely timed, powerful blows with the short club.

The panther leaped away; leaped back, always with that sickening scooping motion.

Above the beast's savage screaming, Peter heard Dekka's booming laughter.

A tooth that looked, close up, as large as an elephant's tusk, raked Peter's shoulder. Down came the club. Another scream. Another backing away. Another scrimmage. Horrible yellow confusion.

At close quarters, Peter brought the club down with

savage energy three times. The panther sagged. Glazed eyes peered at Peter from drooping lids.

"Climb out," Dekka ordered.

Peter did so.

"Well?" he said, slapping blood from the gouge on his shoulder.

"Lousy!" Dekka said. "Supposing I hadn't clipped his claws? You'll have to do better than that."

In his strange, savage heart, Dekka enjoyed these contests hugely. To him, they were full repayment for all his labors. And there were many strange contests. During the six months, Peter fought nine or ten panthers, and the claws of the last five were not clipped. There were savage brown bears, there were wild boars with vicious tusks.

Dekka said he selected the bears because of their savage slyness, their unexpected modes of attack; the boars to teach Peter footwork. Peter had always heard that a man facing a wild boar is facing one of the most dangerous of all wild animals. After a few bouts with boars, he preferred panthers. The boars were swift, not so clever as the bears, but possessed of a maniacal intent to kill. His only escape when a boar charged was to leap into the air—to strike with the club as he leaped.

The Tibetan, lounging at the top of the pit, watched with huge enjoyment Peter's mad dances as he avoided the charging boar.

The bears were savagely dangerous foes, too. Their little eyes would turn almost blood-red as the fight progressed; and they would vary their attacks so swiftly, so cunningly, that on several occasions Peter was almost defeated.

Quite as dangerous a foe was the python. Peter learned

not to be so much afraid of their steely coils as of their hammer heads. They used their heads as a man uses his fists—drawing them back swiftly, striking with the speed of lightning and the power of a battering ram. One such blow might readily crush a man's skull. You had to work fast with a python.

BUT THE COBRAS were the worst of all. Peter awoke one morning to find Dekka sitting cross-legged beside him with two cobras coiling about him. They were roaming over Dekka's naked anatomy, yet he was apparently unconcerned.

Peter, staring at these, the deadliest of all known reptiles, suddenly tasted a discharge of electricity from his teeth and felt the hairs at his nape bristle, while icy chills having nothing to do with the dawn wind rollicked down his spine.

"I won't fight those!" Peter protested.

"The hell you won't!—But don't worry, fellow. You'll fight this one. He's been de-fanged. We'll save the other fellow for later. It's a case of 'Pete be nimble, Pete be quick, or Pete will join the dead or the sick.'"

"Where'd you get them?"

"Jungle," laconically.

"How?"

The invariable answer, "Yogism, my lad!"

"How do I fight them?"

"Small pit. *Parang.*" Dekka arose and slung the snakes about his neck as carelessly as a woman adjusts a fur piece. "I've dug the pit."

Peter followed him along the lake to where Dekka had made a small, box-shaped excavation. It was no more than six feet square and about four feet in depth. The cobras seemed to be eight feet long, but were hardly five.

"The trick is this. The cobra and you will go in, as usual, at the same time, I will strike the cobra with a switch to make him sore. He will think that you did it. He will attack you. What could be simpler?"

"Yeah," Peter dryly agreed, "but it's really a game for small children."

"You hold the *parang* point down, as if you were going to stab yourself in the stomach," Dekka explained. "All you have to do is strike it into the base of his brain, just after you have dodged his lunge. Ready?"

Peter grunted. "Be sure you toss in the de-fanged one. I may be slow at first."

"Ready?" Dekka roared.

"Ready!"

Peter grasped the *parang* and jumped as the writhing black snake fell into the pit. Dekka, leaning down, struck it sharply on the hood with a leafy branch cut from one of the pepper trees.

The great hood of the serpent was swollen. Venomous little green eyes focused a split-second on Peter Moore, then the wickedest of all snakes launched its attack. In the open, a cobra is dangerous, for the cobra is the one serpent inhabiting the earth which will follow a man—aggressively attack him. This infuriated specimen was cornered, and madly he coiled and struck, coiled and struck, coiled and struck; so rapidly and with such horrible accuracy that Peter was paralyzed. Had he struck at the snake, he surely would have stabbed himself.

DEKKA DID NOT laugh this morning. He watched, and in a monotonous voice, counted off the seconds.

At the thirty-fifth second, Peter struck the cobra at the base of the hood and the fight was over.

Climbing out, he met Dekka's scornful glare and withering criticism. "If that snake had not been de-fanged, you would have been dying for the past thirty-two seconds. You must learn to be nimble. You must learn speed—speed!"

"Shall I go up against cobras in the contests?"

"You may."

"Let's see how fast you are!"

"You bet!—And this fellow is not de-fanged. Give me that *parang*."

Peter relinquished the *parang*. Dekka tossed the cobra into the pit. He struck it with the switch, threw the switch aside—jumped!

The instant his heels struck the bottom of the pit, the cobra struck. Peter watched breathlessly—and felt sick with discouragement at Dekka's wonderful agility.

The wicked curved steel blade in Dekka's hand came down like a flicker of light as the cobra sprang. The swollen hood, with the writhing black snake behind it, dangled—as if on a roasting spit—from the point of the *parang!*

"Just like that!" Dekka said lightly as he climbed out of that pit of horrors. "Easy does it."

"I'll try it again," Peter said grimly.

"Are you telling me?" the young Tibetan jeered.

A FEW DAYS later, Peter went into the pit again with another cobra, likewise de-fanged. This time he killed it in twelve seconds—ten seconds too late. But that was better than thirty-two seconds. On subsequent mornings he bettered that record. The time came when Dekka trusted him in the pit with a cobra from which neither fangs nor poison sac had been removed. The instant the reptile, with bloated hood, struck, Peter brought the *parang* down in a swift, sure thrust—and instantly killed the snake.

"Good!" Dekka shouted.

That was the first word of commendation he had given Peter since this fantastic period of training had begun, over five months previously. But Peter was neither thrilled nor gratified. He had come to grasp the meaning behind Dekka's jeering attitude. Dekka had had a terrific time, he said, in winning that contest to the high priesthood.

Therefore, if Peter could not beat him in any contest, what was the good of Peter's entering the contests?"

"But I am as fast and as strong as I can ever be," Peter said disconsolately. "In the past month I haven't improved. I can hold my own with you in almost any contest—but what of that?"

"Yes," Dekka agreed. "What of it?"

"What am I to do?"

"Wait. That's all. It will happen or it won't happen. Something inside of you."

"Yogism?" Peter said skeptically.

"Nope. Yourself. Your powers of coördination. They haven't clicked yet. If it doesn't happen, you'll stay as you are. If it does happen, you'll know it. That's all.—A click. But it hasn't happened yet."

It sounded vaguely logical, and at the same time it sounded fantastic. In all his life, Peter had never approached such perfect physical condition as he had now achieved. In any form of combat he was virtually tireless. He could run miles, climb mountains, swim for hours, fight any of the animals which Dekka magically produced, or even fight Dekka himself, without perceptible fatigue. He enjoyed what few men in the world ever enjoy—a full realization of his physical possibilities. His body was a magnificent machine now. The muscles' under his satiny, golden skin were like lazy snakes—ready on the instant to meet any challenge. He was hard, tough, yet not the least muscle-bound or overtrained. Dekka's magical massages attended to that.

In spite of his perfection, Peter was no more than Dekka's equal. At wrestling, he was a match for Dekka. At free-for-all fighting—without weapons—he won as often as he lost. His swordsmanship had improved tremendously, as had his use of the *parang*.

With Peter's improvement, they had taken to using dulled blades and crude armor made of wild bullock hide which covered their chests and abdomens. They wore masks of hardened hide.

It was inevitable that in the more savage of these contests both men suffered innumerable slashes on the arms and legs, even when dulled blades were used.

These cuts were healed overnight by an application of Dekka's magic-working herbs.

By the beginning of the sixth month, Peter could hold his own with Dekka in all forms of combat. Once, Peter would have been delighted with such progress. Now he was disgusted, for he knew that equaling Dekka was not enough; he must excel in every form of combat.

IT LACKED ABOUT a week of the full six months' training period when, one morning, Peter was aware of a curious sensation which took place simultaneously in every part of his body. It was as if, suddenly, a strange chemical had been added to those of which he was composed. As far as his brain was concerned, it took the form of a sharp and amazing clarity, a sense of unbounded vitality. In that same moment, it was as if his muscles were suddenly filled with a strange, exciting new vigor.

In all his life, he had never experienced such a sensation.

At the moment when it occurred, he and Dekka were fighting—a free-for-all. No holds were barred. Anything was fair—hands, elbows, feet, teeth and knees. Peter had been trying to master a feat of Dekka's which had eluded him all along. It was an attack with the feet—hurling the body, feet foremost, through the air, striking at the opponent's head and chest with the soles of the feet. It was a dangerous maneuver for the other fellow, if it was carried out successfully, for the soles of their feet were now almost as hard as rock. A blow struck by a foot so hardened was like a blow from a club.

The new sensation occurred in Peter Moore just as Dekka launched himself through the air. Instead of attempting to sidestep, which was the prescribed defense for such an attack, Peter held his ground. As the Tibetan came hurtling through the air, Peter grabbed each foot. He stiffened his powerful shoulder and back muscles. His biceps stood out like coiling snakes. He heaved.

Dekka went sailing on over his head, high in the air. He landed with a thump on his back, gave a terrific grunt, leaped up and came charging with blazing eyes.

Peter grasped his shoulders. With a sudden heave, he again sent the Tibetan hurtling through the air. Then he closed in. Blows by fists and feet rained on him. He seemed not to feel them. It was as if he had tapped a source of unlimited strength, of inexhaustible endurance. Closing in, with swift blows of his fists, he knocked Dekka unconscious.

When Dekka recovered his faculties, he looked at Peter strangely. "Get the scimitars!" he growled.

Peter got the scimitars, and they put on their hide armor. In six seconds, Peter disarmed Dekka.

"Now the *parangs*," Dekka panted.

It was the same with the *parangs*. They had hardly closed on each other, when Dekka's *parang* went sailing through the air and clattered to the stones.

"Tired?" Dekka gasped.

"No."

"How's your wind?"

"Okay."

"Come on!"

They went to the lake, dived in.

Peter went to the bottom and began counting. Even at the end of five full minutes, on a second-by-second count, his lungs did not frantically demand air. He stayed under four hundred and twenty-five seconds—five seconds over a full seven minutes—before he let go his rock and rose slowly to the surface.

His lungs were not bursting, his heart was not hammering.

Dekka was sitting on the shore, a wry grin on his face.

The young Tibetan brought up his hand to his right temple in a salute.

"You're a better man than I am, Gunga Din," he said. "It

has happened—I saw it happen in your eyes. You're now fit to enter the contests. Maybe you'll win, maybe you won't. But you'll make them know they've been in a battle. I've done all I can for you. You're a superman, Pete. The question is—will I meet you aboard the Luchow—or will I have the job of burning incense over your corpse?"

10

TEMPLE OF THE COILED SERPENT

SEVEN MILES TO the west of Dekka's cave, at the foot of the mountains, was a jungle road which led to the Temple of the Coiled Serpent. When Peter came down from the mountains, this road was thronged with pilgrims, all traveling in the direction of the temple. Tomorrow the fun would begin; that is to say, the elimination contests to determine who would be the new high priest would get under way.

Orientals do not take their temple festivities solemnly. To them, such occasions are holidays. Lu, the genius, knew this, and took full advantage of it. The pilgrims to his temple were going to have wonderful fun, watching men slaughter each other—and later, the sacrifice of a beautiful girl.

With a woven-reed package slung over his shoulder, Peter joined the throng. Most of these pilgrims were from southeastern Asia—Siam, Malaya, Cambodia—but there was a sprinkling of Burmese, East Indians and islanders.

Barefoot, wearing nothing but a deerhide loin covering, Peter strode along the road toward his greatest adventure. His muscles were like spring steel. His eyes were as clear as sapphires. His body had long since ceased to need artificial stain, so tanned was he from head to foot. Dekka had shaved and stained his eyebrows, lashes and hair, had "nicked" the little muscle which gave his outer eye corners an upward twirk, so making him look definitely Oriental. After a week or two, Dekka declared, his eyes would lose that Oriental look and would resume their normal appearance. As for the color of his eyes, Peter had agreed with Dekka that he need not worry, for many Orientals betrayed distant white ancestry by their gray or grayish-blue eyes.

Peter did not permit himself to think of the dangers which lay ahead. It is hard to be in any sense a pessimist when healthy blood is fairly roaring through one's veins. His feeling of tirelessness, of illimitable strength, gave him a sense of zest that was almost intoxicating.

People along that well-traveled road stared at him. Many of them asked, in almost as many languages, "Do you enter the contests?" Among them were bright-eyed young women, traveling with their parents, some with amahs—the Oriental equivalent of American chaperones. Some of the pilgrims were afoot. Others rode donkeys or horses; and whole families rode in two-wheeled carts drawn by oxen or donkeys. A privileged few traveled in supreme Oriental state—on gayly caparisoned elephants.

The reek of strong Oriental perfumes rose from most of the young women. They were in their brightest holiday finery—silks from the hand looms of the Irriwaddi, sarongs from Java, bright jackets and short skirts. Vivid colors—emerald green, royal purple, sapphire blue, blood red, yellow and orange, clothed—or partly clothed—their golden-brown bodies. A happy, singing throng.

PETER FELL IN with an old fellow from Saigon who was

limping along with the aid of a staff. The old man had snow-white hair and a patriarchal snowy beard.

His little black eyes stared at Peter's magnificent shoulders, inspected his powerful biceps, ran on down his lean hard body to his powerful legs.

"Are you entering the contests?" he asked, in Tonkinese.

"Yes, father."

"Blessings of Lu!—Blessings of Buddha!"

"A hundred ripe years to you, father!"

But a cloud had passed over Peter's fine optimism. Blessings of Lu! That master charlatan!

They climbed a rise in the road. Suddenly, in a hollow in the hills below them, the Temple of the Coiled Serpent materialized, as if, by some trick of Oriental magic, where there had been nothing was suddenly reared an architectural monstrosity of blue stone. The structure fairly took Peter's breath away. It was terrific, fantastic, grotesque, obscene.

It stood on an eminence a hundred feet above the surrounding jungle; a natural or artificial hill measuring at least three-quarters of a mile across at the summit. On this eminence, this plateau, stood the most infamous, most notorious of all Oriental temples. An architectural replica, on a gigantic scale, of a coiled snake.

Flat coil on flat coil, it rose up into the amethystine sky, each coil perhaps forty feet in diameter, and of pale blue stone so intricately laid that the individual stones could not be detected. Twenty of these monstrous coils!

Descending the hill toward it, Peter counted them. Twenty times forty! Approximately, eight hundred feet into the sky the Temple of the Coiled Serpent reared its fascinating ugliness. Eight hundred feet above the artificial plateau poised the gigantic and incredible head of the stone monster, its mouth agape, its titanic fangs exposed, its eyes glittering. These eyes were composed of great sheets of precious stones, glittering and gleaming with all the evil of those cobras' eyes which Dekka had tossed into the pit for Peter to fight.

It was almost unbelievable, the close similarity of this coiled solid mass of stone to the vicious jungle serpent after which it had been copied on such a gigantic scale.

Had it been a live snake, it would have stretched out, uncoiled, to a length of over thirty miles!

About the circular base, on the plateau on which the temple stood, roved lean and hungry black leopards— guardians of the temple door! They were ringed in by a fence of tall bronze spears set in a masonry floor. And about this ring was another ring where countless people roved about, staring at the temple and watching the leopards.

This whole arrangement became more understandable under closer inspection. The base of the temple was circular. Surrounding the base was the circular fence of bronze spears. In the ring-shaped space between temple wall and fence roved the black leopards. And in the outer ring-shaped space, which extended to the edge of the plateau, the public—the pilgrims—were free to roam. A dozen stairways of white marble led up the slope of the hill to this plateau.

Peter, staring, thought: "In that temple—in the very heart of it—is the sapphire skull. Shall I succeed in stealing it?"

Again he wondered what the skull contained. Dekka

did not know. Dekka had spent a year with that skull, and he did not believe it had an opening. To tamper with that skull, of course, meant instant death. And Dekka had not then been courting death.

11

THE GLADIATORS

AS PETER DESCENDED the hill, other wonders developed. The greatest of these was an arena. Dekka had mentioned it, but Peter was not prepared for its magnificence. The stadium was of white stone—perhaps white marble—white as snow against the deep, lush green of the surrounding jungle. Within, once the pilgrims had comfortably seated themselves, the priesthood contests would be held.

In the small and large clearings all about the hill on which the monstrous temple stood were small structures of stone and wood. At first Peter thought that these, in imitation of the great Buddhistic pagodas, notably the Schwe Dagon in Rangoon, were smaller shrines. They proved, on closer acquaintance, to be *salas*—rest houses, where the pilgrims lived during the time consumed by the contests and the ceremonies.

Again he returned his eyes to the temple, to the plateau on which it stood. There must have been at least thirty black leopards in that ring-shaped enclosure. Except for secret, underground entrances, no man could enter the temple, under the present arrangements, without climbing over the high bronze fence and crossing the leopard enclosure. The spot was as practical as it was fantastic. A man who ventured into the leopard enclosure would be swiftly annihilated by those savage, starving black beasts.

Peter followed the crowd and ascended the hill to the round plateau. The area between the leopard enclosure and the edge of the hill was wider than he had estimated. Thousands of pilgrims could stand here and watch the ceremonies.

Through the bars, he studied the temple entrance. It was a huge arch, easily one hundred feet in height by two hundred in width. A bronze grille covered the opening, so that the leopards could not intrude into the temple. Beyond this grille, within the temple, was a round pit in which charcoal smoldered. Glancing at it, Peter shuddered.

Into this pit the dead girl whose throat Lu had cut, at the climax of the ceremonies, was to be thrown by the newly appointed high priest!

Men in flame-red robes moved about the pit of fire.

Peter wrenched his eyes away, still shuddering. He was standing near a wide gate, now closed, which gave upon the leopard compound and faced the temple entrance. Approximately halfway between this gate and the temple entrance was a perfectly round pool of water about six feet in diameter. He presumed that this was the leopards' drinking water. Dekka had not mentioned it. But Dekka had warned him that each year there were many changes, many innovations.

He returned his eyes to the pit of fire. Beyond this pit the famous marble stairway began. From where Peter stood, he could easily see to the top of it—one thousand and one marble steps which led to the platform on which Lu, the

Blue Scorpion, sat within comfortable view of his thousands of worshipful subjects.

The last of Peter's optimism ebbed away. For a moment, the folly of his expedition forcibly impressed itself upon him. Changed as he was, wouldn't Mr. Lu recognize him?

Then his courage, his feeling of exuberant recklessness returned. Nothing, he vowed, would prevent him from taking his revenge on Mr. Lu!

FROM DEKKA PETER Moore had learned what he must do now. He must present himself to the retiring head priest and announce his intention of entering the contests.

The contestants lived apart from the other pilgrims, in a large teakwood *sala* on the western side of the temple mound. Peter found this *sala* without difficulty. It was filled with young Orientals. Most of them, like himself, were clear-eyed, tall, wide-shouldered, muscular young men—men in the pink of condition.

In the center of the *sala*, Peter found the head priest, a man no older than himself, a young Chinese who somewhat resembled Dekka. He was several inches taller than Peter, and he had a physique which reminded Peter of pictures he had seen of Roman warriors.

Shrewd dark eyes scrutinized Peter. These eyes ran from his forehead to his ankles. Firm lips parted to reveal large white teeth. He said, in Tonkinese, "You are a contestant?"

"Yes."

"You are aware of the dangers?"

"Yes."

The eyes hardened a little. "Last year, of one hundred and nine men who entered, seventy-three were killed. This year, the contests are even more dangerous. Do you still wish to enter?"

"Yes."

"What is your name?"

"Lak-Ching."

"What is your city?"

"Hai-Phong."

The high priest wrote these answers on a sheet of parchment.

"Who is your father?"

"Lak-Yan."

"Occupation?"

"Cobbler."

"Your occupation?"

"Cobbler's apprentice."

The high priest asked other questions, rapidly, as if he were interested in Hai-Phong. Peter answered them glibly; but his heart was beating a little more rapidly than was normal. He was entering the first danger zone.

AT THE CONCLUSION of the questions, the high priest clasped his hand firmly.

"My name is Lao Li," he said. "I welcome you to the contests. I hope you will win."

With a sigh of relief, Peter watched Lao Li approach a group of grim newcomers.

The *sala*, open on all sides, was the object of much curiosity. Men and women, young and old, were strolling about under the trees, or boldly approaching the young men, examining them as if they were cattle.

Peter suffered this same indignity. Men and women

came up to him, pinched his muscles, prodded his chest and back, commented as if he were deaf and dumb.

But he was pleased to hear a very old man say of him, "This fellow has a chance. He is made of tempered steel."

"It is all luck," an old woman said, laughingly.

"But it is all fun."

"Hai-yah!" the old man crowed lustily.

PETER THOUGHT HE knew a great deal about Oriental human nature, but he was destined to know much more before many days passed, and not all of it was pleasant.

Among those who came to look over the crop of contestants were many temple priests.

There were two classes of these, the ordinary priests who wore gray robes, and the priests of the holy fire, in their flame-red robes. As though they were the representatives of some aristocratic class, the priests of the holy fire treated the common priests with contempt. But all were young and powerful looking men. Peter knew that they were really little more than watchdogs—chosen for their ability to guard the precious sapphire skull.

Wandering about the *sala,* answering impertinent questions, letting himself be poked, pinched and prodded, Peter suddenly saw, lounging against a roofpost, the most powerful looking man he had ever seen anywhere in the world, in all his life.

This, he promptly decided, was a sweeping assertion. He took another look—and verified it.

The fellow looked Mongolian, with his broad upper cheeks, his close-set eyes, his unruly thatch of blue-black hair—similar, in some respects, to the stranger whom Peter

The monster had broken the backs of five other men.

had discovered hiding behind the vermilion wall piece in the private room of Hong Kong's opium king.

A boy whispered, "His name is Chang Kong."

A woman who accompanied the boy answered, "Chang Kong will easily win."

Peter looked over Chang Kong very thoroughly, and was forced to admit that, if appearances counted, he must share this opinion of the man. Chang Kong was approximately six feet five inches in height. He looked as strong as a tree, as powerful as a water buffalo—and as dangerous. Unlike most Orientals, he was hairy. His arms, legs and chest were fairly matted with coarse, curly black hair, almost like fur. His arms, like logs, were folded over his massive, swelling chest. Peter had never seen shoulders so broad, a chest so thick, muscular development so perfect. Here was, indeed, the super-perfect human animal. His eyes, under heavy lids, were scrutinizing Peter Moore as one fighting dog might scrutinize another before the fray. In these eyes was insolence—and contempt.

As he stared at Peter, a probable foe, his thick, coarse lips parted and he grinned. It was more of a sneer than a smile, and there was nothing in the least amiable about it. Nothing but contempt—conceit—mockery.

People surrounded Chang Kong, frankly expressing their admiration of a man so powerful, so wonderfully made. The hairy giant made gestures with his eyebrows, smiled complacently, and even nodded at some of the expressions of flattery. He was a wonderful figure of a man—and he knew it!

A voice beside Peter said, in Siamese, "That fellow could lift a mountain by the roots. What chance have we?"

Peter turned and looked into a sad young face, that of a young man whom he had seen talking a few minutes previously with the high priest. Another contestant, of course. His skin was a rich golden brown. His features had the calmness, and something of the conventional Oriental beauty of a carved Buddha; and his eyes were the sad, dreamy eyes of Siam. He was as tall as Peter, and he was magnificently built.

IN HIS MUSICAL, liquid voice, this man said, again in Siamese, "Do you chance to speak my tongue?"

Peter answered, "Only a little."

"My name is Para Khan."

"Mine is Lak-Ching," Peter said.

"I come from Chengmei."

"I, from Hai-Phong."

"May Buddha bless you with abundant luck!"

"Luck," Peter answered, "will consist of not being matched against that fellow."

Para Khan sighed. "I have been training for two years to enter these contests. Why, I do not know. My heart is not in this. I am obeying the commands of a prince. I am strong, I am quick, I am clever. But you cannot teach a frog to leap a mountain, or a snail to swim across the sea."

The high priest approached them. He carried over one arm a cluster of sapphire blue silk cords.

"You are to wear one of these cords," he said, "to indicate that you are contestants."

Each of the young men accepted a cord and knotted it about his wrist.

The high priest approached the hairy giant, who showed his great white teeth in a grin. Peter heard him say to the priest:

"Lao Li, you waste time giving these cords to anyone else. I am already the winner. There is not a contestant here that I cannot whip with a single hand. I am faster, stronger, cleverer than any contestants on your lists. These contests will be a waste of good time."

"You can prove that in the arena," Lao Li said, unperturbed.

The giant laughed. "What a treat I will give these pilgrims!"

Once again, Peter carefully examined this creature of wonderful perfection; his splendid shoulders, his massive hairy chest, his magnificent biceps and leg muscles. Across the giant's chest and stomach were ridges of muscles like the corrugations of a steel roof. Each little movement of that tremendous body brought into play masses and layers and coils of powerful muscles.

Thoughtfully, Peter left the *sala*. He wanted to get the hairy giant out of his mind; also, he had been saddened by the attitude of the young man from Siam.

The sun had set. A rosy light now inflamed the sky and colored the world. Peter strolled toward the arena where the contests would be held. It was a great oval of white marble, with seats sufficient to accommodate perhaps eighty thousand spectators. There were many people wandering about. Many of them would sleep on the marble benches, to make sure of a good seat for tomorrow's activities.

It all brought to Peter's mind stories he had heard of the old Roman gladiatorial combats. Young men pitted against young men in the arena, in fights to the death!

As he went here and there, people spoke to him, openly admired him. These girls he saw were of various nationalities. The sapphire blue cord at his wrist marked him as a contestant—a man of importance. There were many speculations as to whether or not he would be alive by this time tomorrow night. And these speculations were uttered in a gay mood. He was, after all, nothing but an entertainer. He would kill or be killed!

NIGHT CLOSED DOWN with tropic swiftness. Brilliant stars and a moon appeared; and with them, the released fragrance of the jungle flowers, a perfume so sweet, so intoxicating that it made the brain whirl.

Peter sat down on one of the marble benches and looked at the arena, drenched with moonlight. A girl approached him, faced him, looked down into his eyes; a girl slim and golden, who wore little except the bright orange *sarong* which fell from her waist to her slim, pretty ankles.

Peter glanced at her. She was a Shan girl, from far away Burma. Her walk was a graceful gliding—the "elephant walk," so-called, and infinitely more graceful than its name would indicate—a smooth, voluptuous motion in which the body softly, slowly sways like a young palm tree in the trade wind.

But she was, he presently discovered, not a Shan girl. She was Annamese—a golden thing from Hai-Phong, as he learned to his immediate embarrassment.

She pronounced, in a silvery low voice, the Tonkinese, "What is thy name?"

"Lak-Ching."

"Mine is Zari. Is that not a pretty name? Is it not like music?"

Peter made the proper answers. Then she said, "Whither art thou?"

"Hai-Phong."

"*Aie!* Not truly! That is my home, too. Strange, I have not noticed a man of such nobility. I thought you were a prince. You must have kept yourself hidden in a cistern!"

She slipped into the seat beside him. Her bright lips were parted, her teeth were pearl-white, her eyes were brighter than the stars they reflected. The brilliant moon lighted the curves and roundnesses and hollows of her slim, graceful little body. Shamelessly, she inclined toward him. Parted lips breathed the perfume of cinnamon seed into his face—a hot and alluring scent, issuing from lips as ripe, as luscious as these.

Zari cuddled against him, whispered, "Now I am not

afraid." Yet she was trembling, shivering. "You will be a high priest, and I will be chosen, too. I have followed you about since you came here. You never gave me so much as a sidelong glance. Am I not beautiful?"

"Yes."

"That is why I am afraid. I am too beautiful. I will be chosen."

"Why did you come?"

"My grandfather forced me to come. He wishes me to be chosen. If I am not chosen, he will kill me! Tell me what to do! You are brave and strong and clever. Give me strength, too. Give me courage!"

Zari's golden body was shaking.

Peter said, uncomfortably, "You may not be chosen. And if you are not, you should run away from your grandfather."

She stiffened. "Can there be the slightest doubt of my being chosen? Am I not the most beautiful girl among them all?"

Peter looking at her little upturned face in the moonlight, willingly and honestly answered, "You are very beautiful."

She cried, "There is doubt in your voice! Is not my presence as soothing as shade after heat? Is not my form as graceful as a young tree? Are not the palms of my hands like lotus blossoms?"

"Yes," Peter groaned.

"*Hola!* Now you groan! I think you are a *bilu*. You have red eyes and you cast no shadow!"

Zari jumped up, angrily.

Peter was learning something new about Oriental feminine nature.

"I come to you for courage—you give me scorn! I offer you my love, because in a few days my throat may be slit from ear to ear—and you mock me! *Bilu!*"

ZARI STALKED AWAY. Zari had been grossly insulted!— As if there could be any question of her winning the coveted privilege of having her lovely young neck slit from ear to ear!

Peter was sorry. Zari was very beautiful. Perhaps she actually was sufficiently beautiful to have her throat slit from ear to ear. But there might be others more beautiful. Peter, denied the sight of women for six months, had been dangerously stirred by the closeness of that golden young body to his. It was as well that he had said the wrong things. Beautiful girl and feats of physical endurance do not mix.

Yet he was incredulous. Never, assembled in one place, had he seen so many beautiful Oriental girls. It was as if the East had been combed for its loveliest maidens. And the threat of death hanging over them made them reckless. So soon to die, as they felt, why not make the most of love now? That seemed to be their theme.

Others approached him with languishing eyes, with frankly displayed charms. In one sense, they were moths to so many flames—the perfect manhood of Asia, assembled here for the bloody contests.

All this was in the very air, with the perfume of the jungle flowers, the drenching moonlight—"tomorrow, or the day after, you and I may be dead. Let us make the most of love and life now—tonight!" It was Oriental fatalism.

What Peter found hardest to understand was the willingness of these beautiful young girls to enter a monstrous form of beauty contest—for the privilege of having their throats cut. Not willing—eager! Jealous of each other for that supreme privilege. One who did not know the Orient would have found it hard to understand. Peter Moore, however, knew the Orient, but even he found it very hard to understand.

Yet almost as difficult to grasp was the willingness of the young men to enter contests from which only a few would emerge alive. It was safe to say that none of them were motivated by an ambition at all similar to Peter's. These handsome, physically perfect young men; these lovely, slim, golden girls; were all moths attracted to the flame of Lu's fanatical religion—worship of a sapphire skull supposed to contain a living human brain—a thing of magical powers! It was fantastic, monstrous, unbelievable.

Where women were concerned, Peter was romantically faithful to an ideal. He could not be otherwise. For him, there was but one ideal of feminine perfection, and he would have matched Susan O'Gilvie's beauty with any of these delicious Oriental maidens. He had never seen a girl lovelier in every respect than was the girl whom he had so determinedly put out of his life on that night, months ago, in Hong Kong.

IN A TINY *sala*, on the outskirts of this strange jungle settlement, that very girl was arranging her belongings. Fearful of being recognized by some of Lu's men, the richest girl in the Orient had reached the environs of the Temple of the Coiled Serpent late that afternoon. With her was an elderly Chinese woman, her *amah*, her chaperone. This woman, Chula by name, had been selected by the owner of the jade shop on Brah Basah Road, in Singapore, to accompany the trouble hunter on her expedition into the very jaws of death.

Chula, richly rewarded for her pains and the risks she ran, had been admirably selected. She had once been a pilgrim to the Temple of the Coiled Serpent. She knew on just what points the girl for sacrifice was chosen from among the hundreds of over-willing maidens.

So close to her goal, Susan was in a state bordering on terror. From afar she watched the large *sala* of the gladiators.—If she could have known that the young man whose death she was planning to avenge was here—alive—healthy beyond the health of normal men—almost within earshot of her voice!

But she did not know. She could not guess. For six months now, she had mourned his death; and in her heart burned the unquenchable flame of determination. To avenge his murder! To stab to the heart of the cruel Mr. Lu, with the thin, wicked little dagger which she carried!

The excitement made her restless. Gladiators and maidens all about her in the moonlight, love-making! A stream of curious pilgrims came to look upon her, to judge her prospects of winning the opportunity to have her beautiful throat slashed, just as they judged the chances of the gladiators to die by tomorrow night or the night after!

Weird, fantastic, horrible! But it accomplished one important object. It gave her courage. It fired her anew with her fierce determination to end the life of the man who had become her mortal enemy!

12

PREPARATION FOR BATTLE

PETER DID NOT sleep in the large *sala* set aside for the contestants, but on the hard stony ground under a gnarled old ebony tree nearby. By now, he was unaccustomed to a mattress or coverings. Dekka had told him solemnly that by sleeping close to the bare ground he was brought into contact with the mysterious mother-earth currents, the great life-building, energy-restoring power.

A hard-headed skeptic, Peter took little stock in many of these fantastic theories of Dekka's. But he had learned to like sleeping on stony ground, with no coverings and no mattress, and he followed his usual custom tonight.

He had hardly thrown himself on the ground when a voice said, in Siamese, "Do you mind if I sleep here, too?"

It was Para Khan, the young Siamese who was entering the contests so much against his wishes. He carried a number of long grass mats, and when Peter welcomed him, he arranged these in a neat pile for a mattress.

Peter understood Para Khan was lonely and unhappy. He considered Peter a friend, and Peter devoutly hoped that he would not be matched against this tragic young man in any of the contests.

Para Khan brought word that more than a hundred

young men had entered the lists, and that more would arrive during the night. Peter fell asleep with the musical voice of the young Siamese in his ears murmuring a Buddhistic prayer.

"Great Mercy, Great Mercy, save from misery, save from evil, O, broad, great, efficacious, responsive Kuan Yin Buddha!"

Peter slept soundly the night through. He was awakened by the deep clanging of the temple gong, tolling in wide-spaced, tremendous strokes. Even in this slight detail, the genius of Lu was manifested. There must have been a great amount of silver in the content of that mighty bell, for its voice was not harsh, not strident, but a deep musical booming. Yet within its massive vibrations there was a note like a threat, a warning. Peter had heard most of the great temple bells of the Orient, yet none he had heard could equal in grandeur the stirring, rounded booming of this.

Para Khan was not yet awake. He was sleeping on his side, his lips parted, his hand curled up under his cheek like a sleeping child. In spite of his magnificent physique, he looked so harmless and so innocent that Peter was suddenly aware of a terrific rising resentment against Lu.

With his package over his shoulder, Peter followed a path down to a brook that leaped and sang over moss-grown stones. Here, he rubbed himself with the purple lotion from one of the three jugs he had brought along. The sky was still black, but pierced by radiant stars. Dawn came, a swift, bloody flush on the eastern sky, as he was finishing his brisk rub-down. His skin, as always, began to sting and burn; and this stinging, from the magical liniment, entered his veins until his muscles burned and swelled and the mists of sleep swiftly evaporated from his brain. He felt, after the preparation had begun to take effect, even more irritable than usual, and his indignation against Mr. Lu increased.

Breakfast, at the gladiators' *sala* was identical with last night's meal—great bowls of steaming rice, quantities of boiled fish and raw meat.

AFTER BREAKFAST, THE contests were to begin. The line of march lay between avenues of people—mostly young girls in their finery, for today was the real beginning of the holiday—the fête of blood and sacrifice to Lu and the sapphire skull. These girls were exotically and excitingly beautiful in the gorgeous blue and golden satins of north China, the *panungs* of Siam, the *longyies* and *engyies* of Burma, the brilliant *sarongs* of Malaya, Java and the archipelagoes—a gay, bizarre, perfumed, powdered, chattering throng of golden-skinned beauties calling out blessings and messages of luck to their favorites.

As he neared the gladiators' entrance to the arena Peter saw the little Annamese girl of the previous evening. Zari was indeed beautiful—a slim, golden goddess. Her eyes, as she stared at him, were blurred with tears.

"*Bilu!*" she shouted, but without venom now. "I hope you are brave enough!"

"Mango blossom!" he called back. "I hope you are beautiful enough!"

She screamed, "Die with my name on your lips! It will bring me luck!"

A jeering voice behind him cried, "*Hi-yah,* brave one! Die with the name of Chang Kong on your lips! A fit ending!"

It was the hairy giant, striding along, clad, as were all of the other male contestants, in nothing but a loin cloth. His massive arms were folded on his chest. In the strong glare of the tropical morning sunlight, he was a brown god who strode the earth—magnificent, with the air of a man whom no one could defeat.

Peter recalled Dekka's doubts. "You will be up against at least a hundred of the toughest, smartest lads in the whole Far East—human gorillas who have been training for this, some of them, for years—since they were kids!"

There were, Peter understood, a total of one hundred and thirty contestants. And the lists were now closed.

The great marble stadium was apparently filled to the very last seat; packed with men and women, old and young, who had made this pilgrimage from every part of the Orient, from most western Turkestan to farthest Mongolia. Tens of thousands of them. The sight filled him with a species of awe.

Glancing up and about at the thousands of yellow and brown and black faces, he saw the tremendous power of Lu—and appreciated his wonderful showmanship, his publicity genius. Lu had given these people a perverted hideous religion—given them what they wanted, for it satisfied their queerly twisted Oriental brains.

Peter marvelled again at this gathering of beautiful young women, all jealous of the chance to be selected for sacrifice.

Once again, he felt the boiling waves of fury at the diabolical genius of Lu. But his brain was clear—clearer, he was certain, than it had ever been in his life. This horrible religion, built upon the legend of a man's fall from a cliff! If he could only possess the sapphire skull, make off with it, destroy it, he would break Lu's hold forever upon these fanatical worshippers. For what they worshipped, in their strange Oriental minds, was not the man Lu, but the human brain in the sapphire skull!

By the time the sun was high enough to be warm, the contestants were assembled at one end of the great arena. It was covered with fresh, hard-packed white sand, free of even the smallest stones—white sand, no doubt selected because it would show spilled blood the better!

THE HIGH PRIEST was striding about in those snowy satin robes which these young men were to fight, and many of them to die, for the privilege of wearing. He was gathering the contestants about him in a semicircle, giving instructions.

The first contest was to be a fight without weapons, the entrants to fight in pairs. No holds were barred. Nothing was barred. Each man strove to vanquish his opponent as best he could, with the weapons nature had given him—hands, feet, knees, elbows, teeth, fingernails.

Peter Moore's heart was beginning to hammer with the excitement of the approaching moment; his muscles to swell and harden with the anticipation of primitive conflict. Most of the contestants, he saw, were pale. Some were trembling. All were grim.

Then he saw the hairy giant, with his grin of supreme self-confidence. Chang Kong was looking at him, baring his teeth. Peter met his eyes steadily, then glanced on to Para Khan, the sad young Siamese. Para Khan, with arms at sides, was staring into the clear, sapphire blue of the heavens with a faraway expression, thinking Buddha only knew what melancholy thoughts. And once again, Peter hoped that Para Khan would not be his opponent in any of these contests.

The high priest was giving out short bamboo sticks, one to each contestant. Each stick was numbered, and for each number there was a duplicate. Each man, upon receiving his stick, was to find the holder of the same number. This man would be his opponent.

Peter drew Number 36. He considered this a good omen. Twelve, or any multiple thereof, had always been a lucky number, he believed. He went about the crowd, calling his number.

Presently he found his opponent—a lean, hard, wiry youth of about his own age, and perhaps an inch taller. He was a slit-eyed Chinese, with knife scars on both cheeks.

"Thirty-six?" Peter said.

"Thirty-six?" the Chinese snapped. "And the thousand curses of En-Zann upon you!"

Lao Li, the high priest was giving last-minute instructions above the impatient calls and laughter of the crowd. It is a mistake to assume that Oriental peoples lack a sense of fun, though it is true that this sense of fun is quite different from that of men of Western civilization. Orientals love to see a man killed; they will watch a man drowning, will laugh until he is breathless, and will not throw him so much as a stick of wood to save him.

Peter was listening to the high priest with increasing nervousness. The contestants were to line up, facing each other in two rows which were to extend the length of the field—each man facing the man who had drawn the number corresponding to him.

The opponents faced each other a dozen feet apart. Each pair was separated by about fifty feet. They were to watch the high priest, who would stand at one end of the arena holding a red handkerchief. When he tossed the handkerchief into the air, they were to engage in a fight to the death.

The rules were simple: when a man killed, rendered unconscious, or sufficiently crippled his antagonist, the victor was to notify one of the temple priests, who were to act as referees or supervisors. As soon as possible the priests would match the winner with another triumphant gladiator. There would be no rests, either during or between fights. No appeals for quarter would be listened to.

"Remember," the high priest said, "once a man is entered in these contests, withdrawal or refusal to continue means instant death!"

The two rows of young men were lined up. The crowd was beginning to roar now. All eyes were on the high priest, in whose hand was the fragment of flaming-red color.

He looked down the lines. He lifted his hand. Peter took a deep breath. He was not afraid or uncertain. He knew just what he intended to do to the slit-eyed Chinese facing him a dozen feet away. He was conscious of a bristling feeling along his spine.

Down the line, halfway between him and the high priest, he again saw Chang Kong, the hairy giant. Chang Kong's thick lips were skinned back from his teeth in a grimace which reminded Peter of pictures of wrathful Oriental gods. His powerful hands were curled. He was poised for a running leap.

Out of the corner of his eye, Peter saw the fleck of flame-red in Lao Li's hand toss into the air. That instant a roar like the breaking of a titanic tidal wave crashed upon the air from the throats of the crowd. The contests were on!

13

THE BACK-BREAKER

PETER SPRANG FORWARD. His opponent did likewise. They met with a crash of bones on bones, flesh on flesh. They separated. Talons raked down, missed Peter's face, clawed into his chest, sank in, as if his opponent would tear out his flesh by the handful. That was obviously his intention.

Peter simultaneously learned that his opponent had no skill. He was a powerful brute, savagely intent on killing by sheer strength. Peter disengaged himself from the raking talons, and as the Chinese lunged, he struck him with killing blows in the face—the nose, chin, eyes.

His antagonist was screaming with rage. He sprang back from that fury of fists, and in his rage, leaped up and down like an infuriated ape, screaming, spitting blood. Then he charged again, and in the same style, with fingers distended, mouth open, his brain fixed on only one plan of action—to tear his enemy to shreds with those powerful, hooked fingers, those long, sharp talons.

Blood was streaming from the long gouges in Peter's chest. He varied his own attack this time—leaped at him feet foremost—drove the rock-hard soles of his feet like battering rams into Slit-Eyes' face. The Chinese staggered and reeled.

Peter, at the completion of that attack, landed on hands and feet with the springiness of a cat. He was instantly up, following his smashing attack with swinging, smashing fists.

He did not hear the roar of the crowd, but he remembered it later. In lulls, however, he heard the sounds of the sixty-four fights taking place all about him. Already, there was plenty of blood. The hard-packed white sand was spattered and blotched with it. Men were shouting or screaming with rage and agony. Men were down, limp, broken, unconscious, dying, dead. It was as fantastic as it was horrible. From a corner of his eye, he saw one man get his neck broken; heard the snap of it, and the victim's short, awful scream as he died.

But Peter had no time to be a spectator. His Chinese antagonist was a thing of rawhide and steel. Groggy, he still fought for holds, for areas of Peter's face or body to rake with those horrible claws.

Peter was trying to finish him off, but it appeared for a time as if he would never succeed. His chance came when the Chinese lifted both hands above his head with the intention of making another rush. Peter leaped in, and with all the strength of back and arms he sent terrific smashing blows into Slit-Eyes' jaw. In swift succession, he delivered more than a dozen such slugging hits before the Chinese collapsed limply in the bloody sand at his feet.

The Chinese was down and out—eliminated! And Peter had won his first victory.

LOOKING ABOUT HIM for a priest to whom to apply for

his next match, he became aware for the first time of what was happening, had happened, in the arena about him.

It was as if a nightmare were being enacted here. All about him, men were lying in the sand, unconscious or dead. He saw men tearing at each other like fiends with their claws. He saw horrible, fantastic things; a man having one ear torn off; a man in the grip of a jujitsu expert having his arms and legs systematically broken at the joints. Worst of all, he saw a man deliberately gouge out an opponent's eye—rip it out of the socket by the roots.

It was gruesome, unbelievable. Steam seemed to rise from the arena as from a hellish cauldron. The faces of the tens of thousands of spectators were specks which emitted a continuous terrible roaring.

One of the gray-robed priests tapped Peter on the shoulder. He spun about; caught a momentary glimpse of a dark brown man, gleaming and glittering with sweat; bleeding from a gash under one eye. He was panting. With a sudden wild gleam of the eyes, he hurled himself on Peter.

Taken by surprise, Peter crashed to the ground. He was on his back. But before the brown man could move, Peter had jerked up his knees to his stomach and kicked. His new opponent went hurtling backward, falling on his side.

Both came to their feet at the same time. Another headlong; head-on rush. A crashing impact of bodies. Peter stepped back, and once again resorted to his fists. With fists, he had a certain advantage, because scientific fist fighting is practically unknown in the Far East.

He slugged the brown man in the jaw once, twice, three times, so swiftly that his fists were like flickers of light. The brown man staggered, went to one knee. He was out.

Some spark far within him was fighting to send him back to his feet, to fight on. But that inner spark could not rally his powers. He was out. His eyes rolled up. He fell face forward, lay limp.

Peter's next opponent was a thick-shouldered Burmese. Once again, Peter fell back on the use of his fists. And once again, with terrific in-fighting, he knocked his man out.

The next was a tall, pale yellow man with incredibly long arms, and large hands with knobby knuckles. They were powerful hands—the hands of a strangler. Strangling, in fact, was the mode of attack he favored. He clutched Peter's throat in his hands, and tried to hold him off.

Peter brought up both feet with smashing blows to his enemy's ribs. The strangling hands let go. Once again, fists. One-two to the belly. One, two, three, four to the jaw. The strangler sat down, feebly waving his hands, and fell gently over on his side.

Peter stepped back as this one fell, and for the first time since the fighting had begun, saw Chang Kong. The hairy giant was in the act of killing a man. His victim was a smear of blood from head to feet.

As Peter watched, Chang Kong grasped this man by the neck and the knee, brought him slowly down, face upward, through the air to a bent knee. One of the hairy hands remained at his victim's neck. The other slid up to the man's thigh. Chang Kong began to bend him down, forcing his back into an arch. The obvious purpose of this was to break the man's back.

The victim began to scream. His eyes bulged, his tongue protruded as he feebly tried to extricate himself from that agonizing position. Chang Kong was laughing down into the helpless man's face. He increased the pressure at neck and thigh, bringing his knee higher, into the small of the man's back. There was a sharp snapping sound as the man's backbone broke.

CHANG KONG TOSSED the feebly convulsing body to the sand and clapped his hands together. Peter was striding toward him, but Chang Kong did not at first see him. His eyes were bloodshot and wild. Saliva was drooling from his lips. Here, indeed, was a man drunk with the lust to kill. Peter later learned that Chang Kong had broken the backs of five men in this same manner.

At the moment, Peter was possessed only with the idea to kill this hairy monster. In all his life, he had never been so boiling mad. He wanted to consult no priest.

He snapped at Chang Kong, "Come on, you ape, and break my back!"

Chang Kong brushed a hairy fist across his eyes, blinked, stared. His eyes steadied. His grin became wolfish. *"Hai— yah!"* he said, and sprang.

Peter met that attack with driving fists. He twisted to avoid a sledgehammer knee intended for his groin. Powerful hands seized his shoulders, spun him about. A hand clasped the back of his neck in a vise-like grip. A great brown thumb came up swiftly toward Peter's left eye. Chang Kong's simple and primitive intention was to gouge his eyes out before he did anything else to him!

For a moment, Peter was helpless in the terrific clasp of that hand on his neck. He could not writhe free. As the thumb swept up, he closed his eye and struck out simultaneously with fists and feet—feet to the shins, fists to the heart and solar plexus. All the power he possessed went into those blows. Each of them brought a grunt from the hairy giant.

Chang Kong let go Peter's neck, stepped back. Unhesitatingly, Peter followed. He slugged Chang Kong six times on the chin—and the giant, backing away, merely laughed at him.

Peter followed. One fist went smashing into Chang Kong's mouth, another into the pit of his stomach. This time the man snarled and stopped backing away. But his laughter was gone; his grin was wiped away. Tight-lipped, he sprang at Peter, suddenly enfolding him with his hairy arms, hugging him to him in an embrace as deadly as the famous death grip of the grizzly bear.

This was the preliminary to his back-breaking maneuver. He would render Peter helpless, weaken him with that crushing squeeze, then grasp his neck and one leg and force him down over his knee.

But Peter did not tolerate that bear-hug, and he knew the tricks of infighting. He rained blows so vicious on Chang Kong's unprotected middle that the giant quickly released him. Once again Peter followed this attack with his iron-hard feet.

Chang Kong, frustrated in his attempts at a quick victory, now adopted Peter's methods. He doubled up his fists and came charging. One mighty fist struck Peter in the shoulder. It spun him completely about; but he was in time to fend off a similar blow with an elbow.

Then they settled down to an exchange of fists. This was the method of fighting with which Peter was most familiar. It was not Chang Kong's way of fighting; but conceit made him adopt it. He would show this upstart that he could defeat him by any method of fighting he might select.

Perhaps it was fortunate for Peter that the hairy giant was so richly endowed with vanity, for it levelled off inequalities. In spite of his physical perfection, Peter was not the muscular equal of this giant. He was David, face to face with Goliath; and what he lacked in strength must be made up in cleverness. Goliath did not appreciate that his most violent blows were falling on elbows and shoulders where they did no damage; but he was not weakening. **SWEAT WAS STREAMING** into Peter's eyes, mingling with the blood streaming from the gouges in his chest. He was not tired, not breathless, not seriously hurt. But he was growing discouraged. It seemed to him that he had been fighting Chang Kong forever, and he was depressed by the most disheartening sensation that can come to any fighter—the knowledge that his hardest blows were accomplishing nothing.

Chang Kong was tireless. When Peter struck him in the midsection, the hairy giant grunted, but he did not waver, and in spite of Peter's most powerful, most carefully placed, most accurately timed blows, he did not seem to be slowing down. It was like trying to knock down a great tree with one's fists.

A terrific blow knocked Peter off his feet. He fell to the sand, quickly sprang up. Now he called upon every ounce of strength he possessed. The determination to kill this hairy monster had not for a moment deserted him. He sent mighty blows hammering into Chang Kong's stomach, heart, face. The giant began to back away, absolutely unable to turn aside this furious assault.

Peter became aware now of a strange note in the roar of the crowd. And he became aware that, save for his combat with Chang Kong, the fighting was over. The priests had drawn the other surviving contestants off the field.

But only subconsciously was Peter aware of this, and of the fact that the crowd was roaring with laughter. Every cell of his brain, every fibre of his powerful, muscular body was concentrated on the single purpose: to kill Chang Kong, the backbreaker.

Down the arena Chang Kong backed, trying to fend off those blows as best he could, his eyes somewhat dazed, his jaw hanging, his long hairy arms flailing about with futility. At the end of the arena, priests pounced upon them, dragged them apart. Peter tried to fight them off, but there were too many of them. They clung to his arms and laughed.

He was furious. He had tapped a deep reservoir of strength—of inexhaustible vitality. He was certain that, if he had not been interfered with, he would, in a little more time, beat Chang Kong to the ground. But the fighting was over. The laughter of priests and mobs was the laughter of delight, applause. The mob was spilling down into the arena. Madly delighted people were surrounding him, pawing him.

But it didn't make him happy. He was, in fact, furious. He had been prevented, at the last moment, from giving a fine beating to the hairy monster who broke men's backs.

14

KING OF KINGS

CHANG KONG WAS not eliminated. That fight was a tie—
the only tie, so the head priest informed Peter, that had
occurred in such fights in many years. Peter carried away
from that fight the image of Chang Kong laughing at him,
jeering, and of Chang Kong's boast, "I would have broken
your back in another moment!"

Peter returned to the gladiators' *sala* to repair damages.
He was bleeding badly from the gouges in his chest
received during his first encounter of the morning. From
his woven grass package, he removed the magical ointment
which Dekka had brewed for him. He applied this to the
gouges, then he threw himself on the ground under the
gnarled old ebony tree to rest.

There, Para Khan found him. The sad-eyed young
Siamese was badly scratched about the face and shoulders, but he was intact, and fit to go on. He had won five
hard victories.

From him Peter learned the results of the morning's
fighting. Seventeen men had been killed, thirty-one were
seriously crippled—with broken hands, arms, legs or other
bones, and thirty-three had been rendered unconscious.
A total of eighty-one men had been eliminated from the

original one hundred and thirty, so that there were now a total of forty-nine contestants.

Peter lay on his back, his hands clasped behind his head, his eyes fixed on a small brown spider that was industriously spinning a web from limb to limb. He was reminded of the famous story of Bruce and the spider—the disheartened warrior who received new strength, new inspiration, from observing the patience with which a spider spun its web.

For a moment, he was obsessed with a feeling of futility for what he was trying to accomplish. It seemed to him there was nothing brave about all this; nothing but folly. He might lose any of these matches by losing his temper; he was disgusted, almost sick, because of what he had seen in the arena—men brutally, cruelly killed—for what? So that eighty thousand blood-lusting Orientals might enjoy themselves! Why? So that Lu would retain the power he had over them! The master showman, the genius!

What lay at the bottom of Peter's rage was the fact that the man at whom he was really striking was so inaccessible.

The man he really wanted to kill was Lu—not these young fanatics. But he could not kill Mr. Lu; and in order to strike at Mr. Lu—at the source of Mr. Lu's power—he must go on killing or be killed.

He muttered, in English, "I ought to be ashamed to look at a respectable spider!"

He had forgotten that Para Khan was still squatting there, near him, like a tragic Buddha.

"You are ill!" the Siamese said, quickly.

Peter rolled his eyes and grunted. "I am sick of it."

Para Khan sighed. "My only hope is that we never have

to fight each other. We are friends. It we are matched against each other, one of us *must* die. We can show each other no mercy."

"That is true," Peter quietly agreed. He, too, hoped that Para Khan would not be matched with him in any form of contest; yet he feared that sooner or later it would be unavoidable.

He realized that he must get a grip on himself. His anger at Lu's grotesque, monstrous ceremonies, at his nauseating feast of human blood, had almost betrayed him. He must keep one thing in mind: that stealing and destroying the sapphire skull was a worthy accomplishment. And he must bear in mind Dekka's repeated advice, "Keep your head, fellow."

PEOPLE CAME AND went, to stare at Peter lying under the tree, to question him about his fight with the big fellow, to guess at his chances for surviving the other contests.

An old woman said, "You should carry a strong luck charm."

The little golden girl from Hai-Phong, elbowing through the crowd, cried, *"Hola!* I am his luck charm! I am his goddess of good luck! He took my smile into the arena!"

Then she kneeled beside Peter and whispered, "I watched you every moment. Not one little instant were my eyes on anyone else." She pitched her whisper lower, sent darting glances from the corners of her eyes to the pushing crowd. "You are a greater liar than a fighter—You are of the nobility." She sent a sharp glance at Para Khan. "You, too, are of the noble blood. What is your town?"

The Siamese looked displeased. "Chengmei."

"A prince from Chengmei!" Zari mocked. *"Hai! Hai!*

Prince Para Khan, of Chengmei—with the blood of Rama in his veins! But you are doomed! I read your fate last night in the dragon stars. You will end violently and soon, prince Para Khan!"

"We are to each other," Para Khan answered, "as burning poison falling into a man's eyes."

"Doomed!" cried the girl.

"Brimming goblet of vinegar!" said the scornful prince of Siam.

Zari snuggled closer to Peter. "He is but a Siamese prince," she whispered into Peter's ear. "You are a king of kings. And I am as fair as the *malla* flower when it perfumes the forest. But what is your kingdom, oh, king?"

"Annam!"

"What is your town?"

"Hai-Phong!"

"Liar!" One slim, golden arm was about his shoulder. Her eyes and mouth were laughing into his face. "You have not the Hai-Phong accent. You are a *ngat* who comes to earth in the form of a man!"

There was dangerous mischief in Zari's eyes, in her laughter. Peter wondered how many others suspected—or knew—that he was not the son of a Hai-Phong cobbler, as he claimed to be.

Her lips were pressed into his ear. "You are a god. I am a goddess! And you will see me die. I shall be proud to have you carry me, dead, down the white stairs and cast me into the pit of fire. I have looked all about. There is no girl here half so beautiful as I. I am doomed! Tonight I die! *Hola!*"

A temple priest in gray robes approached and said, "All

contestants are summoned to the arena for the afternoon contests!"

Peter growled, "What are they to be?"

"Tests of skill!" was the evasive reply.

"More killings," Para Khan said bitterly. "By the tooth of Buddha, may we be alive and smiling this evening, my friend!"

The priest laughed. "If fortune smiles, who doesn't? If fortune doesn't, who does?"

15

THE COBRA PIT

SUSAN DID NOT attend the morning contests. She was afraid to be seen, recognized; and in spite of her thrill-loving nature, she had no stomach for such hideous amusement as these bloody combats. Men thrown together like beasts to kick and punch and claw, to kill and maim—such entertainment was not for her.

On the night when she had learned that Peter Moore was dead, Susan's zest for living had died, too. Only one thing kept her living—the terrible desire to avenge Peter's death. And when that was accomplished, she would die, gladly. Nothing else existed for her now.

But her *amah* sounded a warning note. "By trying to hide, you attract more attention than if you were one of the crowd. There are dozens of beautiful girls here.—Perhaps none so beautiful as you, yet a beautiful face here is but a drop of water added to a sea."

"I won't watch such horrible performances!" the richest girl in the Orient proclaimed.

"You do not have to watch. But you must attend. We will attend the afternoon contests."

"What will happen?"

"No one but the priests know."

"Something horrible!"

"Always something horrible."

Susan shuddered. All morning she had listened to the roar of the mob, and to the shrieks of men in agony. It had made her want to scream. She had thought her nerves would be shattered. Six months of unceasing suffering over Peter Moore's death had undermined her nerves. Now, at the least excitement, her heart hammered with painful rapidity. She had lost her grip. It was taking every ounce of her courage to face the ordeal for which she had come here; and she was in constant dread of being recognized by Lu's men before her moment came. In her distracted state, she could not undergo the horrors of the contests. She went to them nevertheless.

It was fortunate for Susan that she withheld her consent to Chula until the last moment, for when they reached the arena, the only unoccupied benches were high up on the outer rim of the great stadium, facing the sun. From that distance it would be impossible to see the agony in the contestants' faces. Down below her—far below—the assembling contestants were so many insects, not men.

In anguish, she whispered, "Chula! What is going to happen?"

"Look! The pits!" her amah said.

WHEN PETER MOORE and Para Khan entered the arena, the contestants were already swarming about the high priest. Fresh sand had been spread. The dead and injured had been removed. But these were not the only changes. All about the great white sand, square pits had been dug. These pits were about seven feet square by four in depth. Each was lined with fresh clay, so that the sand would not cave in. Peter quickly counted them. Forty-nine! A pit to each remaining contestant!

Stacked up behind the high priest were a number of teakwood boxes or crates about two feet square, and stoutly bound with brass and rattan. There were, Peter estimated, about fifty of them—or one box for each contestant. Near the boxes was stacked a neat pile of short, square lengths of black wood—ebony.

Peter saw Chang Kong standing near the high priest, his arms folded on his glistening brown chest, looking none the worse for his morning's exertions. He saw Peter, gave him a wolfish grin, and lowered his head. An epic hatred burned in his eyes.

Seeing the two young men glaring at each other, fairly bristling to leap at each other's throats, the priests laughed. They would see to it that these two had another chance to spill each other's blood!

Para Khan was saying, at Peter's side, *"Aie!* A delightful surprise, my friend. Cobras!"

Peter had already made that guess—when the breeze carried to his nostrils from the pile of boxes a reptilian stench. Cobras! Forty-nine of them! One to each man!

The high priest was outlining the procedure. There were forty-nine pits, forty-nine cobras, forty-nine contestants, forty-nine priests. A contestant to a pit, a cobra to a pit; a priest to a pit. On signal, the priest standing above each pit would release from its box a cobra. But the man was not to jump into the pit immediately. He was to give the cobra time to accustom itself to the blazing daylight—time to get its bearings and to be prepared to defend itself, to avenge its outraged dignity!

So there would he a second signal, fifteen seconds or so after the first. At this signal, the contestants would leap into the pits, each man armed only with one of the ebony clubs. He must not leave the pit, the high priest said, until the cobra was stretched out, lifeless, at his feet—unless, as it chanced, the man lost the bout.

At this expression of Oriental humor, the crowd roared with laughter. To many of the pilgrims, this particular contest was a familiar spectacle—always a delightful one, because so many of the brave young men never left those pits alive, but died swiftly, in horrible convulsions, from an injection of cobra venom.

Peter listened to the uproar of mirth, and looked at the short, square, ebony clubs with misgivings. If it hadn't been for those clubs, he would not have felt so apprehensive. Except for the weapon used, this contest was one with which Dekka had painstakingly made him familiar. But he had always given Peter a *parang;* never so clumsy a weapon as a club.

The high priest was assigning the contestants to the pits. Perhaps, to amuse the crowd, Peter and the hairy giant were assigned to adjoining pits so that they might stand and glare at one another, to the great delight of the pilgrims.

Peter accepted one of the clubs, hefted it, tested it with a downward swing through the air. It was about the size and weight of the clubs which Dekka had had him use in fighting panthers, bears, wild boars. But Dekka had never dared, even at the height of Peter's training, to let him enter a cobra pit armed with a club.

Peter had never overcome his fear, his primitive hatred,

of cobras, with their great bloated hoods, the swift fury of
their attack, their murderous, savage aggressiveness. This
was the only snake in the world that would deliberately
and unhesitatingly attack a man! And he was once again
obsessed by the diabolical unfairness of this contest. Fair-
ness had so far played no part in these grotesque compe-
titions. Their purpose was to eliminate the unfit; to select
a man braver, quicker, stronger, cleverer than all the rest—
and to amuse the pilgrims!

TO BE MATCHED with a cobra was, at this time, cruelly
unfair. All the contestants had spent a strenuous morning.
No matter how perfect their physical condition, it was
inevitable that their muscles would lack freshness, that
their powers of coordination would be below par. Dekka
had never permitted Peter to enter the cobra pit unless he
was absolutely untired, fresh.

Facing the pit, Peter could see, above the head of the
priest across from him, that architectural monstrosity, the
Temple of the Coiled Serpent—coil upon coil of pale blue
stone rising to the gigantic stone head, with its jaws agape,
its gemmed eyes glistening in the tropical afternoon sun.

Such a contest as this one—man against reptile—was, of
course, in keeping with the cherished spirit of the temple.
Presumably it was regarded as fitting that the next high
priest of such a temple should show his skill against a
deadly serpent.

A hush had fallen over the spectators. Far away in the
jungle, Peter could hear the measured, maddening bell-like
strokes of the bird-that-beats-on-gold.

In the silence, the hairy giant near him shouted, "Pig of

an Annamese!—May your opponent sink its fangs into the veins of your arm!"

"And yours, flea-bitten rat," Peter retorted, "into the vein of your neck!"

The crowd roared its appreciation.

"Attention!" snapped the priest across from Peter.

Peter's wrathful eyes returned to the two-foot-square teakwood box. The priest was holding it at a slanting angle on one knee. The side toward Peter had a hinged lid. The hinges were at the bottom. At the top was a metal hasp through which a wooden plug was thrust. The priest had his fingers on this plug. At the signal from the high priest, he would pluck out the plug and the cobra would slide down, tumbling into the pit. Behind the priest, on the sand, was a thick, five-foot club with which he would, presumably, kill the cobra if the cobra first killed Peter.

The high priest was lifting his hand containing a fragment of red silk. A hush like death had fallen on the eighty thousand spectators.

The red fragment left the high priest's hand. In the deathly silence, the scraping sounds as the priests' freed the wooden plugs from the hasps were loud and sharp. Next the thuds of squirming black and brown and tan coils sliding down out of the boxes, tumbling into the pits, hissing. Instantly the crowd began to chant, counting off the seconds in a score of languages and dialects, to the fateful fifteen.

Peter, with steady eyes, grim mouth, was watching the box in the hands of the priest across from him. The priest's face was flushed, either with exertion or embarrassment. The plug was stuck? He could not pull it out of the hasp!

The chanting voices had reached the count of ten. Still the sweating, flushed priest struggled with the obstinate plug. It would not yield.

OF A SUDDEN, the chanting voices stopped. Fifteen! Peter, with icy claws at his heart, the club gripped ready in his hand, was aware that all about him, men were leaping into the pits. The swift and horrible results of these unequal combats were demoralizing. He saw one bloated head reared up from a nearby pit, saw the flicking tongue, the long, curving white fangs; saw a man strike at it and miss; saw those fangs strike deep into the man's cheek, just below the eye. Then a hideous scream.

The crowd seemed to hold its breath. The hush in the stands continued. Above the mob's silence were these nightmare sounds; men roaring, shouting, screaming; the thuds of clubs on vicious black heads, or the thuds of these heads striking and striking and striking, driving needle-like fangs into men's flesh and injecting deadly poison into their veins.

Few snakes are satisfied by striking at an enemy but once, and the king cobra is no exception to this general reptilian rule. Again and again, those fangs would strike until the victim would collapse from the sheer power of the blows alone—this and the horrified realization that all his life had been cut off as if with a knife, that his veins were carrying swiftly to his brain and heart the deadliest of known animal venoms!

All about Peter, this hideous tragedy was occurring. Death, death, death! The priests were clubbing to death cobras which had killed men.

He was beginning to tremble. His mouth, tongue, finger

tips were as dry as charcoal. His throat was parched. His heart was laboring in a sudden panic. Sweat stood out in a glistening band on his forehead. Fascinated, horrified, he saw a cobra in the pit beyond the hairy giant, saw it striking, striking at a screaming, doomed man.

Then the hairy giant was climbing out of his pit, with the club in his hand, a triumphant grin at his thick-lipped mouth. He was sweating—but the ebony club dripped blood.

Here and there Peter saw other men climbing out of pits. He saw several of them take a few steps and collapse. How few they were—these who emerged!

Chang Kong was running toward him, gripping the club. He ran around to the other side of the pit and snatched the box out of the priest's hands. Others of the priests had gathered around. All the other pits had told their stories. Peter alone had yet to meet his cobra!

Cold, sweating, completely unnerved by suspense, he saw the hairy giant grasp the wooden plug with a mighty thumb and forefinger, give it a slight jerk!

Down fell the lid, and out sprang the largest cobra Peter had ever seen. Into the pit it tumbled, a writhing black monster—an infuriated, coiling messenger of death! Black—more venomous than the cobra of any other color! A king cobra!

The chanting had begun again. The hairy giant was directing it with sweeping gestures of his arms, as if he were the conductor of an orchestra.

"—five—six—seven—eight—nine—ten—eleven—twelve—"

Peter gripped the club. The great cobra had retreated

to the side of the pit farthest from him, as if instinctively realizing that the man was its enemy—coiling tighter and tighter for the terrific, convulsive spring with which it would greet him.

Sweat running into his eyes. A pain at the back of his tongue. His grip on the club weakened. It all but slipped from his sweating palm. He couldn't whip up the courage to jump into that pit! He couldn't face that waiting monster!

THEN, AS IF in actuality, he heard Dekka's gargantuan laughter. His voice, projecting itself into Peter's brain across the miles, "All you have to do is strike it at the base of the brain, just after you have dodged its lunge.—Ready?"

"Ready," Peter whispered.

"—*Fifteen!*" chanted the mob.

The great hood of the serpent was so swollen that the black skin gleamed like the facets of a gem. It was vibrating on the thin stem of the reptile's neck, preparing to strike with death-dealing accuracy wherever the enemy landed.

A thousand thoughts, images flooded through Peter's mind in the fraction of a second which measured his descent into the shallow pit: Dekka—Susan O'Gilvie—the shadow of the Blue Scorpion. It was as if his life, reaching its completion, was unreeling before a remorseful inner eye.

Then his feet struck the clay. He was no longer weak or nervous or afraid. It was as if, far away, Dekka with his strange magic was infusing into him a superhuman agility and fearlessness. He was no longer a man. He was a piece of wonderfully coordinating machinery. Every fibre of him was in tune with every other fibre.

As the hissing black monster shot out that great bloated

head with its long white fangs, Peter stepped lightly aside, brought the club down with a tremendous smash at the base of the snake's mad brain, jumped into the air and over it.

He had delivered a death blow to the cobra, yet the serpent was returning to attack again! Then Peter saw, as he prepared to drive in another killing blow, that the mass of steely muscle was only carrying out, in reflex, the attitude of life. Beyond death, it still struck to kill—but without aim now, without purpose, without result.

Peter hit the dead serpent once again. As he did so, the jaws opened and from the hollow fangs, fine jets of spray squirted out.

None of this venom fell on or close to Peter, however. Now, on the floor of the pit, the powerful black coils writhed and threshed with lessening vigor. Beyond death, it might twitch and convulse in this way for hours.

Peter leaped lightly out of the pit, to hear Chang Kong say:

"Pig of an Annamese—you have made me happy! My ears are hungry for the music of your death-rattle—but at my hands!"

Peter waited for the laughter about him to subside, then he retorted, "Flea-bitten rat, if that small, feeble worm which you fought just now had struck its immature fangs into you, I should have been robbed of the joy of killing you myself! By whiskers of Buddha—may it be soon!"

16

TOMORROW WE DIE

THERE WERE, THE high priest announced, to be no more contests until the following morning.

Peter hardly heard him. He had been looking anxiously about for Para Khan, and he was conscious, when he saw his Siamese friend walking toward him, alive and intact, of a surge of relief—a kind of emotional explosion that shot through him and sent foolish tears into his eyes.

It was hard to explain his attachment to Para Khan. It was partly a mixture of understanding and pity. The heart of the Siamese prince was not in these monstrous doings. Para Khan, with the soul of a poet and the eyes of a dreamer, ought never to have entered these contests. Yet his survival, so far, was a thousand times more admirable than the success of such a powerful, blood-lusting animal as Chang Kong.

"I missed my snake three times as he struck," Para Khan said. "But Buddha was on my side. In my eyes, I lay dead a dozen times—yet I left the pit without a puncture in my cowardly hide!"

They could talk no more for the moment. Once again, the stadium was spilling waves of uproarious humanity into the arena. The surviving contestants must be patted, hugged, slapped, pinched, worshipped. Above the noise rose the thin, heartbreaking wail of a girl whose lover had been killed in the pit.

Peter saw Zari's little golden face tossing about at a distance, like a flower in a gusty wind. She screamed at him, but he could not hear her voice. All about him, in the mob, were other golden faces, staring at him, big-eyed, awed. He did not know, of course, that a rumor had been spread— no doubt by Zari—that he was of the highest nobility, at least a prince, and probably a sultan or a king from some southern land.

He was striding along with his arm locked with Para Khan's, unaware of this awe, this adoration, or of the flames he kindled in maidens' hearts. Truth to tell, his feelings at the moment were of the sourest order. He had just learned that of the forty-nine healthy, powerful specimens of manhood who had entered the cobra contests, but eighteen had survived! In a matter of swift, hideous seconds, thirty-one young men had been struck by cobra fangs, had quickly died in the most exquisite agony!

The news of this sent Peter's brain and his emotions flying down forbidden paths again—his hatred of Mr. Lu, who could conceive and execute such monstrous exhibitions for the amusement of a mob!

He and Para Khan fought their way out of the pawing, delighted crowd and slipped off to the brook which trickled over moss-grown stones in the jungle behind the gladiators' *sala*. Here, in quiet and tranquillity, they lay in a shallow pool and let their blood cool off.

Presently Para Khan said, "That little Annamese girl with the tongue of a viper told the truth. My name is written red across the stars. My time has come to leap the dragon gate."

Peter heartily disagreed with these sentiments, yet in his heart he was uncertain. If contestants were matched against contestants many more times, it was a mathematical certainty that he and Para Khan would face each other in some kind of battle to the death. He did not know what he would do. He would rather give up, drop out, than kill this young man. It was the strangest and most difficult problem in friendship that Peter had ever been called upon to face.

PARA KHAN WAS talking dreamily of his native city, Chengmei. His princely father was an eccentric, a religious fanatic who had discarded Buddhism for the worship of the Sapphire Skull of Mr. Lu. In so doing, he had incurred the wrath of the king and of the king's brother, the head of the Siamese branch of Buddhism. By royal edict, Para Khan's father had been deprived of his lands, his elephants, his palace; he was reduced to poverty. But in his heart still burned the exalted flame of worship for the Sapphire Skull.

"I wanted to become a scholar," Para Khan said. "I would have been sent to foreign lands—to England and America—to learn. But all this was lost when my father turned against his king. I have been trained and trained and trained—so that my father might have the honor of seeing his son become the high priest of this wretched temple—the guardian of the Sapphire Skull!"

So strongly was Peter moved that he was almost tempted to admit Para Khan to his secret. Two heads might be better than one, but he dared not. His was a single-handed fight. No one could help him.

PETER, LYING BESIDE Para Khan under the old ebony tree that night, was in the black depths of first sleep when Zari woke him. Her high, angry little voice aroused Para Khan, too. In the brilliant moonlight, even the shadows of trees were robbed of their blackness.

A diffusion of moonlight from shrubbery showed the mouth of the little golden girl to be twisted, her face contorted with fury.

She ignored Para Khan. Her wrath was all for Peter. "You have been avoiding me all day long!" she accused him. "You have made me a laughingstock!"

"Why?" Peter said sleepily.

"I boast that you, my king, are my slave. I boast that you worship my little ears, my little feet, my lovely little hands, that you adore my perfections. Yet where are you when I come to find you? Off roaming through the jungle with this Siamese monkey!"

"A boastful woman," Para Khan said laconically, "is more bitter than wormwood. The walls of the inner hell are ornamented with the skulls of women who lack respect for their superiors. With one word wit is exhausted."

But the golden child of Annam would not go. It was her obvious intention to out-insult Para Khan, and her sharper tongue won. Muttering, Prince Para Khan got up from his mats and wandered off toward the *sala*.

Zari sank down beside Peter and clasped him to her firm young bosom.

"My king, my lord! I bow my horrid little head with shame that I should speak so rudely!"

Her head, however, was not bowed. It was uptilted, and her large alluring dark eyes were sparkling with thrill.

"I have seen it in the stars that you will not survive the contests!" she whispered, her lips softly caressing his ear.

Peter shook his head as if she were a mosquito. "You read too much in the stars."

"But I have read nothing but what the gods predict! You will die in the morning contests. And I shall be chosen—because I am the most beautiful of all the maidens here—and have my lovely little throat slit from ear to ear!"

Peter said wearily, *"Hai!* Let's not quarrel with the stars!"

"But there is a way!"

"You mean, you've been scheming!"

"Oh, my king," she sighed into his ear, "have I any interests but your own in my small, faithful heart? Am I not the very essence of meekness, humility and unselfishness? Do I give thought to anything but your comfort, safety and whole-skinnedness?"

He growled, "Tormentor of men, what is this scheme?"

She snuggled closer to him. Peter believed he detected a new perfume rising from her face, her ears, her shining black hair. She might have been the very embodiment of all feminine enchantment. Her warm, soft slimness, the teasing scents she used, the guiles of her exotic charm—here was danger, powdered, perfumed, inviting!

She brushed his ear tantalizingly with hot moist lips. "We run away! *Hola!"*

"Just like that," he said dryly.

"Have we committed a crime if we do?" she demanded. "We will slip off into the jungles. Your strength and cleverness will find us food. We will wander where we will. With your courage, we will fear nothing—man nor beast!

"We will see the world." Her small hand was softly

stroking his cheek. "We will slip into little villages for sweetmeats. How I love sweetmeats! Then we will find some delightful valley and build our home."

She said sturdily, as if he had made an accusation, "Do you think I am not a good cook? You should taste my sweet purple rice, so nice and sticky, as it comes out of the bamboo! And my recipe for *tamane*—boiled with sliced coconut, sesame seeds, ginger, onions, and pepper. And how deliriously I can fry red ants in fish oil!"

"My mouth waters," Peter said.

"But we will not stay long in one place!" Zari said rapturously. "On and on! Life! Adventure! Just us two!"

It had a familiar ring. Here, he suddenly realized, was another thrill hunter!

"But some day we would settle down, my king, and have sons—nothing but sons! I want a dozen of your sons at my knee! But not before we had seen the great outside world. We would go to America on a great ship spouting smoke and steam! *Hola!*"

PETER, WITH THAT soft, warm, beguiling body so near, decided that this couldn't go on.

"We would not be total strangers there," she said.

At that, Peter gave a slight start.

"I have," Zari confided, "a great uncle in Gee-Gag-Wah."

"Where?"

"Gee-Gag-Wah."

"Chicago?"

"*Aie!* Gee-Gag-Wah! We would see these great cities, with their temples of gold rising a hundred times higher than the Temple of the Coiled Serpent! Where trains made of purest silver run like rats through holes in the ground!

The Tartar brought his blade down like a cleaver.

Where, when you are hungry, mountains of pickled tea and acid plums and winged rice and iguana's eggs are served to you on golden platters!"

So that, Peter reflected, was America!

Zari, clinging to him, was shivering. "My king, why are you so silent?" she breathed. "I am terrified. Tomorrow, so the stars say, we die. Oh, oh—hi-yah! I don't want to die. I am only seventeen. I am too beautiful to die. Pick me up in your strong arms and carry me off into the jungles!"

Peter said, "Zari, you're dangerous!"

"I?" she squealed, "I am a dove! A lamb! Hah! You wish to see me die! And I am sure to die, because I am noted for my beauty, and I am quite convinced that I am the most beautiful maiden here!"

Para Khan's voice said, "Only a file rasping on metal is crueller to the ear than the words of a conceited woman."

Zari jumped up and stamped a tiny foot. "The prince from Siam," she said shrilly, "should be wearing yellow robes and carrying a begging pot and a gourd of holy water from the Ganges!"

"That voice," Para Khan said wearily, "is more painful to hear than the croaking of the brain-fever bird. Put your elephant gait to some good use, and glide far, far away!"

The golden girl slid her angry eyes from him to Peter. "My king, what is your command?"

"Only in sleep," Peter warily replied, "does a man mine the gold of wisdom, and a woman the gems of beauty."

"Very well, my king," Zari said stiffly. "I lied about the stars. Tomorrow night, at the hour of the dragon, when you carry my lifeless body down the long white stairway and throw it into the pit of fire—perhaps you will be sorry!"

A word of encouragement would have halted her; but Peter held his silence. A woman scorned, Zari haughtily strode off.

17

WITH SCIMITARS

IN A SALA on the other side of the temple, another girl noted for her beauty was unsuccessfully trying to cry herself to sleep. Susan had reached the limit of human endurance. She felt that she lacked the courage to go on. Her amah had made the rounds of the salas; had inspected scores of beautiful maidens with the eyes of an impartial hawk. She had returned to report that no girl she had seen could match Susan's radiant beauty of face, her exquisite perfection of body.

"You are a wood-nymph among multitudes of ugly, coarse and clumsy girls," Chula said. "Your slimness is that of the moonbeam. Your face has the beauty of the loveliest flower that grows in any garden. Your teeth are pearls, your eyes are heavenly gems. You need not fear, my child.—However, weeping reddens and swells the skin about the eyes and removes the freshness of morning dew from the rose that is your face. Compose yourself."

Susan was unable to compose herself, however. If she won this fantastic beauty contest, there was but one more day of life allotted to her. Her heart cried out: "If only I could have seen him just once before I died! Touched his lips with mine once more! Held him in my arms just once!—Cruel, cruel, cruel!" Why had Fate given Peter Moore to her, if he was to be snatched away so soon?

The despairing heart of a woman bereaved of the one man in life could find no answers to such questions. In these past six months of suffering, the richest girl in the world had learned much about herself! her weaknesses, her selfishness, her thoughtlessness. She had been a spoiled brat. She had met and loved Peter Moore. Yet she had been cruel and inconsiderate and unkind.

She had, she convinced herself, been responsible for his death. He had not wanted adventure. He had wanted peace and quiet. Had she not driven him, time after time, into dangerous predicaments; had she not urged him, bullied him, tricked him into perilous places, he would not have been caught in the web of circumstances which had brought about his death—the cold destroying fury of the Blue Scorpion!

Susan had seen, from a distance, the hideous cobra contests of the afternoon.

Faint with horror, she had left the arena, had tried to deafen her ears to Chula's enthusiastic description of the most exciting fight of all—of a cobra box that would not open; of a tall, bronzed youth who stood at the pit, holding himself coolly under that terrific tension until all the other fights were over, and had then leaped into the pit upon the grandfather of all cobras and magnificently demolished the murderous reptile!

Susan, weeping on her mats, thought of the other splendid young men who had not been so heroic, or so fortunate—thirty-one of them. And her horror slowly turned into a greater resentment at the human monster who was responsible.

With that thought she could steady herself. If, tomorrow night, she could only find the heart of that monster with her dagger!

Her tears stopped. A waking dream possessed her mind as she stared out into the beauty of the moonlit world. She imagined that she was dead. A tall man, the new high priest, was gently carrying her down the long flight of marble stairs—hurling her into the white-hot pit!

Then this dream was replaced by one in which she sat on a balcony looking down upon the twinkling stars which were the lights of Hong Kong. Beside her sat the young man whom her folly had lost for her forever. In her sleep, Susan sighed happily; in her dreams, she never lost him.

ON THE STONY ground under the ebony tree, with chill night winds whispering about his almost naked body, Peter Moore slept soundly until the clear, deep booming of the temple bell, with its measured strokes, awoke him to the dewy freshness of the jungle morning.

He reached the gladiators' *sala* with Para Khan to find the surviving contestants in a state of turmoil. A rumor had reached them that this morning they were, with their bare hands, to fight panthers. Another rumor in circulation was that they were to fight one another with flaming clubs—clubs soaked in oil. Still another rumor: two men at a time were to fight starved crocodiles, until, of the eighteen, but one survived.

Peter, hearing these rumors, was skeptical. To him they meant but one thing; they were an indication that the contestants were losing their morale. Their nerves were becoming unstrung by what they had already been through. It was fortunate that the contests were ending today, for if they were to go on into another day, most of these men would collapse nervously. And a large part of the nervous strain was contributed by the riddle of the future—what would be the nature of the contests in which they were to engage today?

Dekka had advised Peter, "Keep your head, fellow. Don't let your imagination play tricks. Take things as they come, one at a time."

Chang Kong, at breakfast, called to him: "Eat hearty, O undersized pig! It is your last breakfast!"

Peter thoughtfully studied the close-set little eyes, the ape-like forehead, the coarse thick lips of his enemy and said, "Today, my flea-bitten rat, *brains* are to tell. Take time now to admire your last sunrise."

"Buddha grant me one last wish," said the hairy giant, "that you and I be matched against each other!"

"Bare-handed," Peter added. "With no one to interfere—no one to leap in at the last moment and spare your worthless carcass!"

"Or to prevent me," Chang Kong said, "from breaking the grass-stem that you call your backbone!"

The pilgrims gathered around to stare at them debated and wagered on the outcome of Peter's and Chang Kong's next meeting in combat.

One dark old fellow, a Burmese *mahout*, declared: "I will wager my three fine bull elephants, trained to tiger hunting and to lumber yard labor, against anything of equal value, that Chang Kong will win over this pale-eyed princeling!"

A young Sikh with a white turban wound about his

head said promptly, "I will wager emeralds and sapphires from my mines in Ceylon against your pigs on the one of noble blood!"

Peter grinned up at him and said, "You've won three bull elephants, friend."

"Let me see these gems," said the *mahout*.

But Peter anticipated no such tests of human endurance and nimbleness as he had indulged in yesterday. Actually, he had told Chang Kong what he believed to be the truth—that today brains would tell; that in some way the contests would call not wholly upon brawn, but upon wits. Dekka had warned him that this would doubtless be the order.

Peter had overlooked the mob's thirst for bloody heroics, however, and the Blue Scorpion's understanding of mob psychology. His great temple was a success because he knew what his people wanted.

BREAKFAST OVER, THE contestants awaited the summons to the arena. It did not come. Many of them paced up and down in the clearing outside the *sala*. Others squatted on the ground, knees under chins, powerful arms clasping about legs, eyes filled with worry. The strain was telling. What was to be the next contest—and when?

Almost any fate is easier to endure than suspense. All that morning they waited. The morning, they presently learned, had been set aside for a feast for all the pilgrims, prepared by the temple priests. And it was not until some time afternoon that the crowd, filled with rich food, poured into the stadium and sat back complacently to be entertained by whatever bloody events might be on the program—the bloodier the better!

A happy roar met the eighteen handsome young men in loin cloths who presently filed into the oval of gleaming white sand. The cobra pits had been refilled with sand. Once more, the arena was as smooth as a table top. It looked as if it had been rolled. The sand had been wet down, and was hard-packed.

As on the previous occasions, Lao Li was waiting in his snow white robes at the far end of the arena, accompanied by a number of the gray robed priests.

Peter, wondering what the afternoon contest would be, saw near the high priest a long mahogany box, of the width, depth and length of the average-sized coffin. No animals, reptiles were in evidence.

He heard a shout of approval from Chang Kong when the lid was opened. At first, all Peter saw was a glitter of hot sunlight on shiny metal.

"Scimitars," Para Khan murmured. "We are to have the fun of hacking each other to pieces. But may Buddha spare you and me from each other!"

Before the hairy one could be stopped, he had seized from the box two scimitars. He grasped one by its knobbed teakwood handle and brought it slashing down through the air in a swing which created a loud whistling.

He rushed over to where Peter stood and thrust the handle of the other weapon into his hand.

"Now!" yelled Chang Kong.

The crowd instantly roared its approval of this informality—and of the appearance of scimitars, the most barbarous, most merciless of all long-edged weapons.

But as Peter gripped the ugly, curved sword, the priests

interfered—grabbed him and Chang Kong from behind and disarmed them.

The high priest was angry. "You two will do as you are told! Fight well enough, and your desire for each other's blood may be granted. I am the master here. Lots are to be drawn."

In a little clump in one large brown hand, he held eighteen numbered bamboo sticks. There were two sets of sticks, numbered from one to nine.

From the corner of his eye, Peter watched Para Khan; and Para Kahn, meeting his eyes, slowly shook his head and let his arms fall at his side.

Peter drew Number 6. Had his luck spoken again? After all, wasn't six half of twelve? And wasn't twelve his lucky number?

"Six!" he shouted.

"Six!" echoed a voice. It had seemed to come from Para Khan's direction.

"Eight!" cried the Siamese prince, and Peter gave a groan of relief. He and Para Khan were to be spared each other for a time at least.

"Four!" roared Chang Kong.

PETER'S RELIEF CHANGED instantly to bitter disappointment. He wanted to try that trick of Dekka's on the hairy giant—disarm him, then swiftly swing the razor-like edge down upon Chang Kong's bull neck!

"Six!" repeated the deep voice.

Peter was confronted by the boastful, sneering Chang Kong, who savagely slashed at the air and laughed. "My number is four, but I beg you to fight well, my little Annamese pig! Fight your opponent well, and save yourself for this fine, keen edge!"

"Be careful!" Peter returned, as the giant stalked away. "If you wish to make me the most wretched man in all of Asia—let another carve you to ribbons before it is my turn!"

"Six!" repeated the deep-pitched, insolent voice.

Peter spun about. "Six," he answered. He had noticed this fellow in previous combats—a tall, curly-headed young man with a pale yellow skin that gleamed as if it were coated with olive oil. His large white teeth were bared in a grimace of defiance and hatred. Peter did not know his name, but he understood that he was a Tartar—the young chief of a warlike tribe which roved the Gobi Desert and the mountain passes from the Black Gobi into northern Turkestan, attacking camel caravans. Undoubtedly an expert swordsman! He was a powerful, clean-limbed young savage. In previous contests, Peter had seen him fighting with the joyous ferocity that has made his people so successful in all wars.

The young Tartar said, with venom, "I have always wanted to chop out the entrails of a Southern prince." Then he gave a yell, possibly the war cry of the Tartars.

The priests were giving out the scimitars. The contestants, now that the suspense was partly ended and their fears of starving crocodiles and bare-handed fights with panthers was removed, were slicing the air with gusto. All were swordsmen. Each had the look of a man indomitable.

Peter tested the scimitar allotted to him, and he also slashed at the air. He was seeing Dekka again; hearing Dekka's wise counsel.

The high priest gave the order, "Line up!"

The eighteen young men, armed with scimitars, were lined up in nine facing pairs, after the order of the previous morning's contests, when one hundred and thirty valiant young men had faced each other in weaponless combat.

Farthest from Peter was Para Khan, waiting, with an expression of Buddhistic patience, for the signal to start killing. Of them all, he was not excited; his attitude was that this sword fight was a business to be gotten through with. Peter was not deceived by this attitude into pity. He knew that the Siamese prince hated these contests and their whole fantastic purpose, but he knew now that in any form of combat Para Khan would give an excellent account of himself.

Chang Kong, however, was not calm. He was executing a mad, savage dance; leaping into the air, spinning about like a dervish, brandishing his scimitar, roaring, as if he were whipping himself into the needed murderous fury to assure a swift and bloody victory.

EIGHTEEN PAIRS OF eyes were staring steadily at the wisp of blood-red silk in the high priest's hand. The red silk leaped up and fluttered away on the breeze. Eighteen young men intent on murder went into action. There was a rattling clash as nine pairs of curved, bright steel blades met, then this was drowned in the roar from eighty thousand throats.

Peter fought coolly, as Dekka had taught him. Dekka had said, "In sword work, remember, the madder they get, the easier you'll take them. Let them turn into howling fiends—but keep your head."

The Tartar had run toward him with a blood-curdling

yell. Flecks of foam were at his lips, and in his eyes was a mad look.

Peter parried his attack; thrust swiftly, side-stepped. The Tartar's blade cleverly met his on each parry, turned it aside, leaped in attempting to score. They were evenly matched. They settled down to grim swordplay. Parry, thrust, parry, thrust.

All about them, this clashing went on. When the crowd was not roaring, Peter could hear the clashing of steel and the yelling of the fighters. He could not spare a moment to see what was happening about him. He hoped that Para Khan was not out-matched; and he hoped that Chang Kong would not settle with his man too soon.

A stream of curses, in the Tartar's native tongue, issued from the foam-flecked lips of Peter's adversary. The Tartar was trying new tricks—rushing in from the side, leaping into the air, gripping the scimitar in both hands, bringing it down like a great cleaver, in an attempt to smash Peter's blade from his hand and disarm him.

At the end of one of these bloodthirsty attempts, Peter suddenly took the offensive, and executed the "spinning arm" trick which Dekka had taught him. He flicked the scimitar's point this way and that until the blades were crossed, then, with a swift upward lunge, he twisted his arm, holding the muscles tense, so that it was as if the scimitar and his arm were of equally unyielding substance. Then he brought his arm driving down.

The Tartar yelled. The scimitar went twisting out of his hand. Before Peter could draw back his own blade, his opponent had rushed face-down along the razor-keen edge. In his forward plunge, he stumbled, and his neck fell full along the hair-line edge of steel! The blade slashed into his neck, and his savage lunge did not end until his chin struck the guard in Peter's hand. The Tartar's neck was cleanly severed, to the backbone. Blood gushed from between the snarling lips, jetting through his clenched teeth. No more would this wild young chieftain plunder caravans on the Gobi. He fell to the ground, rolled over—dead!

18

THE BITE OF STEEL

PANTING FROM THE exertion, shocked by this awful and unexpected ending of the duel, Peter stepped back. About him, six pairs of men were still fiercely engaged, lunging, parrying, thrusting, slashing. Four men lay on the sand, dead or dying. He looked anxiously about for his Siamese friend; picked him out presently, and for a moment watched him.

Para Khan was a magnificent swordsman—as light and quick as a panther, as relentless as a bull, but deliberate and cool. His swordplay was brilliant. And so far he had not been touched. His opponent was bleeding from a number of light slashes. He was not yet vanquished, but his eyes, fixed on Para Khan's flashing blade, had the look of a man doomed.

Another pair of duellists fought into Peter's range of vision. In the same instant, he saw two men killed. One was run through the stomach until the blade protruded several inches from his back, a hand's breadth from his backbone. This luckless fellow dropped his scimitar, and his triumphant enemy, with a tremendous pull, withdrew the sword; and in one swift, terrific blow, severed the dying man's head.

As this swift and horrible butchering occurred, Peter

saw another duel come to an end—a trick of Fate. The victim stumbled against the leg of a man who had fallen earlier. He threw up his arms in a frantic attempt to regain his balance, and his opponent drove a scimitar cleanly into his heart.

The two victims fell. The two victors glared at each other, panting for a moment; then, without hesitation, approached each other. Their scimitars flickered and clashed.

Peter, lacking an opponent, looked about for Chang Kong. Presently he found him, matched, it seemed, with a man who was his physical equal. The opponent was a Japanese of the *Ronin* breed—a lithe, tall man with a shaved skull, an expert swordsman. Behind him, doubtless, were many generations of military ancestors—men who had served the Mikado in wars centuries before the United States opened that small, ambitious empire to Western civilization.

Peter soon saw that the Jap was tiring. He was expert and daring, but he lacked Chang Kong's superhuman strength and endurance. The giant was carrying the fight every inch of the way into his enemy's territory. The Jap, parrying, was fighting a defensive battle. He was alert, ready for the first chance; but Chang Kong was giving him no chances. It was as if the giant's scimitar were merely an extension of his mighty right arm. It flicked, slashed, stabbed—all as if the source of its power was inexhaustible.

Peter now saw that the Jap was actually weakening, that he was carrying on with will alone, and that his muscles were becoming fatigued. Great drops of sweat streamed down his face and magnificent chest. He was biting his lips, and his eyes had a stricken look. He went back and back.

With a savage swing, Chang Kong brought his scimitar down, angling. The Jap, parrying, made the mistake of taking too short a backward step. The slashing blade sliced off his thumb and three of his fingers. The scimitar dropped out of the *Ronin's* hand; and before he could snatch it up with the other, Chang Kong, with an exultant roar, had leaped. He brought his blade flashing down on the Jap's skull as he bent to recover his fallen weapon. The keen edge sank into the skull; but Chang Kong jerked it free and lifted it again. With another lusty roar, he sent it slashing into the Jap's side as he pitched forward on his face.

PETER RAN IN. "When you're through fighting a dead man," he shouted, "try me!"

Chang Kong stared a moment; cried, with joyous gusto, "My little Annamese pig!" Then he attacked.

Peter was not aware that the eighty thousand in the stands, unanimously informed of the epic hatred between him and the hairy giant, at that moment rose to their feet with a heaven-shaking cheer. The fight for which they had been waiting was on!

Peter employed none of the defensive tactics with which he had conducted the first part of his fight with the Tartar; he leaped at Chang Kong, and with all his strength and skill endeavored to annihilate him in three blows.

Chang Kong, being of similar mind, it was inevitable that this phase of the battle should be mutually dangerous. The keen edge in the giant's hand wiped open Peter's left arm from shoulder to elbow, exposing bone. But Peter had scored as tellingly. He had slashed open Chang Kong's chest from shoulder to shoulder, in an arc like a great, ghastly, bloody smile.

Having tasted each other's steel, the two men became more cautious but no less vigorous. Chang Kong was no longer yelling. That deep, wicked slash across his chest had perhaps given him respect for the other's swordsmanship. Blood flowed from the ugly wound and ran in a thick layer down his stomach to the loin cloth. Saturating that, it ran in a thick stream down each thick, hairy leg.

Fortunately, the edged steel that had laid open Peter's left arm had not severed an artery or an important vein; but the wound bled profusely. By holding the arm tight against his side, he could check the gush of blood a little.

Eye to eye, almost toe to toe, they fought. Thrust, parry, sidestep. Thrust, parry, sidestep. Slash, parry, step-back. Peter's concentration was fixed upon his opponent; upon the slightest of his betraying muscular moves, upon his eyes. The real world, for Peter, had ceased to exist, and the world became a six-foot square of bloodied white sand under a merciless tropical sun, peopled only by himself and a giant stinking of blood, a giant who thrust and swung a scimitar like a great machine of bronze built in the semblance of a man. Thrust, parry, sidestep. Slash, parry, step-back.

Silence fell—silence broken only by the clash of steel on steel, of the gasping breathing of two men. A battle between two blood-red gods of the earth. *Clash—clash—clash!* Thrust, parry, sidestep.

Sweat was running down into Peter's eyes; his heart was hammering in his ears. How fast was the blood running out of that gash in his arm? How soon would one of the two stumble, weaken, make the first false move? *Clash—clash—clash!* The stench of blood in his nose.

He was unaware that a deathly silence, except for the clashing of steel and the gasping of burning lungs, had settled over the scene; that the other fights were over; that the high priest had drawn all other contestants and all priests from the ring, to leave those two battlers a clear field in which to have out their heroic hatred.

THEIR BREATHING NOW was in small, hard gasps, hardly more than pain-wrenched grunts. Mouths open, eyes mutually murderous, they fought on and on. It must have been fully an hour and a half. The slant of the sun changed until the blazing ball burned in their eyes. Their blows began to lose force. The keen edges were worn off their scimitars. Great nicks developed in the blades, and threatened to turn them into saws!

Three times now, Peter had attempted the "spinning arm" trick. But it was useless against the superhuman strength of Chang Kong. Peter had other tricks which Dekka had taught him, but these also were of no use now. There was no time, no chance, for tricks. No time for anything but the most primitive swordsmanship.

Clash—clash—clash! Thrust, parry, sidestep. Peter's brain had turned to a hard white coal of fire. On the verge of complete exhaustion, he knew he would, at the very last moment, tap still another well of reserve. In all his scimitar duels with Dekka, he had never fought so long or so hard.

Chang Kong's face had turned to the color of putty. His eyes were dying things, propped between slits of unearthly flesh.

A sullen sound began in the crowd. It grew slowly to a

roar like that which is heard in the throat of a volcano about
to blow off. With a suddenness known only to Oriental mobs, men and women began pouring over the walls
and into the arena, shouting, until Peter and Chang Kong
were surrounded. Men seized the two fighters, plucked the
scimitars from their nerveless hands.

The blood lust of the mob had been satisfied at last. Two
gladiators, thirsting for each other's blood, had become, in
their eyes, two terribly tired young men, feebly going on—
feebly and yet more feebly, yet determined to go on until
one or the other collapsed or met death.

They were picked up and carried limply to the gladiators' *sala*. There was a ticking in Peter's brain. He did not
know how many hours this fantastic endurance contest
had lasted. He had not believed it possible that he could
call upon and count on energy sufficient to carry him the
superhuman lengths to which he had gone.

His wound, which had been roughly bound up, throbbed
and burned. His breath was like fire in his throat and lungs.
He was so weak that he felt nauseated.

Pilgrims and priests surrounded him and Chang Kong
in the *sala*, watching the two of them as if they were two
curious, novel insects. Water was fetched for them. Both
men drank sparingly, after rinsing their dust-dry mouths.
In silence, the crowd about them watched and waited.

Chang Kong presently drew a shuddering breath, fixed
his pig-like eyes on Peter's pale, haggard face and panted,
"Little pig of an Annamese—we will meet in battle again!"

"Flea-bitten rat," Peter gasped, "next time, I will not let
you off so easy!"

WHEN HE WAS rested, Peter tottered out in search of Para

Kahn, whom he had heard was a victor. Seven men, he was told, had survived the scimitar contests. A priest said this.

"And tonight," the priest said, "there will be a contest by moonlight."

Peter walked on.

Para Kahn was waiting for him under the ebony tree. He was lying on his back, staring up through the gnarled black branches at the purple-blue of the late afternoon sky.

The Siamese said, in a tired voice, "He drew blood."

"Yes."

Then Peter saw the folded rag, stained red, on Para Khan's shoulder. "H'm," he said, and lifted it and looked. Blood was welling from a slash five inches in length, bone-deep.

He replaced the rag and said, "Para Khan, come along with me."

He retrieved his woven grass bundle from the bush in which he had cached it, slung it over his shoulder and led the Siamese prince down to the brook. There they bathed their wounds.

With a sigh, Peter said, "I don't know where this is leading us.—Trouble, surely.—I've got magic medicine here that will practically heal that slash by sundown. I'm going to heal this gash in my arm and that gash on your shoulder. Then we're going to rub each other down with some more magic stuff—more Yogi—that will put hell-fire into us."

Para Khan regarded him dreamily. "Why, my friend?"

"Yes," Peter agreed. "Why? We'll merely fix each other up so we can kill each other tonight."

"I would hate to kill you!" said Para Khan, earnestly.

"I may be wrong, but I don't think you're going to have

the chance. I have a hunch that we're through with this kind of contest. There are only seven contestants left out of the original one hundred and thirty. I understand that when the eliminations reach this point, the man-to-man contests are over. It will be some other kind of test."

They had reached the brook. Peter rubbed the healing medicament into the gash on Para Khan's shoulder, and Para Khan administered more of the stuff to the long slash in Peter's arm. When they had rested, they rubbed each other down with the strange purple ointment which Dekka had brewed.

Peter's flesh began to burn. This strange inflammation penetrated his veins, his very bones. His fatigue was driven out as if by an infinite number of little devils. He was wonderfully refreshed and stimulated. But the change in Para Khan was even more pronounced. His lassitude utterly left him. He became mirthful, even hilarious.

Peter recalled that the first few applications of the preparation had had a similar effect on him, mixed with a curious feeling of irritation.

With many gestures and much laughter, Para Khan told the story of a Siamese elephant drive in which an infuriated young bull had chased a prince of Siam, had forced him, howling with fear, into a tree which the furious young bull then attempted to uproot with his trunk.

The prince clung to a branch that swayed and threshed about, yelling for help.

Para Khan and Peter became so uproarious with laughter over the account that the Siamese could hardly gasp out the end of the story.

THUS, RED AND breathless with laughter, they were found

by Zari. That capricious maiden hotly accused Peter of laughing so heartily because he had successfully evaded her. She had seen him wounded; and she was worried. But her indignation changed to wonder when she examined the wound.

"Why, it is almost healed! What magic is this?"

"A goddess in robes of silver, with diamonds and rubies in her hair, emeralds in her ears, and sapphires in her nose," Para Khan answered with mock seriousness. "She came down from yonder cloud and spoke a spell. *Hi-yah*—the cut began to heal!"

Zari regarded him with distrustful eyes, then stared wonderingly at Peter. His face was grave.

"Was this goddess beautiful?" she demanded.

"So beautiful that the most beautiful maidens of this earth," the Siamese answered, "resemble the comic sculpturings made by bullocks' hoofs in mud."

"She was not more beautiful than I!—No woman on earth or in any cloud is more beautiful than I!"

"Little tongue-of-rattling-brass," the Siamese prince answered, "compared to her, you are a withered and toothless hag."

Tears filled the eyes of the golden Annamese girl.

"My king," she said huskily, "say that this is not true!"

"Perhaps he is exaggerating," Peter suggested.

Zari smiled, looked hopeful.

"Alas, no!" Para Khan cried. "She was more beautiful than Amaya, or Madi or Thanbula. Her cheek was more beautiful than the dawn; her eyes were deeper than the river pools. When she loosed her hair upon her shoulders, it was as the night coming over the hills.

"You are a vain and jealous woman, Zari. You have forgotten that liberality is chief among the ten great virtues; it is the second of the three works of perfection; it is the absolute soul of the five renouncements!"

"Siamese ape!" Zari retorted. "The sun may rise in the west; the summit of Mount Meru may be bent like a bow; the fires of hell may languish and die out; the lotus may spring on the tops of the mountains; but the ring of truth is everlasting and pure as gold—and your words are the booming of an empty barrel!"

She slid to the ground beside Peter and shamelessly wrapped her slim golden arms about his neck.

"My king," she said, "I heard two priests whispering. I know what is to happen in the arena tonight. You seven who have survived must walk upon coals of fire!"

19

THROUGH HOT HELL

THE PILGRIMS, THEIR avidity for swift and shocking forms of death being temporarily appeased, were now directing their curiosity upon another kind of contest. The judging of upwards of one hundred Oriental beauties, each driven by the fanatical religion of Lu to the hope that she might be "the little golden lamb" selected to have her fair throat cut and her lifeless body thrown into the pit of fire.

All that afternoon and early evening, following the scimitar contests, crowds had swarmed through the clearings where these *salas* were, comparing the girls as, previously, they had compared the gladiators. It was this inspection which Susan had most dreaded. Of all these thousands who passed before her, staring at her, one might recognize her! Her plan would be ruined, her death ordered, immediately!

She had never mastered any Oriental tongue. But Chula, her *amah*, had found a way around that difficulty, just as she had found a way to give Susan's face an Oriental cast. She had spread a rumor that Susan was a deaf mute. Yet this rumor had certain qualities of a boomerang. Stories had spread of Susan's exceptional beauty; and when it was rumored that one of the fairest of the beauties lacked both

voice and hearing, her *sala* became the very center of interest.

Chula was kept busy answering questions, and she
answered them glibly. Because she was from southern China herself, she had, with all the arts and tricks
of make-up, given Susan the appearance of a southern
Chinese. And she had cleverly made capital of Susan's most
treacherous features—her eyes. The eyes of all Chinese girls
are dark brown or black.

But Chula glibly lied to the curious. "Her name is
Tsi-lo-lan—Violet," she explained. "I beg you, mark her
eyes! Pure, deepest violet! Hence her name. Only once in
ten generations is a girl-child born into a family with these
wondrous eyes."

To all comers, Chula said, "Tsi-lo-lan is from the
village Cho-Kang, on the pearl river. Suitors swarm from
hundreds of leagues around to compete for her favors. But
Tsi-lo-lan is a deeply religious girl. She wishes to be the
little golden lamb.—*Aie!*"

SUSAN WAS AWARE of one person who came again and
again to her *sala* to stare—a beautiful girl with golden skin.
This girl and her grandmother occupied one of the nearby
salas. Chula had learned that she, also, had aspirations to
become a little golden lamb in the selection which would
take place tonight—at the hour of the dragon.

This girl's repeated visits to the *sala* made Susan uneasy.
The stare of the little Annamese was hostile, jealous, scornful. It had all those qualities with which beautiful women
since time immemorial have stared at their rivals. This
slender, golden beauty, lacking modesty or the benefit
of civilizing influences, wore nothing but a bright Java-

nese sarong, which fell from her slim waist to her tiny golden feet. Shamelessly, with an air of utter innocence, the Annamese girl went about thus scantily clad.

Her body was slim, round, beautiful fashioned. She was, Chula declared to Susan, a dangerous contestant. She had no graces—she was a little savage—but she was beautiful. She rejoiced in the name of Zari, and she hailed from the city of Hai-Phong.

Countless times that day, Zari returned to Susan's *sala* to fix her with that hostile, scornful stare. And at each visit, Zari's stare was even more hostile, and Susan's discomfort greater.

Dark fell. Zari wrenched herself from her jealous contemplation of the beauty from South China, and returned to her *sala*.

She said to her grandmother: "Have you looked upon that girl with purple eyes again?"

The old woman testily answered, "Again and again and again!"

"And you still say she cannot match my beauty?"

"No maiden here can compare with you."

Relieved, Zari cried, *"Hola!* Compared to me, does not her face resemble the comic sculpturings made by bullocks' hoofs in mud?"

"Aie! Aie! Well said, my golden lamb!"

AT THIS MOMENT, under the ebony tree behind the contestants' *sala*, Peter Moore and Para Khan were rubbing their feet—soles, toes, tops and ankles—with the magical green liquid which Dekka had compounded.

The thin gassy smell of burning charcoal was in the air, and the light of the rising moon was almost rivalled by the glare from the great mound of flaming embers in the center of the arena, a glare which grew and grew as the temple priests, armed with great hand-driven bellows, fanned this small mountain of coals to higher and higher heat.

The secret was no longer a secret. The pilgrims had learned, to their delight, that the remaining contestants were to be given the trial by fire—unquestionably the cruelest form of elimination so far employed. The survivors of the trials by steel, by cobras, by weaponless combat, were to walk with naked feet across a field of white-hot coals! What a spectacle! What fun! To watch young men walk on white-hot coals in bare feet! *Hai-yah!*

Peter Moore, as he rubbed the magic-working green liquid into Para Kahn's feet, was surrendering to strange, mixed impulses. If, by chance, there was still some form of contest in which he would be forced to fight Para Khan, he might now be defeating his own terrific efforts at reaching an unattainable goal. He had been forced to revise his earlier estimates of Para Khan. The Siamese prince, with all his dislike for these contests and the barbaric purpose behind them, was powerful, nimble, dextrous—skilled in all forms of combat. He would make a dangerous antagonist. So far, only a miracle had prevented their being matched against each other.

From the direction of the stadium there came the muffled roar of thousands of voices. Close at hand, from the little *salas* wherein the pilgrims dwelt, rose a thin, eerie wailing—the high, sad lamentations of women and girls who mourned those strong young men who had died in the arena. Peter shivered.

A priest called out, in the glowing darkness, "Para Khan! Lak Ching! Ready!"

The seven contestants went to the arena, surrounded by priests, to protect them against the too effusive interest of the spectators. The great pile of white-hot charcoal in the middle of the arena gave off an intense light which, playing on objects near at hand, dwarfed the brilliance of the moon. Heat from the flaming white mound, rising into the air, caused that heavenly body to ripple and dance and assume strange shapes, as if it actually shrank from the heat.

The flaming white light danced on the coils of pale blue stone which composed the Temple of the Coiled Serpent, glittered in the jeweled eyes. It was a scene as bizarre, as fantastic, as any conceived in the imagination of *Scheherazade*.

A great iron rake drawn by a dozen bullocks would swiftly spread out the pile of white-hot charcoal into a field several inches thick and a hundred feet square. The seven survivors of the contests were to walk across this field of white-hot coals. They must not run. They must walk steadily, "as if," in the words of the high priest, "you were marching with dignity into the heart of Nirvana"— Nirvana being a form of Oriental heaven.

"As most of us will be doing, anyway," commented Para Khan in a low voice.

"The seven survivors are to watch me closely for the signal," continued the priest. "You must approach the field of fire in a row; not side by side, but four paces apart, so that all of you will begin to cross the field of fire at the same time."

THE SEVEN SURVIVORS looked at the great, white-hot

mound. The heat from it was so intense that even at a distance it dried the sweat on their skin and inflamed their eyes.

They were formed in a line, with a priest at either end. The driver of the bullock teams was given a sharp order. He cracked a great blacksnake whip. The bullocks moved. The chains from their yokes to the great iron rake rattled, clanked, tightened. The rake began to move. White-hot coals tumbled in avalanches down the far side of the mound.

The rake dragged them along and spread them out in a rough layer perhaps four inches thick. The flaming mound perceptibly vanished, and quickly became a thick bed of pink-white coals.

Peter, watching the fiery mountain evolve into a fiery field, with the heat of it scorching his face at a distance of two hundred feet, wondered how he could possibly cross such an inferno. Never, in all his training at Dekka's hands, had he attempted such a large or thick field of fire. His feet were now as tough as rock, and the mysterious green liquid had worked its magic previously.

However, he did not see how human flesh could endure such blistering heat, in spite of Yogi miracle-working medicines.

He glanced about the stadium. Dark eyes glittered in dark faces. Teeth gleamed as if no faces were there. Smiles and expectant laughter! Seven young men to walk barefooted over a field of incandescent charcoal! *Hai-yah!*

It was the most horrible, the most fantastic contest thus far devised. Not believing that he could cross that area of dreadful heat, Peter lifted his gaze to the glittering eyes, almost a thousand feet in the air above him, in the stone serpent's head. The innermost shrine in that monstrous temple was his goal.

Somehow, he must cross this field of scorching heat!

"Ready!" shouted the high priest behind the lines. "March!"

WITH A PRIEST at either end of the line, the seven started. The heat became more and more intense. Blue and purple hues were mingled with the white and pink, as Peter drew nearer and nearer the fiery field. These were unburned gases. Before, the air had been thick with sharp, eye-watering gases; but as Peter approached the fiery area, these gases caused sharp pains in his nose and throat. Almost unendurable they were, and his eyes watered so that he could hardly see.

The man on his left stopped. Priests, in the rear, yelled at him. He took another step, hesitated again. The priests yelled. He went on. The six went grimly, stolidly ahead, shielding their eyes and noses with forearms.

Now the fiery surface was only a few feet away. Heat, in awful waves, beat upward along Peter's legs, attacked his body in a million flaming needles, in waves, in a great and awful reverberation.

He had never imagined such heat. And now he had reached the edge of the field a—swimming, horrible sea of heat.

The man who had hesitated before stopped again. He began to moan. Determinedly, he placed one foot down on the edge of the bed of coals. He shrank back. He was wailing now, in a thin, hysterical voice.

His voice rose to a thin howl of terror. "I cannot! I cannot!"

Suddenly, he turned about. He started to run from that withering blast of heat. Priests seized him before he had run a hundred feet. And Peter, slowly advancing onto the fiery field, heard his scream of terror end in a bubbling gurgle—and knew that a knife had been plunged into his throat.

Shuddering, Peter went on. He felt the heat in feet and ankles; but it was as if this heat came from a distance. It was too hot for comfort; yet, strangely, it was not unendurable. Only above his knees was the pain of it excruciating. There had been only enough of Dekka's magical green liquid to rub on feet, ankles and calves. Originally, there had been enough to permit him to smear the thick, oily green stuff over his entire body, but he had shared it with Para Khan.

On the floor of the miniature hell, he thanked Dekka now. He smelled scorching flesh and leather. The garment about his loins was of leather. The scorching flesh was not his own, but that of less fortunate men.

Through the devilish play of gas flames and heat waves, he could see Chang Kong, out in front. That giant, without benefit of Yogism, was now deserving sympathy.

Near Peter, another of the six was loudly whimpering. These whimperings grew into cries of distress, then of acute pain, finally of agony. This unfortunate was screaming now, taking great exaggerated steps, momentarily in danger of losing his balance and toppling over into the searing pink coals.

Peter, walking more carefully than ever before in his life, watched this man. He knew that the fellow could not go on much farther. He saw him fall to his hands, and his heart muscles tightened at the man's agonized shrieks. Then the unfortunate got to his knees in the pink-hot coals, shrieked again, and again tried to walk. He could not.

The smell of burning flesh was now sickening. The man fell again, this time on his side. Again he got to his feet and tottered on. But he was done for. His feet, unprepared for such an ordeal, were literally baked, charred. With another scream, he fell, and this time he did not rise. A wave of awful, sick faintness went over Peter as little flames burst out at the edges of the man's body, as his screams stopped, as the sound of his broiling flesh crackled above the hissing of the charcoal. It was hideous.

CHANG KONG, PACING along as steadily as an automaton, was now in the center. And, a few feet to his right, likewise keeping up a steady plodding, was Para Khan. Both men had their arms folded over their faces to keep off the blasting heat.

Another man began to scream and to fall, to pick himself up again, to totter, and fall once more. Soon he, too, was but a heap of charring flesh on the embers.

Now there were four of them.

But another was beginning to take those long, strange steps. He was fighting it out in silence, with hands clasped about head, doggedly driving himself on. He wore the white turban of Hinduism, although converts to the religion of Lu were supposed to discard all emblems of previous faiths. Having been a Hindu, it was likely that he knew something about fire-walking. But his earlier practices were not enough now. He wavered. He stumbled, fell to

Searching, malignant eyes were upon her.

his knees. Still he did not cry out; but it was the beginning
of the end.

And because he did not scream, or whimper, Peter felt
sorrier for him than for the others. He saw that turbaned
head pitch down and fail to rise again; saw the burst of
flames as the turban struck the hot coals, and again he
smelled the sickening stench of burning human flesh.

Now there were only the three of them: Chang Kong,
Para Khan and Peter. Peter did not believe that Chang
Kong had the benefits of miracle-working liquids such
as he had. But he did not see how, otherwise, the hairy
giant could go through this fiery hell and not have his feet
charred off to the ankles. Yet Chang Kong went on and on,
together with Peter and Prince Para Khan. The giant was
like a veritable devil on the floor of hell, striding, striding
a little beyond and behind him.

In one way, the very slowness of their gait was an advantage. It permitted the coals to cool. When the seven had

started, the coals were pinkish white. When the three reached the middle, the same coals were an angry red. They became darker.

A howl went up from the stadium when it became evident that the three who had survived thus far would in all likelihood survive to the very end, although whether a cheer of applause or a jeer of disapproval, Peter did not know—or care. How he hated that bloodthirsty mob! *Hi-yah!*

Like three relentless figures in a nightmare of the here-after, Peter Moore, Chang Kong and Para Khan went over the field of darkening charcoal and emerged on the white sand beyond—intact! None of the three had once faltered or fallen.

Chang Kong was first to emerge. Then came the prince from Siam. Lastly, Peter. And they did not stop walking until that hellish heat was well behind them!

ACCUSTOMED TO THE glare, Peter could see nothing for some time. He listened to the roar of the mob with indifference. Once again, the mob was overflowing into the arena, frantic to congratulate the three who remained of the original one hundred and thirty.

But priests fended the spectators off, drove them back. As if from a distance, Peter heard the hairy giant's voice. "Little pig of an Annamese, you did well to survive.—We live to fight again!"

Peter, still breathless from the heat, panted, "It can't be too soon, my flea-bitten rat!" and wondered why the priests about them burst into laughter. It did not occur to him until a little later how foolish might seem such undying hatred between two men who had survived such ordeals side by side. He could not forget how joyously, and with what gusto, Chang Kong had broken the backs of help-less men.

Peter's eyes, now accustomed to the absence of that furi-ous heat, saw that Para Khan's feet and legs to the knees were unblistered, but that the skin above was blistered, and that the hair of arms and face was but a dark char.

Then he glanced at Chang Kong, and laughed.

"The hairy giant is no longer hairy!" he cried.

Chang Kong was growling. "You two must have used a stronger magic against heat than mine. But have you enough magic for our next combat?"

There was a commotion among the encircling priests. One of the mob had broken through—a small person with golden skin and a shrill voice—a golden girl covered from hips to little golden feet by a jade green sarong!

The little Annamese maiden flung her arms about Peter's neck. Her cool slim body squirmed against his burning chest.

"My king!" she panted in his ear. "I watched you! Every step you took was a white-hot iron in my faithful heart! You have the courage of the lion, the fortitude of the water buffalo—"

"Lak Ching!" the high priest coldly interrupted.

Peter unfolded Zari's arms from his neck. A priest seized her and unceremoniously pushed her outside the circle, where her shrieks of fury were drowned in the uproar.

Lao Li said, "The fate of you three who have so far survived is to be decided now within the temple of Lu. We go—alone."

In his voice there was a quality that sent through Peter a sudden chill.

20

THE SLICER

SURROUNDED BY UPWARDS of one hundred of the temple priests, Lao Li and the three survivors made their way through the milling mob toward the steps which led up the face of the mound on which stood the Temple of the Coiled Serpent.

There was a new, electrifying excitement in the air. The rumor had spread that Lu had arrived—was even now within the temple! Peter felt a moment's fear. If his luck held to the end—if he survived the final test—he would, for the first time since the enmity had started, see this grotesque Chinese—Lu—part man, part genius, part monster.

Once again, he devoutly wished that it was somehow possible for him to have a chance at killing this almost mythological figure who had gained such power over the continent of Asia. Lacking that chance, he hoped as devoutly to have a chance at stealing and destroying the infamous Sapphire Skull, thereby destroying a vast part of Lu's imponderable power.

His only fear was that Lu, when they looked at each other through the bars of the bronze grille, would recognize him. Yet he was certain that his appearance was sufficiently Oriental to deceive even such a diabolically shrewd observer as Lu.

The three survivors and Lao Li, protected by the priests, were nearing the top of the great flat mound on which the temple stood. The outer rim of this large plateau was a surging mass of pilgrims. It was supposed to accommodate one hundred thousand worshippers, and it seemed filled to capacity. In the brilliant moonlight, they were staring through the bars of the circular cage about the temple. This was the cage which enclosed the black leopards; and these savage beasts paced to and fro, staring malignantly at the crowd. They had been starved to the point of gauntness.

At the entrance to the enclosure, Lao Li and the three survivors and the temple priests stopped. A priest quickly touched two of the bars with his hands. Slowly, two parallel rows of bronze spikes rose out of the stone floor to a height of ten feet, forming a lane from the gate of the enclosure to the steps of the temple—a lane about ten feet wide into which no leopard could intrude. Halfway down this lane was the round, brimming pool of water which Peter had noticed before.

The gate before which the group of contestants and priests stood sank quickly into the masonry floor, and they entered the safety lane. When the last of them was in the safety lane, the gate rose up behind them again; and as they passed the pool, the high bronze grille ahead—barrier at the temple entrance—sank into the floor.

In all of this, Peter saw the ingenious hand of Lu.

ONCE THEY WERE inside the temple entrance, the great grille there rose up from the floor into which it had sunk. As it did so, the two lines of bronze spears forming the safety lane through the circular cage sank back into their places, out of sight, thereby permitting the leopards once more to roam over that area.

Just ahead in the temple was the pit of fire. It was perhaps twelve feet in diameter, and it gave off a soft hissing. Peter presumed that it was kept at white heat by the injection of air into pipes underneath. Into it the girl chosen by the priests for sacrifice, and then killed by Lu—the little golden lamb—would be tossed by the newly selected high priest.

Peter looked quickly about him as the three contestants were conducted past the pit of fire. From the pit, the wide flight of marble stairs went sharply upward into the gloom. The interior of the temple was lavish—an example of Oriental magnificence. The walls on either side of the stupendous staircase were great slabs of lapis lazuli inset with designs in silver and gold. This staircase was wide enough so that the worshippers, crowding about outside the leopard enclosure, could see to the very top. At intervals, the staircase was closed off by a bronze grille. Thus was any attempt on the life of Lu frustrated. Peter counted six of these barriers—or one at every hundred and fiftieth step or so.

There were other grilles. There was a grille set into the wall on either side of the fiery pit, for instance. Behind these grilles, Peter understood, the priests of the fire, in their red robes, gathered—were virtually prisoners—when the new high priest started down the stairs with the dead body of the "little golden lamb" in his auns.

Lao Li had opened a door beside one of these grilles. The three survivors and the temple priests went through and down a corridor, then up a spiral stairway. They passed through enormous empty rooms, climbed more stairs. Peter impressed this march on his memory—every turn, every twist, every climb.

Presently they entered a spacious room—the last—which was well illuminated with oil lights. In the opposite wall was set what Peter quickly guessed was the last of the tests. It was a perfectly round doorway, about ten feet in diameter. Beyond was gloom. At brief intervals, this doorway was closed by a shining sheet of oiled steel, which seemed to slide out from a slot in the wall.

Then Peter saw that the entering edge of this steel-sheet door was rounded. He realized that it was a disk of steel—a disk slightly larger in diameter than the doorway—and that this disk did not slide across the doorway and then back again, but that it entered from the right and vanished into the wall at the left. It was evident that the upper edge of the disk was bolted to a revolving axle hidden in the wall, and that this axle caused the disk to shoot past the round opening with extreme rapidity—and with extreme irregularity. Sometimes it paused, for a fraction of a second, blocking the doorway, and sometimes it paused in its orbit within the wall, leaving the doorway clear for a fraction of a second.

Peter understood all this without the explanation which the high priest was giving. He knew that the trick was to get through the doorway without being chopped in half—a trick virtually beyond human ability!

THE STEEL DISK came slicing into view from the edge of the round doorway with such rapidity, such speed, and at such irregular intervals that unless one knew precisely how these intervals were timed by the hidden mechanism, he would be instantly cleaved in halves!

Studying this diabolical device, then glancing at Para Khan and Chang Kong, Peter reflected, "How can any of us survive?"

Within the next few minutes, the fate of the three of them would be determined—Peter, his friend, and his enemy.

The three had come far. Of one hundred and thirty men, all but they had been sacrificed to make this moment possible. They had fought through a bloody contest without weapons. They had fought cobras. They had fought with scimitars. They had walked across a field of withering heat. And only the three men remained. Who among them would survive? Para Khan? Chang Kong? Peter the Brazen? Would he lose his friend or his enemy, or both? Or would he, too, be split in halves by that diabolical disk?

Staring at the great steel disk as it sliced across the opening so rapidly, so irregularly, he did not believe that any of them would survive this final test.

The high priest was saying, "You are to draw lots. The first man chosen is permitted fifteen minutes in which to study just how the intervals are spaced. Draw lots!"

He passed out three numbered sticks.

Para Khan drew Number Two! Chang Kong, One; Peter, Three. Peter's heart was beating rapidly with nervous apprehension. His throat was dry again.

Para Khan walked over to him and put out his hand, which Peter grasped. The Siamese prince said, "Blessings of Buddha! If I miss—"

"Good luck!" Peter said, and they watched Chang Kong,

who was staring with wrinkled brow at the doorway. For
the first time since Peter had known him, the giant looked
uneasy. Then his uneasiness seemed to go away. His brow
cleared. He went close to the round doorway, watched the
disk as it came slashing through, and began to laugh. He
wheeled about and roared:

"By the toenail of Buddha, this is a game for children—
not grown men! Anyone but a blind, crippled fool could
leap through this door and escape that meat chopper!"

For the first time, Peter felt sympathy for Chang Kong.

"My advice to you," the high priest said to the giant, "is
to study carefully the timing of that disk. It is not child's
play. The chances against any man's getting through that
doorway alive are one hundred to one!"

The giant jeered at him. "Child's play! Do I have another
chance at breaking this fellow's back, if we both get through
there alive?"

Lao Li said quietly, "First—get through!"

Peter was watching the round doorway and the flashing
disk with its razor edge. There must be, he realized, some
system in the very irregularity with which the blade flashed
through the ten-foot aperture. And every so often, unless
he was mistaken, this system would repeat itself—begin all
over again. Sometimes the disk flicked across the opening
a dozen times before you could draw a full breath. And
twice, within the ensuing five minutes, Peter observed that
the disk remained hidden from sight, leaving the doorway
clear, for fully four seconds—ample time for a man to go
safely through.

Realizing that his very life depended on it, it was difficult to concentrate, to memorize. His thoughts persisted in slipping off to a picture of himself being chopped in halves. **THE VOICE OF** the high priest spoke. "Chang Kong! Your fifteen minutes is about to begin!"

Chang Kong laughed. He glared at Peter and jeered, "On the other side of that door—we will meet again, my little Annamese pig! Your hours are numbered!"

"Unless your minutes are measured!" Peter answered. "Good luck!"

In that fifteen minutes, while the three had stared at the door, Peter believed he had solved the riddle of the disk's timing. It went through a definite routine of irregular halts and slashings *every five minutes!* And twice during those five minutes it halted in the wall long enough for a man to go safely through the doorway. But for a man to go safely through, he must know every one of the disk's hesitations and appearances *in their order!*

Did Chang Kong know this?

The giant strode to the door. He placed his hands on his hips and watched the slashing disk. He watched it for no more than fifteen seconds, then he crouched down. The disk of death hesitated.

As it vanished, Chang Kong leaped into the opening.

The disk instantly disappeared. The razor edge sliced into Chang Kong midway down the side of his body, below the right arm. It cleaved through him with as little effort as a sharp knife cuts through soft butter. His head, shoulders and arms vanished. The lower half of his sundered body fell back from the threshold into the room, gushing blood and spewing entrails. The steel disk appeared again, scattered drops of blood.

Peter's heart gave a sickening thump. A slime of perspiration formed on his forehead. He felt sick and weak, on the very brink of uncontrollable terror.

21

GUARDIAN OF THE SAPPHIRE SKULL

THE HIGH PRIEST said, "Para Khan."

There was a new sensation in Peter's brain, as if horror were sucking the last drop of blood from it. Almost too weak to stand, he watched Para Khan walk to the doorway of suicide.

The Siamese prince turned and looked at Peter. In his poet's eyes was horror at Chang Kong's ghastly, swift death. Para Khan's face, under its rich coloring, was wan. A grin tugged at his mouth. His lips moved, but Peter did not hear any sound from them. His own throat was too dry for speech.

Para Khan turned about and faced the doorway. The Siamese prince waited for fully two minutes, crouched, ready to leap. The disk clicked quickly four times, then hesitated, then seven times. Another hesitation. Two clicks.

"Now!" Peter breathed through clenched teeth.

Para Khan leaped, his head bent down and to one side. Peter clearly saw his profile. Para Khan was looking down; an expression of horror occupied his pale face. He vanished. The steel blade slashed down. Para Khan had gone through safely!

But what lay beyond? What had brought that look of horror to his face?

"Lak Ching, you must wait."

Why must he wait? What further demands could be made upon him beyond that dreadful disk? What was happening to Para Khan?

A tense and terror-filled ten minutes passed. Then there was a stir at the doorway behind him. A grave-faced priest came in. He murmured a message to the high priest.

Lao Li came to Peter and said, "Para Khan did not emerge."

"From what?" Peter cried.

"He is dead. It is your turn, Lak Ching."

Sick and weak with horror, Peter walked to the door. His legs hardly held him up. There was an awful emptiness at his stomach. Para Khan—dead! What monstrous fate had ended that tragic young life?

Peter faced the doorway, waited, crouched, forced his brain to concentrate on the routine of the deadly disk of steel. It sliced through the air with a hissing sound. He, too, would go through on the first of the four-second hesitations.

Beyond was gloom, almost black. Peter's mind was counting like a machine. The disk clicked four times, hesitated; clicked seven times. Another hesitation. Two clicks. Now!

Peter leaped, counting the seconds. One—two—three—
Below him was absolute nothingness! Four! He heard the steel disk hiss past behind him, missing him by inches.

He was falling! His heart beat frantically. Far, far, below him was a light. It rose toward him with the speed of a rocket. He was falling—It might have been a hundred feet; it seemed a thousand—inside a great, vertical tube, eighteen or twenty feet in diameter.

What was below him? Water! He caught the glimmer of it. Then, just as he plunged into it, he saw, floating upon it, the upper part of Chang Kong's body.

THE INSTANT PETER struck the water, he spread arms and legs to check his descent. The impact knocked the breath out of him. Forcibly, he struck a smooth stone bottom at a depth of perhaps fourteen feet. He kicked himself back to the surface, gasping for air.

An oil flame, burning in a niche perhaps ten feet above the water, afforded the only illumination. For perhaps half a minute he floated, taking deep breaths, trying to calm the uproar of his heart.

Then he examined the wall of the tube. He swam about it, testing the stones. No escape there. Presently he took a deep breath and swam back to the bottom. There he found a round opening about thirty inches in diameter. Through this, presumably, he was to make his exit. He swam quickly down this tube. It ran horizontally. It turned, doubled back, went off in another direction.

Dekka had taught him to stay submerged for long intervals, but in those submergings Peter had never moved about. He had remained inert at the bottom of the little lake, counting the seconds. Staying under water depended solely on the endurance, the capacity of the heart. Terrific nervous strain such as this diminished the heart's capacity, and the energy, the oxygen used in the exertion of swimming, of pushing and pulling and kicking himself along the water-filled tube, was already heavily taxing that painfully built-up endurance.

While he swam along the tube, following its turns, he was counting the seconds. His limit was a few seconds over seven minutes. He had already counted off one hundred and eighty seconds—half the limit of his capacity. And suddenly he received a shock which all but proved fatal. Unexpectedly, his hands came into contact with a man's body. And in the next instant, as he slid on, his hands struck the end of the tube—a dead end!

So terrific was the combined shock of these almost simultaneous discoveries that he let some of the precious air supply escape from his lungs in an involuntary gasp of horror.

Rapidly, he ran his hands down the body of the dead man. And his horrified suspicions were verified. Para Khan! The Siamese prince had reached the dead end, and had either lost heart or exhausted his lung supply so that he had drowned!

Even in that moment when his own life depended solely upon his immediate retreat down the tube, Peter lingered seconds, filled with a mingling of hatred and grief over his friend's unfair and violent fate. Then he realized that he had lost count of time; had, in his horror and bitterness, neglected to tell off the seconds. His lungs were beginning to burn. He was conscious of the growing, suicidal impulse to exhaust the used air in his lungs at any cost. His heart was beating painfully.

The question was, was there enough time left for him to return to the tank and to get another lungful of fresh air?

As rapidly as he could, he began pushing himself backward down the tube. And these vigorous exertions, added to the strain already imposed on his heart by his previous efforts and his shocking discovery of his friend's dead body, drained his capacity to the point where he thought his lungs must surely burst.

He had the frantic, trapped feeling which comes in its worst form to a man who is trapped under water.

Back—back—back. In spite of his self-command, bubbles of air were leaking out of his nostrils and the corners of his mouth. And when that involuntary relinquishment of air begins, a man's doom is written.

HE CAME ABRUPTLY to the end. He had emerged from the tube into the great round tank! But long before he reached the surface, his lungs were gasping forth the used and reused air.

He reached the surface almost completely spent. He had, with the narrowest of margins, survived. For minutes he lay on his back, gulping in fresh air, giving his laboring heart a rest. And when he was certain that he was sufficiently refreshed, he took the deepest possible breath, and dived again.

This time, he explored the bottom of the tank thoroughly; and although he examined every foot of the bottom and the sides, he could find only one more opening. He wondered if this, too, had a blind ending—or if he had overlooked a more subtle way of escape? The second opening led into a tube that was larger than the other—perhaps forty inches in diameter.

Peter did not at once enter it; he rose to the surface for a brief rest and another supply of fresh air, then he swam down and into the new tunnel. This time he would not make the mistake of losing count of the elapsing seconds.

He swam and pushed himself along the slimy walls of the tube with the least possible effort. This tube, like the other, curved and twisted this way and that. Occasionally, there was a sharp right or left turn.

He did not grow concerned until he had counted three full minutes. And at that moment, the tube forked. Two tubes of the same size—one to the left, the other to the right! Which fork should he follow? He had no means of knowing in what direction he was supposed to be travelling, or even what his objective was; and there was no time to waste on reasoning. He would have to depend on his luck, therefore.

He decided on the left fork; and as he started along its slimy surface, he wondered if this final test did not call upon such superhuman qualities that an ordinary man could not possibly succeed. By strategy, skill and strength, he had so far survived—one man out of a hundred and thirty. But did he have the necessary stamina to win this last test, the most gruelling of them all? Chang Kong had failed because he was stupid. Para Khan had failed because his endurance, in the final analysis, was insufficient. But did Peter possess enough of both brains and endurance?

He was thinking thus, automatically counting off the seconds, when his head encountered a wall.—A right turn or a left turn? Neither! Another dead end!

The elapsed time from the beginning of his submergence was 272 seconds! Slightly more than four and one-half minutes!

In other words, there was left to him less than enough

time to return to the tank! If he tried to return to the tank, he would reach the limit of his heart capacity, more than two minutes before he could possibly reach the surface!

And for the first time since he had adventurously entered the contests, he felt utterly hopeless, defeated. He saw no possibility of escaping this death trap. He would die as Para Khan had died—because he lacked sufficient endurance!

HE WASTED NO time as he returned to the fork. Reaching it, he counted off the three hundred and sixty-fourth second! Already, more than six minutes of his seven and a possible fraction were exhausted!

Now he started swimming and pushing his way along the right fork—and his faltering hopes received another blow. The tube was inclining sharply downward! It continued downward at an increasing angle, which sharply increased the demands on his swimming strength. He could feel the greater pressure on his eardrums, on his lungs, and in the heavier laboring of his heart.

And once again, in spite of his efforts, little bubbles began to escape from his nostrils and the corners of his mouth. Torturing pains began again in his heart. The necessity for freeing the used air from his lungs became almost imperative. He could not retain that burned-out air any longer.

Four hundred and twenty seconds! *Seven minutes!* He was clawing frantically at the water now, using his last ounce of strength in a final, despairing spurt of speed. No longer could he withstand the pressure, the heart strain. He *must* release the air—gulp in water—drown!

The tube inclined sharply upward. It became vertical. In spite of the air dribbling more and more rapidly from

Peter's nose and mouth, he was shooting upward. A ruddy light shone down through the water. And all at once his head shot above the surface!

He expelled the spent air from his lungs, inhaled deeply. He looked dazedly about him, too bewildered at first to recognize his new surroundings. Oil tapers flickered. A familiar roaring sound filled his ears—roars of the mob!

Then he discovered that he had emerged in what he had supposed to be the leopards' watering pool. The bronze spears, forming that safety lane, were up, so protecting him from the black brutes.

Priests were swarming out of the temple toward him. At their head was Lao Li. Staggering with weakness, Peter climbed out of the pool and threw himself on the ground as the high priest approached.

Above the roaring of the mob he heard a familiar sound—a feminine shriek.

He saw her standing there against the bars of the outer gate—the golden girl from Hai Phong. Her face was pressed close to the bars. Her eyes were glowing with adoration. They were misty with tears of delight. And her smile was rapturous.

Gasping, shaking with exhaustion, he gave her a wan grin. The next moment Lao Li began to strip off his snow-white robe, and the uproar made it impossible for Peter to hear what he was saying. Peter did not know that the mob was roaring its approval of his victory—that he had become, by virtue of his fights with the giant Chang Kong, the mob's hero.

The high priest helped Peter to his feet, ceremoniously draped the white robe about Peter's shoulders—a signal to the mob that this young man was the victor in the series of terrific contests in which one hundred and thirty young men had entered—that he had become the new high priest of the Temple of the Coiled Serpent, the guardian of the Sapphire Skull!

22

THE SECRETS OF THE TEMPLE

WITH THE WHITE robe draped about him, the new high priest, staggering wearily, entered the temple with Lao Li, who now wore only a white loin cloth. Lao Li was talking, but it was impossible for Peter to hear him above the noise made by the crowd.

They passed the pit of fire. Lao Li led the way to a door to the right of it. They entered a large empty room of white marble. Here, the uproar of the mob was a far-away droning.

Peter's breathing gradually returned to normal. But his heart still pained him. He felt sick, and not in the least exultant. That he had proved himself the strongest, cleverest, most enduring of the hundred and thirty contestants was a triumph that he did not appreciate. Any exultation he might have enjoyed was killed by the shock of Para Khan's death. He had liked and admired Para Khan tremendously. A friendship such as theirs was one that should have gone on for many years. Sadly he told himself that he ought to be thankful that he and Para Khan had been so miraculously spared the necessity of facing each other in some combat to the death.

But this was slim comfort. Para Khan's death completely

darkened the glory of a moment which any man might pardonably enjoy. The shock of his friend's death was like a dash of cold water, awaking him more sharply to the urgency of the task still ahead; namely, to steal and destroy the Sapphire Skull—to strike a death blow at Lu's power over Asia!

Lao Li was staring at him curiously. Peter, studying the lean brown face of the retiring priest, saw the beginnings of a cynical smile.

"All honor and glory!" Lao Li was saying. "Tonight, you are to stand on the right hand of our master. There is much to explain. Perhaps we ought to begin at once."

Peter was returning the man's stare of curiosity with one no less curious. "Lao Li, what is to become of you now?" he demanded.

"I go with our master to the Lake of the Flying Dragon."

"What becomes of you there?"

Lao Li shrugged, still with that cynical smile. "Who knows?" He really was saying, with the fatalism of the East, "Who cares?"

Peter wondered—death, or the oblivion of a slave in that bizarre underwater palace?

Lao Li said, "You should feel glorified. You alone, of one hundred and thirty young men—the flower of the Orient—survived the cruel contests. A year ago, I felt that way."

"How do you feel now?"

"My friend, the affairs of this world are so much duck-weed on the river. I am twenty-four years old. I have lost all my ideals—all my illusions—even hope. My home was the Shan Hills, of Burma. There I was an ironworker. I was to have married the most beautiful girl among the Shans—and they are the most beautiful girls in the world. She wanted luxury. She married a man who owns twenty elephants. She loved me—but a sable robe cannot be eked out with dogs' tails."

Lao Li dismissed his past, his present, his future with a sharp, hard, mirthless laugh; then he said, "We have much to do. There is much for you to learn. First, I will show you such of the plans of this temple as the high priest is permitted to see."

THESE PLANS WERE kept in an adjoining room, under a lock the key to which Lao Li surrendered to Peter. Lao Li explained the temple—such of it as the high priest was given access to. The other plans were in the possession of the warrior priests.

"Actually, this temple is a fortress. At a moment's notice, every entrance can be closed with great slabs of armor-plate. In the turret—to which you are not admitted—are machine guns and French field pieces, to hold off invaders. And when this place becomes a fort, it commands the surrounding country.—Our master thinks of everything.—Of course there are many secret passageways, known only to him. Many attempts have been made to seize the Sapphire Skull. Men have tried singly—and in force. But no one has succeeded, and no one ever will."

Peter said nothing. He was memorizing such plans of the temple as he, as high priest, was given the privilege of seeing; and he saw that it was impossible for a man to enter or leave the temple without going through the leopard enclosure, unless one had help from the outside. It was impossible to raise the double line of bronze spears forming the safety lane through the leopard enclosure, except from outside that enclosure.

In other words, if Peter wished to escape from this temple unaided—as he must—he must take the following route: he must go through the door of death, dive down through the underwater tunnel and emerge in the leopard's drinking pool, unprotected against the leopards! If he could live through the attack of these half-starved leopards, he could make his way in the enclosure to a bronze door set a quarter of the way around in the face of the temple. This led to an underground passageway which had an outlet about a mile away in the jungle.

Peter had knowledge of this passageway. He had proved that he could escape through the door of death and the water-filled tunnel. But—the leopards?

Lao Li was explaining other matters. There were inner and outer temple guards on duty day and night, throughout the year. There were guards whose duty it was to feed the leopards—sparingly—and there were other guards to spy on these. Within the temple was a small army of priests, actually guards, likewise, who were ordered to protect the high priest and to prevent his escape. There were guards over these—and guards set to watch the warrior priests constantly. In short, an intricate system of guarding and spying to prevent any threat against this priceless property of Lu's—the Sapphire Skull.

Peter's year-round task was to guard that Sapphire Skull. He would live in the room where the skull was kept. He would have servants at his command, but during the coming year he would not be permitted to leave these rooms except for a few days, when a new high priest, his successor, would be selected.

"Now, I'll show you the skull," Lao Li said casually. To him that priceless relic was apparently a matter of little importance.

They climbed stairways, went down corridors, climbed more stairways, always going up and up, nearer the very top of the temple.

LAO LI PRESENTLY opened a door. "Here," he said.

Peter, with thumping heart, saw the glitter of the object in the light of the oil dongs. It stood between two dongs, on a pedestal of purest gold; glittering, twinkling, giving off a blaze of blue glamour. It was the size of a man's skull, and he concluded that either it was a human skull studded with sapphires—the largest stones Peter had ever seen—or it was fashioned after a human model, of some substance resembling bone. It was a thing of uncanny, bizarre beauty.

Across from it, and out from the wall, was a low marble bench upon which, presumably, a privileged worshipper might sit and adore the barbaric thing. But the Sapphire Skull was not for ordinary eyes.

Peter dismissed as premature the impulse to overpower Lao Li at once, seize the skull, and make off with it. He had come thus far without fumbling his chance. At this moment, the skull seemed to be unguarded. But no doubt it was being guarded most efficiently.

In one corner of this shrine—this inner holy of holies—was a thin straw mat. On this, Lao Li explained, Peter would sleep. Adjoining the shrine was a smaller room which gave upon a white marble platform on which stood a marble throne. There, at the top of the marble stairs, Lu would sit for the ceremonies!

Peter said, "Have you ever seen Lu?"

"No. No high priest has ever seen the master. This year, for the first time, he reveals himself. Always, in the past, his entrance has been preceded by a glare of blinding blue light—so dazzling that one can see nothing. A year ago today, I nearly lost my eyesight, staring into that blue glare for a glimpse of him. But I saw nothing!

"This year, he has announced that he will show himself to his people. For the first time, the people will see him actually cut the girl's throat. Always, in the past, she has climbed the stairs and entered the area of blinding blue light; and when the light diminished, she was lying on the floor, with her throat cut—the throne empty! Our master had come, cut her throat—and gone!

"In previous years," Lao Li went on, "it was the high priest's task to carry the skull down and show it to the people. This year, perhaps, the master wishes to take greater precautions. This year is the first time he, personally, will take the skull in his own hands and carry it down for the people to see."

Peter's heart was beating faster. For the first time since he had incurred the enmity of this powerful, almost mythical Chinese, Peter would meet Lu face to face!

Lao Li was again explaining the high priest's duties.

A grille, now closed, separated the high priest from the platform on which Lu's throne stood. It was a barrier of small but stout vertical bronze bars. In the center of the grille was a wicket about ten inches square, very much like the wicket at a paying teller's window in a bank.

Peter, thinking how easy it would be to shoot and kill Mr. Lu from this vantage point, recalled what Dekka had said, "Don't try to tote a gun into that temple. That would be absolutely suicidal, for long before you see Lu, you will be searched to the skin."

Peter believed he could have concealed a small automatic pistol in his loin cloth; but much as he would have liked to assassinate Lu, Peter would have hesitated. To kill that human monster would have meant instant death for his assassin, and Peter, having so successfully run the gantlet of death on various occasions, had no longing for death now. Life was too exciting. Beyond this temple, more adventures were waiting. By attempting to steal the Sapphire Skull, he would be running the risk of death, but at least he had a fighting chance.

LAO LI WAS saying, "I will have to ask you to strip to the skin. It is a precaution we always take." Peter obliged. If he had concealed an automatic pistol in his loin cloth, he might have reached it in time to kill Lao Li. But the shot would have summoned guards.

When Lao Li was convinced that Peter was unarmed, he plunged into a description of the forthcoming ceremony.

Lu would come into the throne room through a secret passageway. When he was seated on the throne, the girl who, because of her superlative beauty, was selected to die, would walk up the stairs. Lu would slit her throat with the *parang* which he carried, then Lu would retire.

Next, by hidden mechanism, Lu would cause the grille at which they now stood to open. The high priest would go out, pick up the dead girl, carry her down the stairs and toss her into the pit of fire. Then the high priest would return to this cubicle, and Lu would cause the grille to close again. He would then reappear and come to the grille and open the wicket. The high priest would hand to him—through the wicket—the Sapphire Skull. Lu would walk down the stairs with this skull in his hands, and would display it to the worshippers. Coming back up the stairs, he would give the skull to the high priest and vanish. This would end the ceremony.

Peter, looking through the grille, could see all the way down the marble stairs to the pit of fire, a white-hot eye burning in the purple gloom below. Between the throne platform and the pit of fire were the six equally spaced bronze grilles. He mentioned them to Lao Li, and Lao Li explained.

"They are a precaution for protecting Lu. His claim—and these pilgrims believe it—is that he is absolutely immortal, that he is invulnerable, and that human hands cannot touch him or harm him. When any one walks down this stairway, these grilles are automatically lowered, one at a time, by concealed machinery. As one goes down, the grille ahead of you opens and the one behind you closes.

"Lu is at all times shielded from any form of attack. He is clever. He trusts no one—none of his priests, not even his high priest. The moment the ceremony starts, the priests of the fire will be shut behind the grilles on either side of the fire pit. Did you know that the Chinese engineer who designed the mechanism of this temple was killed at Lu's order the day the last piece of machinery was in place?"

"No."

"Did you know that every succeeding engineer or architect who has made changes in the temple has been killed the day his work was finished?—Our master, my friend, is a thorough man. For example, a year from now, you will not know the interior of the temple—aside from the great stairway. Everything else will have been entirely rebuilt. Once every year the high priest and the plans of the temple are renewed!—Are you sure the ceremony is quite clear to you?"

"Yes."

Peter was looking at a grille across the way. Apparently it was identical with the one behind which he and Lao Li now stood. "What's that for?" he asked.

"Lu's personal guards. They will appear a moment before he does, and they will stand there. In case of any threat to him, he releases them and they come swarming out. Our master—"

"—is a very thorough man," Peter finished. "What now?"

"I surrender myself to special guards. My work is done."

Peter believed he had the situation fairly well in hand. His plans were laid. When the ceremonies began, he would stand at the grille until the "little golden lamb" reached the top of the stairs to have her luckless throat cut. In the excitement attending her killing, he would seize the skull and make his getaway by the only possible route—through the door of death, down through the tank and the water-filled tube, then through the leopard enclosure and to the door which gave upon the underground passage leading into the jungle! He would have to chance the leopards.

23

ORIENTAL BEAUTY CONTEST

ANOTHER STRANGE ELIMINATION contest was getting under way meanwhile. But this had nothing to do with muscular power or quickness of wits; it was a contest concerned solely with beauty, and the girl who won it would have that highest of honors bestowed upon her—the sacred privilege of having her little throat cut! She would become "the little golden lamb."

While Lao Li was explaining to the winning contestant among the men the mysteries of the temple and the duties of the high priest, the maidens were assembling outside the leopard enclosure.

Some hours previously, Susan's preparations had seriously begun. Since an hour before the setting of the sun—the last sunset, perhaps, that Susan O'Gilvie would ever gaze upon—her *amah*, Chula, had been arranging her hair and making up her face.

A Chinese maiden's toilet is a long and tedious process. Her hair must be done according to rules as old as Confucius. Oils and perfumes must be applied in the proper order. Every hair must be in its assigned place. With equal care must the face be prepared.

But coiffure and facial perfection, in this bizarre beauty

contest, were not all that counted in the selection, by the priests, of the little golden lamb. Susan had learned from Hing Sing Joy, in Singapore, that a contestant was also weighed according to the beauty of her costume.

The garment which Susan had had made for the occasion—under the supervision of Hing Sing Joy and Chula—had cost the richest girl in the world somewhat more than $160,000, in American gold. It was of hand woven silk, from the looms on the Irriwaddi; silk so fine, so lustrous that it was more than mere cloth. It was a living texture, of blue in many shades, with a life of its own like that of living skin. It was richly embroidered with precious stones—loops of pearls about the neck, emeralds on cuffs and sleeves, sapphires, diamonds, rubies placed elsewhere to the best advantage.

It was a barbarically beautiful costume—a fitting adornment to the American girl's slim, beautiful body—and in the left side, just under the left breast, was a cunning little pocket in which a small, keen, ivory-handled dagger was hidden. It had been ingeniously designed, that pocket, so that it did not appear to be a pocket at all, and so that Susan would have no slightest difficulty in snatching from it, when the time came, the dagger which she proposed to strike into the heart of the Blue Scorpion. In Singapore, she had practiced and practiced this part of her plan—the culminating step by which the murder of her lover was to be avenged.

She would murder the Oriental human monster who had caused the death of her lover—and then? Nothing else mattered. She would be brutally killed. To achieve this dramatic moment, she had so far spent, in bribing

Hing Sing Joy, Chula and others, and for the making of her gem-studded robe, more than a half million dollars, in good American gold. Yet her fortune was still hardly scratched!

Susan's riches had long since ceased to have any importance to her. She blamed her wealth, in one way, for her loss of Peter Moore. Her millions—and his pride—had always stood between them.

When Susan climbed the steps up the mound to the entrance to the leopard enclosure to join the other girls, she went alone. Chula's work was done. Chula had done everything for her that was humanly possible. Chula would slip away now, vanish.

SUSAN WAS NO longer afraid, no longer even nervous. She had gone over all this so often in her mind. Her thoughts were exalted; and her exaltation marked her with an unearthly beauty.

Surrounded now by other girls, at the gate to the leopard enclosure, a corner of her mind was amazed that so many girls should strive to sacrifice themselves. But Susan had long ago abandoned the attempt to understand Oriental human nature, or the Oriental's weird belief in his horrible gods.

She watched the starved black leopards pacing back and forth in the enclosure, lashing their long tails, glaring with murderous yellow eyes at the faces close to the bars. Now and then, one of the ravenous black beasts, with a screaming snarl, would hurl itself at the bars and strike out with horrible claws at a face that came too close. Then there would be shouts of laughter from the mob.

A priest elbowed his way among the girls to the enclosure gate. As Susan watched, she saw two parallel rows off stout bronze spears rise out of the ground and form a lane from the gate at which she stood to the enormous bronze grille over the temple entrance.

There were shouts from the mob when a leopard was imprisoned in this safety lane. The spears went down into the ground again; and when the leopard had prowled away, the spears again magically rose out of the ground.

The gate into the safety lane was now opened. When all the girls were inside, the gate was closed. Led by the priest, the girls flocked past the round pool. The great grille ahead of them now sank into the ground, and the girls were led up the steps toward the pit of fire.

Susan shrank from the blast of its heat. Would it be her lifeless body that would be carried down the marble stairway and thrown upon this bed of flaming coals?

A dozen of the fire priests, in their red robes, took the assembled girls in charge. The girls, numbering about a hundred, were instructed to form in a line, side by side, on the lower temple step, facing the crowd. Susan, standing near the middle of the long line, looked at the girls on either side of her with growing apprehension. Chula's optimism had made her confident; now her confidence began to ebb. All the girls she had seen so far were beauties, and their costumes were imaginative and beautiful; some of the costumes simply intended to reveal the lovely lines of the figures inside them, others frankly barbaric and striking.

On her left stood a northern Chinese girl in jacket and trousers—a bell-shaped, flaring turquoise jacket and magenta trousers. She wore ear pendants of jade, and jewelled slippers. On her right was a Burmese girl, star-

tling in her costume of coral pink, at neck, wrists and hem
of dress small gold bells which tinkled when she moved.
Because of her shivering, the bells set up a steady golden
sound. In her hair was a cluster of kingfisher feathers.
Farther down the line, Susan saw the small golden girl who
had haunted her *sala* all afternoon. This one wore nothing
but a jade-green *sarong* which fell from slim hips to little
golden feet—naked feet. Evidently she was relying upon
the sheer beauty of her face and body.

The air was heavy and sweet with seductive perfumes.
The soft golden glare of the countless oil torches picked out
glittering jewels in hair, at ears, at throats, and sewn into
the amazingly beautiful costumes. In that strong, steady
glare, they were like girls on a stage, with the arch of the
great temple behind them.

LOOKING ANXIOUSLY AT the girls on either side, Susan
was growing more and more concerned. Never had she
seen such brilliant fanciful costumes. There was one girl
in a gown made of tiny jade beads. Another was dazzling
because of the ropes of large diamonds which were sewn
into her hair. Still another girl's face, hands and feet were
thickly gilded. Her features were sculpturally perfect; and
her face might have been that of a golden statue, so perfect
was its balance.

Here was represented the very flower of Oriental feminine beauty—girls who had come from the remotest parts
of Asia: from Java, from Turkestan, from China, Siam,
Malaya, Burma.

As the girls lined up, chattering and squealing in their
nervousness like so many birds of brilliant plumage, the
crowd which they faced roared its approval.

Six priests in flame-red robes—the high priests of the holy fire—were moving slowly down the line. The eliminations were under way!

Susan, watching, felt cold waves of fear dancing up and down her spine. Why, she asked herself, should she have believed that she had the slightest chance of winning this fantastic beauty contest? All her life she had been told that she was exceptionally beautiful; but she was not vain, and she was cynical. Chula had declared that Susan was by far the most beautiful girl in this year's contest, but Susan had paid Chula enough gold to permit the *amah* to live luxuriously for the rest of her days—and why, after all, should Chula care?

Moreover, Susan argued, as the priests came closer and closer to her, her beauty was that of the Occident, not of the Orient. By Oriental standards, her beauty was entirely synthetic. These other girls were true Oriental beauties; she was a beauty who had made herself over according to Oriental requirements.

The mob was rearing its approval or disapproval of the priests' decisions. If some girl who was a favorite of the mob was told to drop out, the mob snarled its displeasure. If she was permitted to remain in the line, the mob cheered.

As for the rejected girl, when she was told to drop out of the line she generally did so reluctantly, and under great protest. She screamed, or she sobbed, or she argued. But there was no appeal from the priests' decisions. If one of the contestants was told to drop out she went, or was forcibly taken by priests in gray to stand at one side of the arch.

The high priests of the holy fire had stopped before the girl on Susan's right. Susan would be next!

The little golden bells which adorned the costume of the Burmese girl were now setting up a musical din. Suddenly their tinkling stopped. The Burmese girl screamed. Eliminated!

Now the six priests were considering Susan. Glittering black eyes in a brown square face peered into hers. It was as if she were an insect under a magnifying glass. The little black eyes studied hers for so long an interval that Susan began to feel faint. Her tell-tale violet eyes! Had Chula made that story of her eyes sound convincing?—The black eyes roved about her face, her hair, her ears, her neck.

In an instant, another pair of eyes, this time greenish-brown, in a thin, bony yellow face, replaced them. These eyes came within inches of hers. The man bent closer. His eyes came so close that his eyelashes almost touched Susan's. She wanted to scream. In those eyes, it seemed to her, there was something malignant; it was like staring into the eyes of an octopus.

Then came a third pair of black eyes; close-set, inscrutable, likewise terrifying. This man put thick, sticky fingers to her lips and parted them. He bent close and looked at her teeth.

IN A SURGE of hysteria, Susan wanted to shriek, to laugh, to sob. The eyes went on—and still another pair replaced them. Susan steeled herself, but her terror grew. Since she had been in China, she had often been in danger, but never had she been quite so unstrung as she was now.

Even when she realized that the first inspection was over, and that she had not been eliminated, she experienced little relief. She felt ill. She was afraid that she would faint; and a girl who fainted, Chula had told her, was automatically eliminated.

The priests were going on down the line. Girls shivered; one of them screamed. Priests in gray behind the line seized this girl and carried her, struggling, to the growing throng of the unsuccessful.

In that first inspection, the priests had eliminated more than three-quarters of the contestants; and only about twenty-five girls remained. Among these, Susan, the girl in the green *sarong* and the girl with the gilded face, hands and feet, remained.

Now the next stage of the elimination began. Susan, as the priests once again started down the line, told herself that she could not longer stand it. Her stamina was used up. Her grief for the past six months had left her weak, and the strain of the past few days had used up what little nervous reserve remained. She knew that under her powder and paint her face was white and haggard. She knew she must look ghastly, with her glittering eyes and drawn mouth.

There was another shriek of hurt pride, of insulted vanity or awful despair. One by one, the priests were deciding against the girls who remained.

But the protests of the losers came faintly now, and the crowd was voicing its partisanship more lustily. Large groups of young men had their favorites, and when these favorites were told by the relentless priests to withdraw, the groups angrily protested.

Susan knew that most of this tumultuous mob was drunk tonight on *lehpet*—"pickled tea"—which was not so much an intoxicant as it was an irritant which attacked the lining of the stomach, causing an intense inner excitement and producing hysteria.

The priests were now inspecting the little half-naked girl from Hai-Phong. She met their eyes unflinchingly, with her chin up, her shoulders back, her fists resting impudently on her hips. Susan saw her suddenly smile, excitedly. The girl in the green *sarong* had survived the second inspection!

Now the priests had reached Susan again, and this time their scrutiny of her was more thorough. They came close, they stood off. They inspected her as carefully as if she were a slave on the auction block. Greater attention was paid to her costume. The gems were examined. One priest even got down on hands and knees and examined her diamond-studded blue sandals.

Under the mingling stresses of hope and despair, her heart was thumping. That she had survived the first inspection seemed a miracle. That she had entered such a contest at all was a presumption.

Susan told herself that the girl in the green *sarong*, now glaring at her with hatred and scorn, was far more beautiful than she was.

BUT THE PRIESTS went on—and still she survived. The line had shrunk. On her right stood the girl in the green *sarong*. Beyond her was a Javanese girl, in starched black silk trimmed with little raw nuggets of gold. Her headdress was a magnificent confection of gold and emeralds and diamonds. It rose to a peak, like a witch's hat, and at the peak was the largest diamond Susan had ever seen—a stone as large as a pigeon's egg. Susan, who had seen the great Kohinoor Diamond, among the crown jewels of

England, believed that this gem was even larger. She had been told that there existed, in southern Asia, unlisted gems larger than those in any crown collection of Europe.

Her eyes, hot with nervous excitement, went back to the priests. A girl in golden yellow satin embroidered with blue and red dragons was kicking and screaming in the arms of several gray-robed priests. And the priests were considering another girl; a beautiful, sullen creature, tall and voluptuous, with heavily mascaraed eyes and a sullen, sensuous mouth. She tossed her head this way and that, coquettishly; she posed, flashed her eyes from side to side, and ran her long, tapering hands down her sides in gestures calculated to be irresistible.

This girl's fury, when she was informed that she was out of the running, was magnificent. It was as if, within that voluptuous creature, a crouching tiger had leaped to life. She shrieked insults at the priests, beating into the palm of one hand with the clawlike fingers of the other, stamping her feet, tossing her head in a very tempest of fury.

Then priests in gray laid heavy hands upon her, dragged her, kicking and screaming, into the group of unsuccessful aspirants.

The priests had concluded their second inspection. But seven of the original hundred-odd now remained. The mob, outside the bars of the leopard enclosure, had gone mad. Fists flew in excited gestures. The air fairly shook with the uproar of voices.

A gray priest produced a round, red-lacquered pedestal about two feet in height. On this, the girls were to stand, one at a time. Susan went first. She stood on the pedestal and looked out over the crowd. The crowd became silent, and in the stillness she could hear the savage snarling of the starved leopard. Then the crowd roared.

THE JUDGES, HOWEVER, were evidently not to be swayed by the crowd's opinion. Once again, with a patience and care that made their former inspections seem superficial, they studied Susan. They walked about her; they came close; they backed away; they cocked their heads.

Then, after minutes of dreadful suspense, they gathered together for a consultation. At the end, one of them raised his arms, palms up. He was the high priest of the holy fire. He meant that Susan was still in the running.

Next, the girl with gilded hands, face and feet went to the pedestal. Another roar of approval greeted her barbaric, statuesque beauty. The priests considered her, then consulted. The high priest lifted his arms, palms downward.—Eliminated! Priests seized her arms and impelled her, although she did not resist, to the ranks of the disappointed.

Now came the Javanese girl. Her mouth was convulsing. Her eyes were tear-stricken. The magnificent diamond which capped her be-gemmed golden headdress fluttered and danced and flashed like an eye in the head of an infuriated serpent.—Yet she was eliminated, and sobbing, she stepped down from the lacquered pedestal and walked without urging to the large group, while the mob snarled its disapproval.

Then came the girl in the flashing garment of jade beads. She held up her head arrogantly, as though she were a little queen; but her lips, too, were quivering.—Soon she was eliminated.

The fifth girl was Japanese, and her costume was one

of the most beautiful Susan had seen—a court kimono of richest orange, with an *obi* of midnight-blue encrusted with sapphires. Nevertheless her nervous smile gave her an idiotic look, and she, too, joined the unfavored ones.

A Malayan girl, thin, exotic in a purple costume which might have adorned the goddess Siva, followed. Her dark eyes, in a thin face, were enormous, beautiful. She was of the melancholy, the madonna type! Despite that, when she was eliminated she bared teeth, distorting her face with a rage that was anything but saint-like.

Last of all came the girl in the green *sarong*. She went laughing to the pedestal, and struck another impudent pose, with legs crossed, one hand on hip, the other pointing straight up over her head. She looked as if she might, on the slightest provocation, spin into a wild dance. Her white teeth flashed. The ruddy light glowed and gleamed on the perfection of her golden skin.

The priests considered her. They walked about her. Then they conferred. And while the priests consulted, the mob shouted, danced, banged on the bars of the leopard enclosure.

The high priest of the holy fire lifted his hands, palms up! The golden maiden threw her other arm into the air, entangled her fingers, clasped the back of her head and wriggled her hips. The roar of the mob reached a higher pitch. Here was, indeed, a favorite!

She climbed down, and her smile, her animation, vanished. She looked at Susan with thin lips, glowering brows, eyes glinting with loathing. The victory lay between these two.

Like moths, Susan's fingers flitted over the cloth which concealed the dagger lying under her heart.

24

THE MAN OF THE JADE BRAIN

PETER WAS STANDING at the grille in the cubicle adjoining the "skull room" when he saw men in black appear at the grille across the marble platform from him. Tall, silent fellows these were, all in black, with wide red leather belts. From the belt worn by each man hung a leather sheath containing a long knife like a monstrous bayonet! The Blue Scorpion's personal bodyguard! No man in contact with Lu, Dekka had told Peter, was ever permitted to carry a firearm. No one who might wish to betray the master with an unexpected shot was ever allowed within range of him.

The heart of the new high priest speeded up to trip-hammer tempo; he was conscious of thrills along his nerves. Lu—the Blue Scorpion—the most sinister, most mysterious, most powerful figure in all of Asia—was about to appear! For the first time, Peter was to see him as he actually was—shorn of his legendary attributes!

Twice, Peter had had interviews with Lu, but he had never been permitted to glimpse the person of Mr. Lu.

Even as he waited for Lu to appear, knowing that that infamous man must conform, in however distorted a way, to some human conception, Peter felt himself shivering, as if he were about to glimpse some hideous monster—

so realistic were those old legends which Lu had created about himself.

Suddenly, to left and right of the marble throne, dazzling blue light blazed forth.

It was the blue of sapphire—pure, intense, vivid blue flame—a blinding blue glare.

As it appeared, a hush fell on the watching mob on the terrace outside the leopard enclosure, far, far below.

Lu, the immortal, the imponderable, the deathless Oriental genius of evil, was about to appear!

A BLOCK OF lapis lazuli set in the wall to the right of the white marble throne swung inward—a block some four feet in width by eight in height. A deep humming sound, like the premonitory temblor of an earthquake, issued from this opening. A man stepped forth—a tall, powerful man, with a robe of sapphire blue satin falling from his shoulders to his ankles, His face was covered by a mask of sapphires set in silver or platinum.

In spite of himself, Peter felt the hairs at his nape stirring. Here, before him, at last, stood the greatest of living Orientals—the most powerful man in Asia—the Blue Scorpion! Not a twisted and distorted monster; not a caricature, in human flesh, of the reptile from which he had taken his name; but a tall, lithe man in whose shoulders, in whose stride, was expressed a terrible and unconquerable energy.

With no attempt at concealing a devouring curiosity, Peter stared and stared. This man in the sapphire mask, in the robe of gleaming blue satin, was not an old man. According to the legend fostered by Lu he was three hundred years old. He had fallen from a cliff at the age of nineteen, had obliterated his face and smashed his skull. An old surgeon, versed in magic, had repaired his body, mended his bones; had given him, in exchange for his battered brain, a brain of purest kingfisher jade; had, at the same time, magically endowed him with a deathless spirit.

Such was the legend. Here was reality—a man some inches over six feet in height, with the springy step, the carriage, the build of an athlete—a youthful athlete.

The tall man in the sapphire mask paced slowly out on the platform with the confidence, the importance, of an emperor; and to Peter it was again made very clear in just what direction Lu's greatest vanity lay. He saw himself as a Cæsar, an Alexander, a Hannibal, a Napoleon—an Oriental conqueror of the world!

Then Peter saw, with shocked amazement, that this man had no hands, that where his hands should have been were stumps, and that these stumps were capped with some white metal—silver or platinum, or some alloy developed, perhaps, in his own laboratories. Into these metal wrist caps sapphires were set, large ones—as large as marbles. To his right wrist was clamped by metal bands a gleaming sharp *parang*.

Moving about the platform, Lu gave an impression of tremendous, inexhaustible nervous energy. He was making sure that the situation was to his liking. For a moment, the sapphire mask was turned fully toward Peter, and Peter knew that he was being given a thoroughgoing scrutiny. Wheeling about, Mr. Lu stared for a moment at the opposite grille, behind which his personal bodyguard stood. Then he went to the head of the stairs and looked down, far down, at the awe-stricken, silent crowd.

Evidently satisfied with the arrangements, Lu went to the stairs and descended six steps. He stopped, moved quickly to the wall on the right hand side and touched a spot on it. Instantly a small cube of lapis lazuli swung outward, revealing an aperture about six inches square. He placed his mask to this square opening, and for some time remained motionless.

Bright golden light streamed past the sapphire mask—and Peter could see, under the thatch of inky black hair at the back of Lu's head, the gleam of a triangle of white metal. Peter shivered again. That was the mark of a brain surgeon—a silver plate built into the back of the Blue Scorpion's skull!

25

THE SACRIFICIAL LAMB

THE GIRL IN the green *sarong* was now standing, with hands on hips, staring out, laughing, at the mob, encouraging their persistent roars of enthusiasm by wriggling her lips, making grimaces, clowning.

Susan supposed that the contest was over. In all her life she had never seen, in any country, a girl who could match the beauty of this little golden one. She was not only beautiful, she was delicious. She had the supple grace of a young tree, swaying in the wind, and she had the vitality of a playful pantheress.

At this moment a sudden hush fell on the mob. Susan turned and looked up the great marble stairway and into a dazzling glare of sapphire blue light. She saw there, dimly, a figure moving about; knew that it must be Lu—the Blue Scorpion! The palms of her hands turned icy and her lips tasted salty.

The crowds beyond the leopard enclosure had prostrated themselves, she saw.

One of the priests touched Susan's shoulder and jerked his head toward the pedestal. She was to stand there once again and be judged. She saw that the crowds were getting to their feet. Yells of excitement were breaking out again.

Unsteadily, she climbed upon the pedestal. This, she knew, was the moment toward which she had been planning, plotting, plodding all these months. Her heart seemed to stop beating. Her throat was paralyzed. Was she, then, to fail so close to her goal? That she had survived the eliminations thus far was little short of miraculous; but when she looked at the little golden girl, all hope left Susan. She felt that she hadn't a chance.

In the confusion of complete discouragement, she had forgotten the mob, and it suddenly struck her that all this uproar was for her—that she, too, was popular. Why, she could not guess. Comparison of herself with so many beautiful girls had given her an overwhelming feeling of humility. She had seen herself as a synthetic Oriental beauty. She did not realize that beauty can rise above racial preferences; that her own beauty would have caused excitement anywhere.

The roaring of the mob beat against her in palpable waves, in a steadily growing reverberation.

Another red lacquered pedestal had been fetched. On this the girl in the green *sarong* climbed. She planted her small bare feet apart, until each leg pressed tightly against the confining *sarong*. She planted her fists on her hips, tossed her head, flashed her eyes.

The priests considered first one girl, then the other. And each time they gave their attention to one, the mob roared, stamped, howled, until the very pedestals on which the two girls stood were vibrating.

Susan's throat was paralyzed. Her spine seemed to freeze.

The high priest of the holy fire was standing between the two pedestals. He turned his head to look first at one girl, then to contemplate the other. Finally, his two hands went up. For the girl in the green *sarong*—a palm turned downward. For Susan—a palm upturned!

With a frantic lurch, Susan's heart began to race. She had won! She had not believed she had a chance to win against this beautiful Annamese girl. But the priests had decided—and the mob was giving its tumultuous approval. She had won!

Then she became aware of a commotion beside her. A priest in gray was forcibly holding the Annamese girl by the shoulders. With the tactics of a cat animal, she was straggling to free herself. She sank her perfect pearl-white teeth into one of the restraining hands. She swung about and scratched the priest's face.

The priest let go his hold. As he did so, the golden maiden from Annam sprang at Susan. Hate and fury made flames of her eyes. She was intent upon killing this beautiful creature in her gem-crusted gown! But before she could reach Susan other priests in gray had pounced upon her. She tried to claw her way free. Her lips worked as she shrieked abuse, but her voice was drowned in the tumultuous applause of the mob for the girl who had been selected. Screaming and kicking, the golden Annamese maiden was taken away.

Once again, Susan's fingers, like white moths, fluttered over the dagger's hiding place. Her eyes were shining with a light no less zealous than the light she had seen in the eyes of these religious fanatics. She was no longer afraid.

BACK IN THE temple, Peter, standing close to the bronze grille, saw Lu close the peephole and start back up the stairs; and he was amazed once again at the man's lithe-ness, his apparent youth and muscular power. The glimpse of that metal triangle built into the back of Lu's skull had shocked him. He wondered if there could possibly be truth in that legend that Lu, three centuries ago, had been healed by a magic-working surgeon—and had been endowed with perpetual youth.

Lu had seated himself on the throne, in the blue glare.

Above him, Peter heard the deep, somehow sinister voice of the great temple bell as it began to toll. The ceremony was about to start. The time for his plan to go into execution was but a few minutes away. The instant the girl chosen for her beatify reached the platform Peter would dart back into the shrine and seize the skull.

With his face pressed against the grille, his heart hammering high in his chest, Peter looked down the staircase. He could see the leopards pacing about in the enclosure. He saw the unsuccessful contestants filing out through the safety lane.

Then came the priests in flame red. They formed a cluster about a central object in blue—the winning girl. He saw the priests conduct this girl to the steps of the temple, saw them form in a line behind her. The last of the unsuccessful aspirants—a small golden-skinned girl in a jade-green *sarong*—filed out of the safety lane, and the gate closed behind them, the bronze spears sinking back into the ground.

Even at that distance, Peter had recognized the girl in the green *sarong* as Zari. He would have recognized those slim, perfect shoulders, that sleek, beautiful golden back anywhere. His little maiden from Hai-Phong was not to be granted the inestimable boon of having her lovely throat cut!

He felt a moment's sadness. He was sure he would never see Zari again, and hers had been a delightful friendship. Her warmth, her fiery nature, her young impulsiveness had been endearing. Her love for her own beautiful face and her perfect little body was appealing.

The priests of the holy fire were bringing the winning girl into the temple. At the foot of the great marble staircase they left her, and withdrew to the grilles on either side. When they had passed through, the grilles, operated by the magic of Lu, closed down, barring them from the staircase.

All the priests were now within the temple. The safety lane through the leopard enclosure could be operated only from without. So, for another year—until the annual messenger of the Blue Scorpion came to operate the safety lane from outside—the priests of the Temple of the Coiled Serpent were prisoners in that fabulous structure.

The winning girl approached the steps. Peter reflected that she must be rarely beautiful to have won her privilege over so many other beauties, to deserve such uproarious approval. Beautiful, indeed, if she had won over Zari!

Even at that distance he could see, from the very manner in which she held herself, that she was poised, proud, unafraid. He could also see that her blue costume was rich—could detect the glitter and twinkle of the precious stones embroidered into its living texture. She was a small girl, and she carried herself with a grace that bespoke a supple, well-trained body.

As she passed the pit of fire, he wondered just what her thoughts, her emotions were. At the top of those stairs

*The starved black
leopards crept closer.*

which she was just starting to climb, lay death, swift,
certain, terrifying; and he fell to pondering the heights of
religious fervor to which she must have attained to give
her the strength to climb these thousand and one marble
steps—to have her poor little throat cut!

THE ONLY THOUGHT in Susan's mind as she started up
those thousand and one marble steps was the determination—burning like a pure white flame—to achieve her
purpose. Her blue satin sandals made a whispering sound
on each step, and this whisper seemed to say, "I must not
fail—I must not fail!"

Through the bronze grilles ahead of her, up the unbro-
ken flight of marble, she could see the figure of Lu sitting
between two ghastly glaring blue lights which sent vibrant
shadows of blue and black through the bars of the inter-
vening grilles and down the stairs. On Lu's right, she could
see still another grille, and the vague form of a man who
stood behind it. He was, of course, the newly selected high
priest—the Oriental youth who had won his priesthood

through a series of hideous, bloody combats in which one hundred and twenty-nine of his fellows had been killed or eliminated.

As she approached the first grille, which blocked her way, it silently, gracefully arose, as if by some trick of magic; and when she had climbed on, it swiftly, silently slid back down into place.

She climbed slowly, steadily, with eyes alert. Her program was complete. She did not know about Lu's stumps of arms, but she had learned from Hing Sing Joy, the jade seller in Singapore from whom she had bought many of Mr. Lu's secrets, that when she reached the platform—the thousand and first step—Lu would arise from the throne and come toward her with a *parang*. He would push back her head with one hand, and at the instant he did this—before he could bring up the *parang* in his other hand—she must strike! Deep—deep! Quicker than thought, the dagger must leap from the little pocket under her left breast. Quicker than thought she must plunge it into Lu's monstrous heart! Then let them do with her what they pleased.

She might have been disturbed had she known that Lu had no hands; that the *parang* would be attached by means of an ingenious metal band to the wrist cap he wore. But she did not know that the Blue Scorpion had no hands, and therefore she could not realize that his very lack of them might confuse the issue.

She passed under another grille, and another, and continued to climb. Her heart was beginning to beat more rapidly, though this was not due to fear.

Another of the grilles slid upward as if on wings, to permit her to pass; came down behind her with a soft clang. **ZARI, PRESSING CLOSE** to the bars of the leopard enclosure, watched her successful rival steadily climbing the white marble staircase, and the heart in her little pagan bosom was sick. There had not been the slightest doubt in Zari's mind that the dramatic privilege which Susan had won would be conferred upon herself. Glaring through the bars with eyes which glowed and burned no less malevolently than the eyes of the hungry black leopards, she watched the chosen girl, hated her—hated the cruel fate that had disappointed her. It should be she, so gracefully mounting the long white staircase—she, so beautiful, with a form so heavenly!

In her queer little Asiatic mind, Zari had long ago decided that Lak Ching, the newly selected high priest, was actually not a man of this earth, but a god. How could he have resisted her virginal loveliness, if he was merely a man? Her desire to be this year's little golden lamb had been exceeded only by her desire to possess Lak Ching forever—to bear him numerous wonderful sons!

Denied Lak Ching, because of his godhood, the next best thing was to die under his eyes, by the knife of Lu; to be carried, dead, in his arms down the steps and cast into the pit of fire.

She had been denied both. Her heart was broken. Her life was ended. Her naïve self-love rebelled in a very welter of fury and hate and malevolence for the winning girl—for fate—for life. Zari now wanted only to die.

BEHIND SUSAN WAS a death-like silence. She was

unaware of the thousands of eyes in pilgrims' faces, greedily watching her—some of them bitterly envying her!

Then, as if for the first time, she looked again at the figure behind the slender bronze bars at the right side of the throne platform. Somewhere behind that figure a light was shining, and as Susan climbed, the head and shoulders of the new high priest came more clearly into silhouette.

Something—something about that head, the shoulders—was familiar. For an instant, her step faltered. It was not—of course it could not be—! A girl deeply in love is apt to make such a mistake—to see in other men the features, gestures, postures of the one man she loves. She had always admired Peter Moore's head and shoulders—the head so erect, so well proportioned; the shoulders so wide, so powerful. But she had been tricked before in these past six months of her bereavement. In her present high-strung state, her eyes might well be expected to play such tricks.

Yet she was so startled by that silhouetted head, by those shoulders, that she involuntarily betrayed her excitement by a gesture of her own—a flight of a clenched fist to her cheek.

As she hesitated and stared, the head of the high priest sharply jerked up. She had never known another man to make quite that gesture, in quite that way; and as the realization began to dawn, her heart leaped with a surge of unutterable joy.

Then it went sick and cold. A full realization of what this meant swept over her in a wave of utter horror, obliterating all joy in the discovery that Peter Moore was alive. That figure behind the bronze bars was unquestionably Peter

Moore! The report of his death had been a trick to blind his enemies to his purpose! Somehow, with superhuman courage, strength and stamina, he had survived all those barbaric contests—won his way to the high priesthood as part of some plan—a plan no doubt ruined now by his recognition of her!

As her eyes swung back to the man in the sapphire mask, it was as if, in her brain, terror reverberated like the voice of a hideous brass gong. On previous occasions she bad plunged Peter Moore into perilous predicaments, but from this predicament there was no possible escape!

MARVELLING AT FIRST at her poise, Peter had watched the chosen girl start up the wide stairway. She was a little thing, and as she climbed and climbed, steadily, without once hesitating or faltering, his admiration and his pity grew.

When she came close enough for him to discern her features, he ceased wondering how she had come to win over Zari and all her other beautiful rivals; her beauty had a quality of its own.

Where Zari was alluringly lovely, this girl, the winner, was exquisite. She was smaller than Zari, more delicately made. Even at that distance he was aware of a certain fineness, of a certain daintiness, which Zari lacked.

The chosen one was breathlessly beautiful. Her loveliness might have been the supreme accomplishment of a great race, yet there was a freshness, a dewiness about her that marked her, not as a goddess, but as a woman—young, warm, passionate, tender. This unknown girl set up in Peter strange and stranger sensations. Her costume revealed a slim, gracious body.

Suddenly his very masculinity rebelled against the destruction of a girl so alluringly perfect. This girl was meant to love and be loved.

As she came toward him, so gallantly, so fearlessly, he too experienced the dawning of a horrifying realization. All along—ever since she had started her climb—vague, formless premonitions had been hovering on the border-land of his conscious mind. Little by little the girl's manner of climbing the stairs seemed familiar.

For moments, it was as if he were seeing a figure in a dream. Then these formless thoughts began plucking more insistently at his attention. How many times had he seen Susan walking up other stairways toward him; how often had he marked the daintily decisive way she put her little feet down!

As the chill sweat of apprehension prickled on his fore-head, he told himself, reasonably, that a thousand girls might have that distinctive manner of walking up stair-ways, of holding their heads in that certain gallant way.

She looked toward him, and she faltered. Other girls might walk like that, but no other girl he had ever known had that trick, when startled, of sending her hand up, in that certain way, to her cheek! This girl, despite her gemmed costume, despite the Oriental aspect of her face, could be no one in the world but Susan!

Catastrophe! She was not a dozen steps from the plat-form now. His plan to make off with the Sapphire Skull was to have been executed within the next ten seconds.

Now, he dared not move. He could not move. It was as if the thin bronze bars he grasped were charged with a high voltage current, freezing him there. But not for a moment did it occur to him to blame Susan for this sudden, complete destruction of the plan on which he had worked with such care, such tremendous sacrifice, for more than half a year. The only thought in his brain was the ghastly knowledge that it was not humanly possible for him to help her! Imprisoned behind these thin, stout bars, he could not save her. He must stand there, utterly helpless, while Lu slit her throat!

Staring at her eyes—those telltale, beautiful, deep violet eyes—he realized that she must have come this far along a road quite as dangerous, in its way, as the one he had followed. He realized that her choice had been far braver than his, for not for one moment had he entertained the thought of sacrificing his life. And he knew that whatever her plan was, she had adopted it because she believed the reports of his death.

In any event, their ironical meeting here, at the end of their roads, had utterly spoiled all plans; had reduced to ashes the brilliance of their individual achievements. He realized, too, in this fearful moment, as recognition dawned on each, that nothing mattered to him but this courageous girl; and he saw in his whole adventurous undertaking, from the careful establishing of his death in a Hong Kong hotel to his superhuman final efforts at winning the high priesthood, nothing but folly.

He and he alone was responsible for this inescapable predicament!

Then a harsh, inhuman whisper was saying, in English, *"Miss O'Gilvie, why do you hesitate? Mr. Moore is waiting for you."*

26

INHUMAN HUMAN

PETER'S STUNNED AMAZEMENT quickly passed. The sarcasm embodied in that short utterance sent boiling through him a wave of such fury, such murderous hatred, as he had never known. The genius of the man in the sapphire mask was beyond all human comprehension. How long had Lu been aware of their identities? How long had he been laughing behind that mask at their intentions?

Susan had stopped, four steps from the platform, in horrible amazement.

Again this man of many legends whispered, "Miss O'Gilvie, why do you hesitate?"

Susan's eyes, dazed by shock, traveled from the sapphire mask to the man behind the bronze bars, then back to the glittering blue mask. She did not answer. She seemed to wilt. The high courage, the fearlessness of certain death, had suddenly left her. She was a helpless, terror-stricken girl.

The Blue Scorpion bent forward to whisper, "Is it that there are too many eyes upon us? Perhaps you would prefer a private audience?"

Lu stood up with that. The *parang*, ingeniously clamped

to the sapphire-studded wrist-cap, fell with a singing clang to the marble at his feet.

Peter was holding his breath. It could not be said that his brain was thinking usefully, but one department of it had been occupied with conjecture. He had instantly visualized Lu freeing the men in black, behind the grille across the way—instantly making Susan a prisoner and spiriting her forever from his sight. But nowhere in his mind was a thought of his own fate.

He waited for the grille across the way to spring open, for the black-garbed personal bodyguard to spill forth. But although the armed men in black pressed against the grille, they were not released. And the man in the sapphire mask was slowly walking toward Susan.

"Come!" he whispered. No longer mocking, there was a new note in his voice—a harshness—anger—fury!

Susan hesitated, then slowly advanced to the platform. She stood facing him, staring up into the glittering blue mask with horrified eyes. Compared to his great height, she looked like a child—a child on the verge of screaming, collapsing with terror.

"Come!" Lu repeated, and there was the same note of savage, terrible fury in the whisper. He strode majestically to the grille behind which Peter stood, transfixed. The wrist-cap on Lu's right arm ticked against the wall. The grille sprang open.

Susan, driven, though not by fear, sped past him. With a strangled little cry, she threw her arms tightly about Peter's neck, hugged him and shook with sobs. Still fiercely hugging him, she kissed his cheeks, his mouth. She panted:

"I thought you were dead!—They said you were dead—Oh, my darling! My darling!"

"Love!" said Lu, the whisper bubbling with fury and hate. "The ecstasy of love!" As he uttered this, in the grotesque reaches of fury, he clicked the metal wrist-caps together. His tall, powerful body was a-tremble, as if he were undergoing a series of convulsions which fairly shook his flesh on its bones.

The hatred of this Oriental giant, this man of weird and fanciful legend, was like a poisonous broth which, boiling in his very veins, was distilling into the room invisible clouds, black, dire, horrible.

"A lovers' meeting!—The ending of journeys! Ah—you two! Revel in it! Clasp each other! Drink the sweetness from the cup!—Love!"

SO VIBRANT HAD that harsh whisper become, so poisoned with the chemicals of loathing, that Susan, freeing herself from Peter's arms, shrank back, staring with shocked fascination.

Their enemy, his blue velvet sandals planted far apart, was facing Peter. The sapphire-studded wrist-caps were no longer clicking in that long spasm of rage. Lu was as stiff, as motionless, as a sculpture in lapis lazuli. The tempest of unbridled hatred was now past. His whisper, when it issued from the mask again, was no less hateful, but his emotions were under control.

"Mr. Moore, this has gone far enough. My patience is exhausted. This time I shall deal with you myself. For upwards of two years you have, with your petty annoyances, tempted my displeasure; but this time you have gone too far. This time you have trespassed upon the sacredness of my own temple; you have violated the sanctity of my shrine! You have soiled both with your presence—you have mocked my dignity. You have thrown the lowest of insults into my very teeth. This time, I shall not be lenient. This time I shall kill you.—

"I am unarmed; and I am going to kill you myself. Not with my bare hands, for I have no hands, but with weapons. I could summon a thousand men who would tear you to shreds; but I need no assistance. You have proved, by contests, to be superhumanly powerful. Perhaps you feel that you are the most powerful man on earth. Let me correct that mistake! In the past, I have shown that I am your mental superior. Now I descend from my exalted throne for the satisfaction of proving that I am also your physical superior!"

Peter was slowly moving toward him. He did not believe that the Blue Scorpion, weaponless, intended to fight him. But he was not afraid of Lu. His sensations were very similar to those which he had experienced just before the first combat—a sense of power, like a chemical, flowing into the muscles of his arms, back and legs; a sense of these muscles swelling and hardening; a sense of warlike bristling along his spine.

The whisper went on, harsh, cold, hateful. "As for you, Miss O'Gilvie, I might let you die, also. I might stake you out in a pool and let starved fish pluck the flesh from your bones. I might kill you by slow, agonizing poison, until your brain rotted in your skull. I might place you at the mercies of leprous convicts who have not set eyes on a woman in years. I might order your death by any one of a thousand methods of torture.

"But I do not want you to die. I want you to live on with the memory of your lover's death at my hands forever in your heart. Instead of ordering your death, I shall present you to my friend Gung Chou, who appreciates lovely women. He is fat and old and ugly—but he loves slim, tender, beautiful young women! He loves to fondle dainty young women like yourself with his fat, coarse hands, to feast on their kisses with his thick, gross lips! Therefore, Miss O'Gilvie, I shall—"

Peter leaped at him. The first blow, with his right fist, smashed into Lu's heart. With his left fist he sent the sapphire mask spinning, to crash to the floor, beyond the golden pedestal on which stood the infamous Sapphire Skull.

And for the first time in history, the face of this mysterious Oriental, who was supposed to have fallen from a cliff three hundred years ago, was seen by a fellow man. So horrified was Peter that for a moment he could not follow up that attack; he could only stand and stare.

THERE WAS NO face! The Blue Scorpion, the Oriental genius whose power was felt over all of Asia, was a man without a face! Where a face should have been there was nothing but a gray, flat surface of hideous scar tissue. There was a lipless gash for a mouth; two small holes lined with white metal where the nose had at one time been; higher up and farther apart, two tiny apertures where the eyes had been. From the latter glowed sparks; not human, not eyes, but bits of stark, flaming hatred.

Peter, staring horrified into these bits of flame, realized that this man was neither sane nor insane; he was a creature absolutely apart—a thing of flesh and blood and bone, but inhuman—a human monster activated by a deathless, insatiable hatred!

Peter was unaware that Susan, staring at Mr. Lu, was screaming with sheer horror at that hideous, faceless head. He was equally unaware that yells of fear and fury were issuing from the grille across the platform where Lu's bodyguard remained helplessly imprisoned.

Then his momentary shock of horror passed, and with all the fury of his own hatred he struck at that gray, featureless area in Mr. Lu's head. Other blows drove into the monster's body. But it was as if all of Peter's blows fell upon a mass of coiled steel spring.

Lu met his attack with even greater fury, striking out with the metal-capped stumps of his wrists. These were terrific blows, like the blows of a striking python. They smashed into Peter's body and face as though they were delivered, not by human bone and muscle, but by some powerful machine. Each blow of those sapphire-studded wrist-caps was immeasurably harder than any blow Peter had ever received from a human fist, and each blow bruised and tore his flesh.

Peter, fighting desperately and with all his power, soon realized that his enemy was drawing upon a source of inexhaustible energy. The American sent smashing blows into gray scar tissue and springy, tough body; but they produced absolutely no result. They brought no grunts, no groans, no gasps; it was as if they fell, with all their crushing force, upon rawhide—or some tough substance unknown to ordinary men.

As perfectly timed, as well-placed as they were, they sapped none of the strength of Lu. The metal wrist-caps were deadlier than any fist, and they crashed into Peter's face, into his body, with tireless fury. They were like projectiles.

It was a hopeless, heartless combat. No man, no matter how perfect his condition, could withstand for very long that metallic barrage. One blow sent Peter crashing to the floor with such violence that it knocked the wind out of him. Gasping, panting, he sprang up. Again he was sent smashing to the floor. He was hopelessly outmatched—he, the man who had won through contests which required the strength and endurance of a superman! It was as if he fought a machine of leather, of brass and tempered steel. And the feeling grew upon Peter that this man towering over him was, in truth, the actual creature of those mystic legends; that Lu, despite all skepticism, was actually an automaton, a mechanized giant.

He seemed as irresistible as a mill for grinding scythes. He was like a human juggernaut governed by the same kind of unfailing mechanical intelligence as that which dictates the functioning of a gasoline engine.

For as Lu delivered these smashing blows with unfailing power and unvarying precision, an awful grinding sound issued from the lipless gash which served him for a mouth. In the tiny round holes where eyes had once been remained the tiny glaring sparks of hate!

SUSAN, STANDING BESIDE the marble bench, across from the golden pedestal, watched the unequal struggle with rising helplessness. She saw, even earlier than did her lover, that the Blue Scorpion was indomitable. But after her scream at the sight of that hideous gray scar that was Lu's face, she made no sound. She realized that unless something happened quickly mere minutes—now seconds—intervened between Peter and death. He was panting, groaning at each blow from those terrific metal caps.

She, too, sensed in this unequal fight a strange and terrifying unearthliness. Watching that perfect fighting machine as it beat Peter down and down, she wondered if such a man as Lu might, like Achilles, possess a vulnerable spot.

She was thinking coolly now. The inevitability of death had shocked her into calmness, readiness. The dagger which she had so cleverly concealed was clutched in her hand. But she waited. She knew that one blow from one of those metal-capped wrist stumps would knock her senseless, if it did not kill her instantly; and she knew that Peter's chance lay in her readiness to attack, to strike her one small blow, at some critical moment.

Peter's back had struck the wall. The metal caps were striking him with the precision of shells from a rapid-fire gun. He suddenly sagged. His head dipped forward; his knees bent.

One long, blue satin-clad arm struck out, swept about his neck, snatched him into the crook of the elbow. The droning sound issuing from the lipless gash in the hideous scar-tissue area went to a higher note; it might have been the humming of the wings of death.

Susan, in horror, watched, waiting her chance. She sensed that the Chinese monster had forgotten her very existence. Peter was striking out feebly with fists and feet, being dragged to the white marble bench. His struggles grew weaker. Lu, retaining that remorseless strangle hold, was forcing his back down over the bench.

Susan had slipped around back of the man in the sapphire blue gown. She stared from the dagger clutched in her white fingers to the broad, powerful back. Where should she strike? Then she saw what Peter had seen previously—the triangular patch of white metal in the skull under the blue-black hair.

In his harsh whisper Lu said: "So—I deal with those who defile the shrine to my brain!"

Susan struck once at the white metal plate, with all her force. The point of the dagger skidded off, buried itself in the bone. Blood spurted.

One sapphire-studded wrist-cap struck backward. It caught Susan in the left temple, with sufficient force to have crushed it. She slid to the floor unconscious, with blood trickling from the ugly bruise.

But Lu, an instant later, went limp. His head dipped forward, his arms fell aside. He rolled off Peter, a limp thing, like something suddenly deflated. He struck the end of the bench, continued to roll, and fell, face up, as if dead.

27

DIVING TO FREEDOM

PETER, ON THE verge of unconsciousness, was lying across the bench, with head touching the floor on one side, heels on the other. For a moment he lay there, fighting for recovery, gasping for breath. He struggled up to a sitting position. Presently, the black stain left his face, was followed by a red flush. He clenched his fists, struggled again and, with a superhuman effort, forced himself to stand erect.

For seconds, with feet planted wide apart, he swayed, his eyes swimming, with blood trickling down from the lower lip which he had clenched between his teeth, fighting off the swirling black mists in his brain, driving off the dizziness.

He was staggering about the room now, like a man drunk. His balance was still precarious. The robe was no longer snow-white, but flecked, spotted, smeared with his own blood.

He went to the open grille out onto the platform and stared across the way at Lu's personal bodyguard—now a cage of frenzied, yelling men. He swung drunkenly about and stared at his enemy. Again he clenched his fists. His chest swelled. His stature, his breadth seemed to increase.

A grotesque sound came rumbling from his mouth. Laughter! Deep and awful laughter!

He looked at the Sapphire Skull, on its shining golden pillar. He looked un-seeingly at Susan, at the blood trickling from her temple. He looked at the master of the Temple of the Coiled Serpent, still lying without movement, without sound, where he had fallen.

Peter strode over to his enemy, still laughing, but more softly now. He reached down and grasped the folds of the blue satin robe. With a deep growl he hoisted the Chinese slowly into the air, until Lu was at the end of stiffened arms above Peter's head.

Slowly he walked out onto the platform on which Lu's throne stood; he walked to the top of the stairs. If there had been bedlam before, the noise was like the silence preceding a typhoon, compared to the uproar that was now loosed. Then silence fell again; even in the grilled cubicle across the way, where the black-garbed guards clutched the bars.

Peter's thundering voice filled the temple. "Master of Asia!" He gave a thunderous laugh.

Then Peter heaved. The limp giant seemed to fly from his arms; the body struck the twelfth step down; it began to roll. As it neared the first grille, that bronze gateway magically soared into the air, letting the body roll past.

It had ceased to roll and was grotesquely bounding when it neared the second grille. This, too, opened for it to pound past. Standing at the top of the great stairway, with hands on hips and legs planted apart, the American watched as if with a hypnotized fascination. He did not move until the secret monarch of Asia had bounded and rolled and tumbled to the very bottom of the thousand and one steps.

Then Peter picked up the *parang* which Lu had detached from his wrist-cap, and with it strode back into the room where Susan was.

Red mists now followed the black ones out of his brain, and his brain was suddenly as clear as a Borneo water-diamond. He was safe. He could carry Susan down the staircase, with nothing to worry about except thrown daggers. For not one man who came in contact with Lu—not even his personal bodyguard—was permitted to carry firearms!

Very deliberately, he went about the execution of his plan—so different from the way it had been originally conceived! He lifted the Sapphire Skull from the pedestal, folded it into his robe, bound the bloodstained white sash more securely about his waist, so that the skull could not slip out. He slid the *parang* under the sash.

THEN, TENDERLY, HE picked up Susan. He carried her face up across his arms. Her hair had come undone; it hung loosely down from her upturned face. Blood had trickled from her temple and down her left cheek to her throat. Looking down at her as he went out onto the platform again, he was shocked at the resemblance of that course of blood to a slash. Lying there, across his arms, she might indeed have been the "little golden lamb," with slashed throat.

His reappearance was greeted by another thunderous outburst from the maddened thousands below. But they could not reach him. No one could reach him! That was the beauty of this altered plan! On either side of the staircase were grilles behind which priests stood helplessly and stared and screamed. But they could not escape from those grilles until Lu, with his magic, wished them to be released!

As Peter neared the first of the six grilles guarding the descent of the stairway, the grille rose to permit him to pass, as it had risen moments before, when the master of the temple had bounded so grotesquely under it.

Silence gradually fell as Peter, with the unconscious little golden lamb in his arms, majestically descended. And as he descended, he began to chant, first in southern Chinese, then in Mandarin, again in Burmese, and lastly in Malayan:

"The power of Lu is broken! Gone, gone is the power of Lu!"

As the final grille dropped behind him, he paused.

Priests imprisoned behind the grilles, the mob held back by fear of the leopards, all stared in utter silence, with utter fascination, at this tall young man, the newly selected high priest of the temple.

He glanced down at the limp figure of the Blue Scorpion, sprawled face down at the foot of the steps. Then, very deliberately, he laid the unconscious girl on the white marble and approached the pit of fire. He plucked the Sapphire Skull from the robe. He held it above his head. A deep sigh, like that of winter wind in naked branches, rose from the hypnotized crowd.

Again he intoned, "The power of Lu is broken! Gone, gone is the power of Lu!"

He repeated it in a loud, clear voice, and in all the Oriental tongues at his command. Then, with a gesture of contempt, he cast the Sapphire Skull into the pit of holy fire! White sparks greeted it. Flames coiled about it. And suddenly it seemed to writhe as though it were living flesh.

There was a hiss, a bubbling sound, as though something was frying. A dark liquid flowed out of it, fell dripping into the white coals, exploded into puffs of steam which rose in the heat.

As the skull disintegrated into little smouldering heaps of sapphires, Peter wondered what it had contained. He would never know, but he did not greatly care.

HE LOOKED AT the pallid, shocked faces pressed against the bars of the grilles, at those pressed against the bars of the leopard enclosure.

He gathered Susan into his arms and walked quickly to the door which he, Para Khan and Chang Kong had entered hours previously—for that final test. It was the only way of escape which he knew. He did not know how to operate the secret mechanism which would cause the great bronze grille covering the temple entrance to lift. He must go the other way—and take Susan with him!

He ran up the well-remembered stairs, passed through several rooms, climbed other stairs, and presently reached the room of the door of death. The disc of steel was still flashing past the opening in its ordered course.

He placed Susan on the floor, placed the *parang* in his teeth and stripped off the white robe. In anticipation of the ordeal by water that lay before him, he began taking deep breaths, to pump his blood full of oxygen long before the ordeal began.

Then he examined Susan's eyes. The bruise on her temple was serious. Whether her skull was fractured or not he could not tell; he did not even know whether she was alive or dead. For a moment, he let discouragement possess him. He was winded and weak, suffering a nervous reaction from the terrific excitement which had already taken place. Was it possible for him to leap with Susan past the disc, to fall at least one hundred feet into the water tank, then to swim that great distance under water with her, unconscious, in his arms?

What then? Leopards! Emerging in the leopard enclosure, provided he safely negotiated the underwater tube, how could he, with an unconscious or dead girl in his arms, fight off those ravenous leopards? Especially armed as he was, with only a large dagger? Another problem tormented him: could Susan withstand that six or seven minutes' submergence without being drowned, even if he closed off her nose and mouth with one hand? It was doubtful. It seemed utterly impossible—an utterly fantastic course. Yet he must attempt it. There was no alternative.

He picked up Susan and strode to the round doorway. It was harder now to concentrate on the hesitations, the reappearances of the steel disc than it had been before. Dared he leap through it and into that tank and attempt to swim through it with Susan, unconscious?

The disc, in its eccentric triming, had reached the period when he must jump—or waste another precious three minutes! The disc clicked four times; hesitated; clicked seven times. Another hesitation. Two clicks.—Now!

He jumped across the threshhold and far out. His heart, as he fell, seemed to climb up into his throat. The light, far below, rose swiftly toward him. He caught the glimmer of the water.

An instant before he struck the water, Peter clamped Susan's nose with a thumb and forefinger, covered her mouth with the palm of the same hand. At the very instant of striking he had himself inhaled deep lungfuls.

HIS FEET STRUCK bottom; sent him to his knees. Holding Susan, he swam toward the opening of the tube through which he had barely reached safety on his last attempt.

His heart beat rapidly, with thin, sharp pains. Automatically, he counted the seconds. He entered the tube and started down it. He was making a last supreme effort, and he knew that he was taking far less time than when he had escaped this strange journey previously. New terrors assailed him, however. He passed the fork, and ahead, just ahead, the tube dipped down and the pressure increased. Could he keep the water out of Susan's lungs?

Then, just as he started swimming one-handedly, kicking with the last ounce of his strength, to drive them downward, Susan began to struggle in his arm! That shock of striking the cold water with such suddenness had revived her!

At first feeble, her struggles were now more violent. He pictured the terrifying sensation she must be experiencing as she recovered consciousness. But he kicked on, clawed at the water with his one free hand. He felt bubbles escaping from her mouth; clamped his hand down more tightly. Would he be able to revive her, once they did reach the surface?

His own lungs were beginning to protest, and his heart was thumping in agony.

Once again, the terror of this hideous underwater invention of Mr. Lu possessed him. If Susan's struggles grew much stronger they would both drown.

His mind went on. Even if they safely reached the pool

in the leopard enclosure, he would be too exhausted to ward off the attacks of those snarling savage beasts!

They were rising now; slowly at first, then more and more rapidly. Could he reach the surface before Susan expired completely from lack of air?

Another danger loomed. In that mob outside the leopard enclosure there were doubtless men with firearms. What chance had he, even if he escaped the leopards, to escape the fury of that mob?

His lungs burning, he forced air in thin streams of bubbles from nostrils and the corners of mouth. The next second his head shot above water. He released Susan's mouth and nose, heard her frantically gasping for air. Could she survive the ordeal they had just passed through? He clung to the edge of the pool, with the world whirling about him, gulping air into his own lungs.

As his head cleared, he became aware of an awful silence. The mob had not moved. He saw their faces pressed against the bars of the leopard enclosure. He saw their eyes fixed on him—thousands of staring eyes. But there was no sound. Nothing but Susan's and his own gaspings for breath.

At that moment of awful stillness the leopards became aware of the two of them!

28

YOGISM

TWO OF THE starved black beasts simultaneously became aware of the pair of humans in their drinking pool; but they did not charge. They came slowly, with glowing, golden eyes, with deliberate steps. Perhaps they too were dazed.

Their deliberation gave Peter sufficient time in which to climb out of the pool, to seize Susan's hands and drag her out. She regained consciousness quickly; enough so that he could place her behind him, and to back part way toward the temple wall.

He had almost reached the wall when the foremost of the leopards leaped, with a squalling snarl. Peter, under Dekka's tireless training back in the mountain fastnesses of the Himalayas, had met this kind of attack in much narrower quarters. That training stood him in excellent stead now, for as the leopard sprang, Peter swept the tottering Susan aside, then stepped quickly aside himself. He brought up the *parang*, and brought it flashing down, with a powerful lunge, into the nearest blazing golden eye. The point of the blade struck deep into the leopard's brain.

Peter jerked the weapon out and stepped clear of the animal's death agonies. There were now at least eight of the long black cats. For a moment, curiosity halted them all. With lashing tails they watched. Then, as one, they pounced on the threshing body of the leopard which Peter had just killed. With snarls, with hideous screams, they fell on their dying comrade.

Others of the hungry black beasts, attracted by the snarling of the pack, came loping up; and for a space of seconds Peter and the terrified girl were ignored. She was now gripping his left arm so fiercely that her fingernails were biting deep into his flesh.

He pushed her along the wall, keeping her behind him, and facing out, watching in all directions, his *parang* ready. In that sullen silence, broken only by the screams of the leopards fighting over their carcass, the two fugitives progressed ten feet—twenty—thirty.

The bronze door for which Peter was making was now no more than seventy feet away. But reinforcements were arriving. A trio of leopards came charging from the rear of the temple, attracted by the snarls and screams of their fellows. Others followed them; loping black shadows with glowing eyes and gleaming fangs.

Then they stopped. They had seen the two humans sliding along the temple wall, and so they abandoned their original plan and started slowly—very slowly—toward Peter and Susan.

The girl made a little whimpering sound.

Peter said quietly, "Stay behind me!" But he was convinced that there was little or no hope. He might have fought these leopards one at a time, as Dekka had taught him; but not a horde of them. At the least count there were fifteen of them; and more were coming!

Shoulder to shoulder, with lashing tails, the leopards

slowly came toward Peter and Susan—a mass of blackness, relieved only by their flaming yellow eyes, the gleam here and there of bared fangs, or the glimpse of a pink throat.

Peter, holding Susan behind him, holding the *parang* ready, swung his eyes from side to side, watchful but hopeless. They would not charge, he knew, until the final moment; then they would charge all together, and he and Susan would be struck down and promptly torn and clawed to shreds.

AS THE MASS of leopards crept toward him, bellies down, tails slowly lashing, he became aware of a commotion beyond. Someone was climbing the high fence which enclosed the leopards—some member of the mob outside. Peter caught a fugitive glimpse of a golden body, then a flash of jade-green cloth.

His heart, which had been pounding with deathly slowness, suddenly thumped and leaped. He saw hands reaching up. He heard screams of fury, saw naked feet and legs kicking. His little maiden from Hai-Phong was climbing the forbidden fence! But for a moment he did not appreciate that she was carrying out a well-deliberated plan of action.

His voice came, choking. "Zari!—Go back!"

She did not answer. She had freed herself of the restraining arms of the mob outside; had reached the top of the fence. For a moment she stood there, balancing, poised, on the inward-curving bars. The light gleamed and glowed on her shining golden body.

He cried again, "Go back!"

She was smiling now—a glorified smile. If he could have read her strange little Oriental mind, he would have known that the golden Annamese maiden, while fully convinced that no beast of this earth could harm her hero, did not know whether or not her hero, with all his godlike attributes, could save from death the girl he had chosen.

In Zari's mind not only had her hero chosen this other girl, but he had brought her back, miraculously, from death. For Zari had seen the traces of blood on Susan's throat, and had mistaken it, as had all in the mob who had noticed, for the slash of Lu's *parang*. Magically, Zari's god-hero had delivered a girl with her throat cut from the very country of death—and now her throat was healed and intact, without the slightest sign of that slash! For Zari did not know, of course, that the water had washed away all trace of blood.

All this had impressed itself on Zari's mind, but she doubted now that her god, with all his magic, could save this girl from being torn into ribbons by the colony of starved black leopards. And, reasoning thus, thinking so clearly, the little golden maid of Annam was prepared to make a supreme sacrifice.

At last she was to be of some use to her god!

So she smiled and, smiling, leaped into the enclosure.

THE WALL OF leopards was within a dozen feet of Peter and Susan when Zari leaped. Landing in a heap, she cried out.

As one, the leopards sprang about, their tails lashing with greater interest. The golden girl had fallen very near them; she had not risen. Lying there, facing them, she uttered taunts at them.

The leopards started toward her. Susan cried out. A whisper arose from the mob—a soft moan—as the leopards, suddenly snarling and squalling, leaped upon golden little Zari.

Peter, with a groan, started toward the fallen girl. But he knew he was too late. By the savage twistings and shakings of the leopards' heads, their feet braced against the ground, as they crowded tightly about the girl, he knew that the golden maiden was beyond saving now.

Sick in his soul, Peter turned. In another moment he had reached the bronze door in the wall, had pushed Susan ahead of him and slammed the door behind them. They had entered an impenetrable blackness, but he was not afraid now.

If Dekka had told the truth, there was nothing more to fear. The last danger was behind them.

Below them, he knew, was a long flight of stone steps leading into a tunnel with smooth walls and floor. It contained no traps, no pitfalls; and it emerged, about a mile away, in the jungle not far from the Baralang River.

He did not descend it at once, however. He took Susan in his arms and kissed her and held her close to him. He was trembling with an uncontrollable nervousness, a reaction from their latest close escape from the seemingly inescapable fangs of death, and with horror at the sacrifice of the girl who had saved their lives.

Susan, clinging to him, shivering, too, could say nothing but "Darling! Darling! I thought you were dead."

Her mind would return to that very often during the months to come, to shock and dismay and terrify her. But she was in his arms now; he was alive, strong, whole.

Peter was thinking, "I'll never let her go again!"

For Susan, alive and in his arms, was more important than anything else in the world.

With his arm about her, they started down the steps in the blackness.

DAWN WAS A saffron flash on the eastern horizon when they emerged from the tunnel into a cave, screened by shrubbery, on the brink of the Baralang.

Peter's last vestige of fear was removed when he saw, anchored in midstream, the familiar low-lying gray form of the yacht called the Luchow. More than six months ago that sturdy little vessel, once a mandarin's pleasure craft, had speeded him up the Pearl River from Hong Kong on the first leg of the most amazing adventure he had ever undertaken.

He went to the shore and sent a hail over the water. "Luchow, ahoy!"

As he turned back to Susan a tall young man stepped languidly out from the ambuscade of an ebony tree. Peter shouted, "Dekka!"

The young Thibetan, grimly smiling, said, "Hello, fellow. You're fifteen minutes late. What happened?"

Briefly, Peter told him of his adventures in the past few hours. At his references to the fight with the Blue Scorpion and the destruction of the Sapphire Skull, the young Thibetan's eyebrows became black crescents.

"But is Lu really dead?" he demanded.

"I don't know. I think so."

Dekka shrugged. "Why didn't you chuck him into the fire, along with his precious Sapphire Skull?"

"I can't kill in cold blood. Besides, I had an appointment with you, Dekka."

"Yeah.—What are your plans now?"

"Marriage.—Susan, this is Dekka Lan Shan. Dekka, this is Miss O'Gilvie, who has just honored me by consenting to become Mrs. Moore."

The young Thibetan gazed at Susan and sighed. Then he squinted at Peter and growled. "Talk about luck, fellow! If it was raining fried eggs you'd be caught out in it with a knife and fork in one hand and a platter of ham in the other! How do you do it?"

"Yogism!" chuckled Peter.

THE OCTOPUS OF HONG KONG

*The most mysterious and dangerous
woman in China challenges Peter
the Brazen in a deadly game*

1

MYSTERIOUS MESSAGE

WHEN THE SWIRLING warm waters of the Canton River meet the cold incoming tide of the China Sea in Lyeemoon Pass, the city of Hong Kong vanishes into fog. Streets become tunnels of wet gray vapor which cling to window panes, trail pedestrians and rickshaws in ghostly plumes, change street lamps to sickly glowing pearls, and give that fabulous Oriental metropolis a quickening sense of mystery.

Thieves and footpads creep into the streets, bold as wharf-rats. Familiar objects become strange and sinister in the damp gray shroud of fog at nightfall. Familiar sounds are amplified or dimmed. The whistles of steamers feeling their way into or out of the harbor are far-off melancholy mooings—the muffled bellowings of lost souls. The very gurgling of the water along Connaught Road, which is the bund of Hong Kong, takes on a sinister meaning.

On this evening, the business life of "The Pearl of the Orient" was drawing to a close, and the gay life of a Hong Kong night was beginning. American and British bars, snug and warmly aglow, resounded to the merry clatter of cocktail shakers, of voices already a little boisterous.

In the native quarters, iron shutters were raised, cook-

ing smells mingled with the fumes of incense from brood-
ing temples and the more acrid pungence of smoldering
spicewood from the braziers of closing bazaars. And China
proceeded about her mysterious nighttime affairs.

The weird harmonics of a stringed instrument, plucked
by the chilled fingers of a Burmese beggar, twanged across
the velvety refrain of the latest American foxtrot played by

Peter stared in fascinated disbelief.

the Colony Hotel's orchestra—smartest hotel, smartest
orchestra in Hong Kong; the West meeting the East on
the common ground of music, meeting but never blending.

The sensitive ears of the tall young American who
emerged from the waterfront offices of a trans-Pacific
steamship agency singled out the foxtrot through the
twanging of the lute. He tucked into an inner pocket a pair
of steamship tickets, snapped up the collar of his raincoat

against the damp chill, and strode through the fog toward the Colonial, whistling.

He was unquestionably the happiest man in Hong Kong tonight. Tomorrow he was marrying a girl who, in his opin-

"Banish them! Make slaves of them!" Susan cried regally.

ion, was not only the most beautiful girl in the world, but the most charming and the gayest. He had reserved the best suite on the *King of Asia* which, at noon, would up anchor and away to America. And the honeymoon of Mr. and Mrs. Peter Moore would have begun!

He was happy on a number of grounds. To marry the most attractive girl on earth, to return to America was enough. But there were other reasons. Tonight was his last night in the seething, tumultuous Republic of China. He was through with China forever; its intrigues, its dark and sinister lure. China was in his blood, in his very attitude toward life. It was time to go. A married man had no business in China. And Peter Moore had been an expatriate long enough. On to America! Home!

Phantoms slithered past him on the wet sidewalk. Rickshaw boys clip-clopped past him on the thin, muddy slime on the cobblestones. Their measured strides ticked out a refrain, repeated it over and over, made it ring above the velvety strains of the Colonial orchestra, the weird melody of the Burmese lute. Go-ing home! Go-ing home!

One of the phantoms brushed the American's shoulder, almost bumped him into the gutter. But this one did not pass on. He was a tall, thin figure in gray, as gray as the very fog. A gray hood cloaked all of his face but the eyes, which peered at the American, bright as a snake's. He might have been a passenger on the grisly craft that crosses the River of the Dead.

Not a beggar. The gray cloth was of too fine a texture for a beggar. The eyes danced over the American's face and a thin, whispery voice uttered in the tongue of North China:

"Those who know do not tell, and those who tell do not know."

Peter Moore gave a slight start. That ancient saying of China's wisest philosopher had once, far in the hazy past, had a dangerous significance. But the actual significance, the time, the place, the occasion evaded him. It recalled suddenly the blaze of an equatorial sun, the whispering of palms, the beating of long, slow waves on a white beach.

The apparition whispered, "I will meet you in your hotel room in precisely ten minutes. It is of the utmost urgency. Leave word that I am to be admitted."

"Wait a minute! *Hai-yah!*" the American called. But the gray ghost had vanished into the fog.

"This," Peter Moore addressed himself, "is damned nonsense." It was a dream in the mist. And yet the man in gray had been there, his voice had been as actual as the sidewalk.

UNEASILY, THE AMERICAN wondered what this might portend. He was sure he had cut off his past as if with a knife. Was this voice from a vague niche of that past—a ghostly tendril linking him with some forgotten obligation, some unfilled threat?

"Those who know do not tell, and those who tell do not know." What was the rest of it? "By many words, luck is exhausted. A little stream if not stopped may become a great ocean."

He was perplexed and a little worried. He walked slowly the rest of the way to the Colony, trying to spur a hazy memory. At the desk he hesitated. He left word that a Chinese caller was to be sent to his room.

He took the elevator to the seventh floor, proceeded down a wide corridor and let himself into his room. He locked the door, opened a handbag and removed from it a blue Smith & Wesson .38 revolver. He loaded it, unlocked the door, left it fully ajar and waited.

Without key to the identity of the man in gray, but highly suspicious, he was taking no chances. Tonight was his last night in China. And he was determined that it would be his last night in China. No forgotten old episode of the past would enchain him!

He heard felt soles padding down the maroon carpet runner and slipped behind the door. The deadened footsteps hesitated, turned into his room.

Peter Moore slipped out from behind the door, held the revolver on his unknown caller, and shut the door.

In the bright light of Mazdas, the gray cloak proved to be waterproof, finely-woven Shantung.

The unknown pulled off the cape, revealing to Moore the head and face of a Chinese some sixty years of age, gray, gaunt, unsmiling. Only the lively eyes possessed youth. Green-black, they glowed and gleamed.

The gray, gaunt, unsmiling face was unfamiliar.

"Master," the old man said, "I come to serve, not to harm."

Peter Moore had lowered the revolver.

The old Chinese said, "You do not know me, master." The green-black eyes were sparkling now. "But you have become, in the house of my heart, the most welcome of all guests. You do not recall what happened in Saigon?"

Moore said cautiously, "Many things have happened in Saigon."

"You saved the life of my oldest son in the Temple of the Nine Hundred and Seventy-Four Winged Serpents. He was left there to die of cobra bite. You tricked him away from his enemies. You hurried with him to the French Hospital. You imperiled your life to save his!"

"His name," Moore said quickly, "is Chay Gah."

"Mine is Chay Quon. I am your slave. I come here at greatest personal risk to give you a warning. My life, the life of my sons and my little grandsons are endangered by this rash visit. I can, with honor, say only this: Your betrothed is in danger. You will meet with bitter disappointment unless you act swiftly."

Chay Quon had backed to the door. His hand fumbled

for and found the knob. His other hand had disappeared into the folds of the gray Shantung robe. It appeared again. The yellow, clawlike fingers clutched a thin white object that softly glowed.

"Take this," Chay Quon said. "It is the key to no riddle, but it may assist you out of peculiar troubles—if you are the man you were."

He thrust the slender white object into Moore's hand, opened the door and departed.

Somewhat bewildered, the American adventurer did not move for a moment. He looked at the white object. It was a phial of white, translucent jade. The contents appeared to be lavender or purple. It meant less than nothing, at present, to him. He dropped it into his pocket and yanked open the door.

He shouted: "Chay Quon!"

The clanging of an elevator door answered him. The corridor was empty. Chay Quon was gone, leaving behind him the very aroma of ominous mystery.

2

"WASHED UP!"

MOORE CLOSED THE door and started across the room with the intention of returning the revolver to the handbag. Thinking better of it, he dropped the weapon into a hip pocket.

Versed as he was in the deviousness of the Oriental mind, he did not know quite what to make of Chay Quon's visit. Moore's fiancée, Susan O'Gilvie, was having dinner tonight at the Luxor with two young women of her acquaintance, an old friend and a new one—Jane Henderson and Marcia Pool. Moore and Miss O'Gilvie had agreed to spend this, their last unmarried evening, separately. After tonight they would never be parted—not for a single hour! They had agreed that she was to dine with Miss Henderson and Marcia Pool, while he was to dine with Marcia Pool's fiancé, Terry Teeple, an amusing young American who was the wireless operator on the ship on which Miss Pool had just arrived in Hong Kong.

What Chay Quon had said perplexed and worried Moore. He would go to the Luxor, make sure that Susan was safe and spend the evening, not with Terry Teeple, but in taking steps that no harm befell her.

The head waiter had once been the steward of a ship on which Moore had made a run as wireless operator.

Moore went to the fashionable night club. It was crowded, but he did not see Susan O'Gilvie or Jane Henderson.

The head waiter came over to him. "Alone tonight, Mr. Moore?"

Moore said that he was looking for Miss O'Gilvie. "I don't see her here. She made a reservation for a table for this evening."

"When did Miss O'Gilvie make the reservation?"

"This morning. She phoned."

"I don't recall it, Mr. Moore."

"That's queer. Perhaps I've made a mistake." But he hadn't made a mistake, and it wasn't, in light of other minor things, quite so queer as it might have been.

Somewhat grimly the young man returned to Queen's Road, hailed a rickshaw and directed the coolie to the Henderson mansion, on Upper Elbert Road, near Government House.

Reaching the Hendersons', he told the coolie to wait, ran up the steps and rang the bell. The Hendersons' English butler opened the door. Moore asked him if Miss Henderson was home.

"No, sir."

"Do you know where she's dining?"

"Yes, sir. She is attending a dinner dance at the Recourse Bay Hotel, with Captain Mac Alister."

"Has Miss O'Gilvie been here?"

"No, sir."

Moore thanked him and returned to the rickshaw. Why

had Susan lied to him? He was uneasy. It was unlike her to lie, to practice deceit in any form. Rather, it had been, until very recently, unlike her. She was frank, honest, sincere to a fault. A girl with her type of courage never resorted to lies or deceit. Yet, in the past few days, he had discovered her in a number of petty lies and little deceits.

Under ordinary circumstances he would have suspected that Susan was up to some mischief. She was a thrill-hunter. Yet he was sure that she was now as anxious to leave China and its intrigues forever as was he. Her recent nervousness and evasiveness he had supposed was natural in a girl soon to be married. But that hardly explained her small lies and petty deceits.

He dismissed the rickshaw at the Colonial and went directly to Susan's suite. He was about to knock when he heard the murmur of voices. He hesitated, then knocked.

THERE WAS A delay of perhaps ten seconds before the door was opened. Susan opened it. She was charming, beautiful in a negligee of orchid. She looked strange. She looked excited. Her eyes were brilliant, the pupils dilated. Her cheeks were feverishly flushed. Her lips had a bright, feverish look.

He was conscious, as he anxiously regarded her, of two distinct scents—the delicate French perfume she used, and an exotic spiciness, not incense, not perfume; a heady smell, a somehow sinister aroma.

She did not fly into his arms. Her eyes, which were not blue but a deep, lovely violet, stared at him almost wildly, as if he were a stranger, as if she were terrified. But he knew that the brilliance in them was anger.

Susan said in a vexed voice, "What do you want?"

He could have been no more surprised if she had slapped him.

"Good Lord, Susan," he said. "What's wrong? You said you were dining with Jane Henderson and Marcia Pool at the Luxor."

"I changed my mind." She was staring at him with defiance. And he suddenly had a strange feeling, a feeling almost mystical; that Susan was gone, that she had slipped away from him forever, that in her place was a strange, soulless woman.

"Who's here?" he asked.

"No one," she answered, in the same defiant voice.

"I could have sworn I heard voices."

"You're mistaken, Peter. I—I wanted to be alone."

"You didn't want to kiss me."

"Not now. Please go."

It didn't quite come off. This wasn't mere nervousness. There was trouble. It was that exotic, spicy aroma.

He said grimly, "Let me in."

Susan stood her ground a moment, then stepped aside. Peter Moore went into the room. It was the parlor of her suite. The spicy smell was stronger. He sniffed it and said, "What is it?"

"I don't know what you're talking about, Peter."

He looked at her, troubled. Lying again. He wanted to take her into his arms, to smash down this barrier, whatever it was, that had come between them. Susan was small, slim, dark-haired. Her size had deceived him before.

"Susan," he said gravely, "you're lying to me. You're up to mischief."

She had not closed the door; was still standing on

the threshold, with arms folded on breast, chin up, eyes strangely brilliant.

He asked, in a somewhat shaken voice, "Where's Marcia Pool?"

"I'm sure I don't know."

"But you had a dinner engagement with her, if not with Jane Henderson. I heard you ask her this noon at lunch if she would have dinner with you tonight. You'll have to admit this is pretty mysterious. What happened?"

"Am I responsible for her?" Susan cried angrily.

Moore shook his head with a baffled air. "I don't understand you, Susan. In a way, it seems to me you are responsible for her. You know China. She doesn't."

"She got away from me," Susan said sullenly.

Moore's blue eyes sharpened. "What do you mean?"

"We did start out for dinner," Susan replied, still with that sullen air. "We took rickshaws."

"To the Luxor?" Moore interrupted in a surprised voice.

"We changed our minds. We decided we wanted to have a real Chinese dinner. We were going to the native quarter. We were going along Tung Road when she suddenly stopped her rickshaw and jumped out. She'd seen some one she knew—an old friend."

"A man or a woman?"

"A man. I think it was an old beau. I don't know. And she yelled at me to go on without her."

MOORE STARED AT Susan O'Gilvie. "That doesn't sound like Marcia Pool," he said. He did not, to be sure, know Marcia Pool very well. He had known her only a couple of days. She was a charming, delightful blond girl of about twenty—very much in love with tall, dark Terry Teeple.

"Naturally," Susan said, "I was furious. After all, we did have a date. And when she dashed off like that—"

"Susan," Peter said firmly, "you're lying again. What happened to Marcia Pool?"

"I told you!" Susan cried. "She saw this man—"

"Nonsense. You're making it up as you go along. You broke your date with her, didn't you? You didn't see her at all this evening, did you?"

"Have it your way," Susan said stonily.

Moore shook his head. "It—it's pretty puzzling," he said. "You—you've changed so. Something is going on that you're not telling me about. Don't you want to talk things over? If I've done anything to offend you—"

"I have no desire to talk anything over."

"But can't you tell me what's going on? When I came to this door a moment ago, I'll swear I heard voices. All this—this subterfuge, all these deceptions—"

She cried, "How dare you spy on me?"

"Good Lord, Susan, I wasn't spying. I was worried. I wanted to make sure everything was all right. An old friend told me there was trouble brewing. He said you were in danger."

As if she had not heard, she said angrily, "You were spying! I'm sick of you!" She licked her bright, dry lips. "You—you fortune hunter!" she cried.

Peter's face went grim and white. Then the crimson of anger mounted into it. It had always been a bone of contention between them, that fabulous fortune of hers, but never before in this sense.

Susan, for two years, had maintained that she was too modern, too sensible, to let love slip by when she was sure she had found it, and that in Peter Moore she had found the one man she could ever love. Until very recently he had stubbornly refused to marry her because of her great fortune. The problem had finally been solved to their mutual satisfaction. They were to live entirely on his income, to touch none of her own.

He said, feebly, "Susan, you're joking, aren't you?"

"Am I?" she cried. "Look at me!"

He was looking at her. And again, he was swept by the feeling that this girl who faced him was a stranger. She had often been angry at him. She had flown into rages. But she had never, at her angriest moments, lost her charm. He had the feeling of mysterious, dangerous fires. She had suddenly become a haughty little princess.

He went to the door and said quietly, "Okay, Susan. The wedding bells are off."

He hesitated. It was very much like a nightmare. In the two years he had known Susan they had shared adventures, dangers, hardships and fine, exalted moments. He knew her only for a charming, delightful, generous gay companion whose only fault was an insatiable thirst for adventurous thrills. He presumed now that she had found an adventure more desirable than himself.

There was no relenting in her eyes. They remained brilliant, hard.

AS HE STARTED down the hall he heard her door close with a sharp click. He hesitated, went on. He was too hurt, too angry, too baffled to think clearly. He went to his room and tried to think it out. He dismissed the theory that he might have done something to offend her.

He gave way briefly to fury. He told himself that she

wasn't, never had been worth it. And he knew he was lying to himself. She was worth it. She was the most charming, most attractive, the most lovable girl he had ever known.

And it suddenly occurred to Peter that he had been a blind, stupid fool. She was in danger! They had been through so many scrapes. She knew the ropes. There had been some one, a dangerous enemy, hiding in the room, prepared to shoot him if she had not done precisely as she was instructed!

It was the only logical explanation for her sudden, complete reversal of character. She had not dared warn him; had trusted to his cleverness to guess the truth, to save her from some unimaginable danger. That explained the murmurs he had heard. That explained her startling change toward him.

He was running down the hall. He passed the elevators, ran to the stairs and took them three at a bound. At her door, he paused and listened. He heard nothing. He decided against knocking and tried the knob. The door was unlocked.

With revolver ready he threw open the door.

The parlor was empty. He tiptoed to the bedroom door, threw it open. The bedroom was empty. The bathroom door was open, the lights were burning. Both rooms showed evidences of Susan's hasty departure. The dresser drawers were pulled out. A powder puff and a few dark hairpins were scattered across the dresser. Otherwise, everything she possessed was gone. She had evidently dressed the instant he had left, had packed and gone!

Where? Why? What had happened?

He stared about the abandoned bedroom with a sickly

thumping heart. His guess had been wrong. She hadn't been in danger. She had meant what she had said.

Peter Moore saw, at that instant, his image in the long French mirror on the back of the bathroom door. He saw a tall young man with rumpled blond hair, stricken eyes, ashen face. He looked pretty awful. He felt pretty awful. He could not believe that Susan meant what she had said. Only yesterday she had impulsively thrown her arms about his neck, clasped him tight, and told him how deliriously happy she was. They were, at last, to be married! Wasn't it wonderful?

Or had it been the day before yesterday? When had the change in her begun? A man in love is apt to be blind.

He felt sick. He thought of the steamship tickets in his pocket. Well, that was off. Everything was off.

He was suddenly aware of the perfume she used. A faint breath of it lingered in the air, made her seem vividly near.

The face in the French mirror was no longer gray but darkly red. Peter Moore gave his reflection a hard, bitter grin. Jilted!

HE WAS ABOUT to leave the room when his attention was attracted by the glint of light on metal or glass under the bedside table. He bent down and picked up a small empty phial of carved crystal with a carved kingfisher jade stopper. No more than a drop of thick, purple liquid remained in the bottle. He pulled out the stopper and sniffed it. And the smell which rose sweetly, spicily into his nostrils was the same that he had detected in the air on his earlier visit.

He held the phial to a light and, with narrow, dreamy eyes, inhaled the exotic fragrance again. Then he took from his pocket the jade phial Chay Quon had given him. He removed the stopper and sniffed the purple contents. It was the same sweet, spicy stuff! Unquestionably, it was a drug, some potent Oriental concoction, more sinister in its fragrance alone than opium!

Peter rejected the impulse to taste the stuff. He had had experience with Oriental drugs.

He placed both phials in his pocket and returned to his room. He tried to think clearly. There was no question in his mind that Susan, on the very eve of their marriage, had fallen under the power of some sinister influence. He had, in the past, helped her escape from a number of dangerous predicaments, but on those occasions he had had Susan's cooperation. Now she was his enemy.

His mind flashed back to some of their past adventures. Their most dangerous enemy had been Mr. Lu, the monstrous genius who lived in a marble palace at the bottom of the Lake of the Flying Dragon in the cobalt mountains of Szechwan. In Annam, a few weeks ago, Peter had succeeded in destroying Mr. Lu's vast power, and had, he believed, killed that mythological figure.

This, he was certain, was not the work of that fantastic giant with the jade brain.

There was a knock at his door. He opened it. A Chinese boy handed him an envelope. In one end of it he felt a small, hard lump. The envelope was addressed to him in Susan's vigorous handwriting. He tore it open. The small hard lump proved to be the emerald engagement ring he had given her. The note was brief.

DEAR PETER:
We are absolutely washed up. I mean it.
SUSAN.

That was all. He was staring grimly at the ring when a sudden explosive shattering of glass occurred at the window. The lower pane had been burst. He flattened himself back against the wall and watched the jagged hole. His room was six stories from the street, four from the roof. There was nothing beyond the window but swirling gray fog.

As he stared, a small white-and-red object fluttered in through the jagged aperture.

It was the creamy petal of a flower. He bent down and picked it up. It was a lotus petal, one end of which was dripping with blood!

3

INTO THIN AIR

MYSTIFIED, PETER EXAMINED the lotus petal for a mark, a symbol of some kind. Finding none, he placed the blood-dipped petal in the envelope with Susan's note and returned the envelope to his pocket. The lotus petal was, presumably, a warning. Presumably, it implied, according to his knowledge of China and its devious methods, that he was to keep his distance. But from whom or what?

The warning, so delicately conveyed, helped to clear and crystallize his thoughts. It was no longer a question of hurt pride, of being jilted on the eve of his marriage. Susan's very attitude was a cloud over the issue, a cloud cleverly devised by Susan's—his—latest enemy.

His job was clear-cut: he must remove Susan from an ingenious, diabolical influence before both their lives were ruined.

Peter descended to the lobby and made inquiries. Miss O'Gilvie, he learned at the desk, had paid her bill and checked out. At the mail desk he learned that she had left no forwarding address. And from the Sikh doorman he learned that Miss O'Gilvie had left in a black sedan chair.

"A public chair?"

"No, *sahib;* a private one."

"Numbered?"

"I saw no number, *sahib.*"

"Did you recognize it?"

"No, *sahib;* it was a strange chair."

That was that. Susan had been called for. A strange sedan chair had spirited her—to what fantastic fate? At all events, the trail was broken.

He watched the tide of vehicles in the street for a moment—wraiths emerging from and vanishing into the sea of fog. Rickshaws, sedan chairs, wheelbarrows with enormous wheels, each having for a cargo a fat, prosperous-looking Chinese. Always fat, always prosperous.

He returned to his room. He wanted to inspect the broken window, to attempt, if possible, to pick up this other trail.

Moore was half out the window, storing upward into fogbound darkness, when his door burst open and a young man's voice cried, "Hey, Mr. Moore! What's going on, anyhow?"

Moore backed out of the window and into the room. A pair of sparkling black eyes in a flushed, handsome young face stared at him. Terry Teeple was a tall man of about twenty-four, with thick, curly black hair.

"I've been waiting down there in the bar for an hour," Teeple said. "Anything wrong?"

"Yes. Plenty." Moore told him briefly of Susan O'Gilvie's strange behavior, her disappearance, and showed the wireless operator the lotus blossom.

He had hardly concluded his account when Teeple interrupted with, "Where's Marcia?"

Moore told him what Susan had said. The sparkle left the young man's eyes. His face became grave.

"That's funny," he said. "It doesn't sound like Marcia. She doesn't run out on dates. And she's crazy about Miss O'Gilvie—thinks she's wonderful."

Moore said: "I don't believe the story. I don't believe Marcia started out with her. But we'll check it up."

He picked up the phone and called Marcia Pool's room.

When she did not answer, Moore hung up the receiver and said, "Something queer is going on. I'd like to have a look at Marcia's room."

THEY SECURED A pass key from the desk clerk, went to Marcia Pool's room and let themselves in. It was in the condition that a pretty, frivolous young woman like Marcia Pool might have been expected to leave a room in. Clothing was flung over chairs. Powder had been spilled on the dressing table. The air was warm and sweet with the fragrance of bath salts and perfume.

Evidently Marcia Pool had bathed and dressed to go out to dinner in the rush and hurry that seemed characteristic of her.

"She went out to dinner with somebody," Terry Teeple said quietly. He looked sad. "Maybe Miss O'Gilvie was right, after all. Maybe Marsh did meet somebody she knew—an old beau."

Peter was thinking rapidly, wondering where would be the best place to begin looking. He was more worried than he seemed. He was sure that Susan had been lying. He was sure that Marcia Pool had not rudely left her and gone off with some old friend, even an old beau.

But he said briskly, "They may have gone to dinner somewhere in that neighborhood. We'll look-see."

The two young men took rickshaws to Tung Road. It was a narrow, dark little road, with street-lamps widely spaced. There were several native restaurants in the neighborhood, but none of them was the kind of restaurant to which you would take the kind of girl Marcia Pool was.

In the fourth of these dank little eating places Moore found a telephone. He called the hotel and asked for Miss Pool. To his great relief she answered the phone.

Her voice was hysterical.

"Oh, it's Mr. Moore!" she cried. "I've just got back here after a perfectly horrible experience! Have you seen Miss O'Gilvie?"

"Yes."

"Is she all right?"

"I believe so. What happened?"

"We started out for dinner," the hysterical girl said. "We were going to the Luxor, but we changed our minds. Miss O'Gilvie thought it would be more fun to go to a place where we could get real Chinese food. She said we knew just the place.

"We went down Queen's Road—I think that's the road—and turned into a dark little alley. Halfway down the block both our coolies stopped. A horrible looking Chinaman stepped out of the shadow of a building and grabbed my hand. Miss O'Gilvie was on the other side of me—I mean, our rickshaws were stopped side by side.

"When I screamed she grabbed my other hand and said, 'Don't yell! It's all right.' I don't know why she said that. I thought it was terribly mysterious. This—this man was trying to drag me out of my rickshaw. There was a closed sedan chair near him—a dark red one. He said something to me in Chinese—and I hit him in the face. I jerked my hand away from Miss O'Gilvie. I jumped out of my rickshaw—and ran toward Queen's Road.

"But I heard this man after me. I think there were several others. I dashed into a narrow little doorway and hid. They ran on past. I don't know how long I hid there. It seemed ages. I was too terrified to come out. I knew they were looking for me, and I was afraid something had happened to Miss O'Gilvie. But I didn't dare move! I was never so scared or bewildered in my life. And finally, when I was sure they'd gone, I sneaked out and ran every step of the way back to the hotel. I only got in a few minutes ago. Where's Terry?"

"Right here."

"Is he all right?"

"Yep."

"But it's so mysterious," Marcia wailed. "Why did Miss O'Gilvie grab my hand? What was it all about?"

"I'll explain everything when I see you," Moore answered. "Terry and I will be up to your room in about ten minutes. Keep the door locked. Don't let any one in. Understand?"

"Yes. But what on earth is it all about?"

"We'll try to clear things up when I see you."

PETER MOORE HUNG up and turned to Terry Teeple. "She's okay now," Moore said. He told Terry Teeple what Marcia had told him on their way back to the hotel.

At the Colony entrance they paid off their coolies and went to Marcia's room. There was no response to their knocks.

Terry Teeple said, in a shaking, husky voice, "They've got her! They got in there and grabbed her! Who is it?"

"I don't know."

Terry Teeple went down once again for the pass key. The two young men let themselves in. Since their previous visit the scene had drastically changed. The room was now in the greatest disorder. Two chairs had been overturned. The dressing table had been pulled out at one end about a foot from the wall. The rugs showed evidences of a scuffle. But what interested Moore most at the moment was the window. It was open. It was open upon a fire escape.

He went to the window and looked out, up, down. He found a shred of jade-green chiffon dangling in the fog from a sharp point on the fire escape railing.

Terry Teeple identified it. "She was going to wear that green dress tonight," he whispered.

Moore said, "I don't know anything about Marcia Pool. You'd better tell me what you can. Is she wealthy?"

"Her father's a millionaire."

"Where is he?"

"New York."

"She was traveling alone, wasn't she?"

"Yes."

"Did you know her before this trip?"

"No. I met her the day after we left Frisco. Look here, Mr. Moore. You know China like a book. You know how these Hong Kong gangs work. I haven't much money, but I'll guarantee her father will pay any price!"

Peter replied grimly, "This isn't an ordinary kidnaping." He suddenly felt sick. There was no question that Susan was somehow involved in the disappearance of Marcia

Pool. That meeting with the Chinese in Tung Road had been, he was sure, a rendezvous. Otherwise, why would Susan have grabbed Marcia's wrist and tried to detain her—and warned her not to yell?

He felt sure that Susan, acting under some one's orders, had attempted to deliver Marcia Pool into the hands of some dangerous and wily Oriental. Moore had, he believed, reached Susan O'Gilvie's room in time to hear her discussing a new plan with some member of the conspiracy—some woman. This new plan had just been executed.

If Susan had been poor it might have been a little easier to understand. But Susan was not poor. She was fabulously wealthy in her own right. Granted that she might have lost her senses through the use of some mysterious drug, why should she take part in any plan involving the kidnaping of another wealthy girl?

No, it was not an ordinary kidnaping.

He began to look about the room carefully, sniffing the air as he moved about. He expected to find a trace of that mysterious scent which, he was now sure, had been Susan's undoing. But he detected no other odor in the room but a faint, springlike fragrance—an old-fashioned fragrance, the one that he had noticed on his former visit here.

"Geranium," he said.

"It's the only kind of perfume Marcia uses," the tall, agitated young wireless operator said.

IN his thorough examination of the room—an inch-by-inch search—Peter had reached the dressing table. It was littered with a jumble of toilet implements—gold-backed brushes, a comb, a hand mirror, a manicure set, several dozen small, gold-topped jars and little bottles.

Half-hidden by an edge of the hairbrush, he found what he had been fearing he would eventually find.

It was a note on a sheet of white rice paper, painstakingly written in purple ink.

> MR. HORATIO POOL:
>
> Your daughter will die tonight of a thousand tortures in a thousand exquisite agonies. Perhaps you will be sorry now for that night in Yokohama in 1914.

There was no signature, but pinned to the bottom was a lotus petal, one end of which was black with dried blood!

Terry Teeple read it over his shoulder, and burst explosively into a seagoing man's profanity. He was going to crack Chinese skulls and fracture Chinese jawbones until the streets of Hong Kong were knee-deep with his victims.

"It isn't going to be as simple as that," Peter warned him. He removed one of the phials from his pocket and took out the stopper. "Smell this," he said. "Is it familiar?"

"It smells dangerous," Terry Teeple said. "No. It's new to me."

"Are you sure you've never smelled anything like it in Miss Pool's presence?"

"Positive."

"She hasn't acted strangely, or differently, in the past day or two?"

"Not a bit. I saw her less than two hours ago. We had a cocktail at the American bar. I brought her here, kissed her so-long. No, she was just the same."

"You say she was traveling alone?"

"Yes. She was making a trip around the world, and

was meeting her brother Gregory in Manila. We became engaged the night before we put in at Yokohama."

"Does she know any one in Hong Kong?"

"Not a soul. Some of her father's old friends live here, but she hasn't looked them up. We've been together practically every waking minute of the time. The *Vandalia* only got in last night."

Peter glanced at the note again. "Was Miss Pool born in China?"

"Yes. In Peking. But her family—her father, mother, an older sister and Gregory moved to New York when Marcia was five, and have lived there since."

"She wouldn't recall any of her father's old friends—or enemies," Peter said thoughtfully. "Has she mentioned any of them?"

"She mentioned a few people he knew in Shanghai and Hong Kong—all old friends. But she didn't look any of them up. We were too busy."

"Know her father's address in New York?"

"No. He has an apartment there and a summer place at Southampton, Long Island."

PETER PICKED UP the telephone. He said to the operator, "Get me Mr. Horatio Pool, in New York City. If he isn't at his apartment try his place at Southampton, Long Island."

While he waited for the call to be put through, Peter looked about the room for further clues. He was still looking without success when the long lines operator advised him that Mr. Pool was on the circuit.

A gruff voice ten thousand miles away said sharply, "Hong Kong? All right, all right. Is it you, Marcia?"

Peter explained himself. At the end of fifteen minutes,

at approximately ten dollars a minute, he was still endeav-
oring to make a frightened, suspicious, angry millionaire
in New York understand that his daughter had been stolen
from her hotel room in Hong Kong, China, and that only
from his lips could the necessary helpful information be
obtained.

The connection was good, Mr. Pool's voice was clear, but
he was almost hysterical.

Peter said: "Think hard, Mr. Pool. What happened in
Yokohama in 1914?"

The frantic father at the other end cried, "Good Lord,
man! I was there a dozen times that year. That was the
year of the War. Nineteen years ago! A thousand things
happened—deals of all sorts. I met countless people under
every possible condition."

"Enemies?"

"I've got enough enemies in the Far East to start a war!"

On an inspiration, looking at the note, Peter hazarded:
"Does the name Lotus suggest anything?"

The man ten thousand miles away answered: "Hold on!
Wait! Let me think! Lotus! Lotus Burma!"

Something clicked in Peter's memory department.
Lotus Burma. Shanghai. Some four or five years ago he
had seen a Lotus Burma, a fascinating, beautiful Eurasian
woman at a party given by a Japanese exporter.

Horatio Pool was saying, "She came to one of our parties
that summer in Yokohama—a party in honor of the American Ambassador. She wasn't invited. She insulted Mrs.
Pool. I had the servants put her out. Lotus Burma was a
notorious woman—one of the richest women in China,
an opium fiend."

"That's all for now," Peter said, cutting the hysterical man off. "I'll report later."

He replaced the receiver and turned to Terry Teeple.

"It still doesn't make sense," he said. "The only incident he can recall happening in Yokohama in 1914 concerned a half-caste named Lotus Burma. This Lotus Burma is a hellion—but it doesn't seem to hold water. We'll get busy. Have you a gun?"

"In my room."

"Get it and meet me outside."

4

THE WISE ONE

PETER'S OBJECTIVE WAS the House with the Black Door on Wing Lok Street, a place known among the select as the Mansion of Divine Contentment, and to tourists and most white residents of Hong Kong, known not at all.

A grimy, one-story stone building with corrugated steel shutters at the window, the Mansion of Divine Contentment gave no indication that it led a charmed life.

Peter told the wireless operator to wait. He advanced to the black door, knocked twice, then once, then twice again. The door swung open. An elderly Chinese in the servile blue of the Chinese lower classes peered into his face and said, "Ah, master, it is you!" and stepped aside for Peter to enter.

He went through a labyrinth of rooms and corridors without hesitation, and came at length to a finely polished brass door, carved beautifully and ornamented with laughing lions and sneering tigers. This he opened without ceremony, entering a room with walls of golden silk and an atmosphere of the finest sandalwood incense.

A fat, living Buddha squatted on a teakwood stool in a corner. He was sipping, from a silver goblet, a decoction which Peter recognized as rice gin flavored with whompee juice and pomello seeds.

He stared at Peter with his tiny, shoebutton eyes and set the goblet down with a clink on the mother-o'-pearl taboret beside him.

"By Buddha's toenail," he cried, in a thin squeal of a voice, "I heard, once again, that you had leaped the dragon gate. Clacking tongues in the heads of fools told me you had entered the holy contests for the high priesthood of the temple of the Blue Skull with the Living Brain in Annam, that you locked horns with Lu the unconquerable and were cast to his black leopards for tiffin! You are a man of rubber and steel indeed. How many lives has a cat of your caliber?"

He peered uncertainly at the American adventurer. "I grovel and abase myself in the muck of this miserable room in the presence of your magnificence. I am flattered that a man of your high purposes has crossed the sill of my wretched abode. I am the slave to your bidding. Command!"

"I'm here for some information, Yat Gow," Peter said crisply. "Let's dispense with the formalities."

"O man of many troubles," Yat Gow piped, "in the Taoist heart there is no place where mercy cannot be exercised; in the Taoist brain no corner that is not illuminated with sympathetic wisdom. Command!"

Peter withdrew the full white jade phial from his pocket. He advanced on the fat, flowery Yat Gow with the phial unstoppered, but he held it firmly in the muscles of his fingers.

"Smell!" he said.

But the pudgy little nose of Yat Gow was already working, wriggling like the nose of an excited rabbit.

"By the whiskers of Buddha!" he squealed, making a snatch for the phial. "One thousand Taikwan taels for that!"

Peter withdrew it from the range of the fat, clumsy hands and dropped the stopper in place.

"Not for sale," he said. "What is this stuff?"

"It is the drug of sublime joy and utter self-fulfillment and magical power!" Yat Gow cried. "Where did you steal it?"

"Tell me more about it."

"A thousand Taikwan taels," Yat Gow cried, "for the name and address of the man from whom you got it!"

"Is it as rare as that?"

"It is rarer than the sixth toe of a dragon! It is rarer than the essence of life! It is rarer than a fleshy appearance of the King Gautama Buddha!"

"What is it?"

"Alas, would I beg for a drop, a merest taste, if I knew what it was? It is a secret. It was lost with the last of the Mings. I tasted it just once. The Grand Eunuch in the household of the Empress Dowager gave me two drops on my tongue years—years ago! In the summer palace, in Peking. I would have given my right and my left eye for two more drops. But the Grand Eunuch was disappointed in the pickled rotten eggs I brought to him. I incurred his disfavor. It was my last taste."

"What was the effect on you?"

"A sense of utter power and dominion, a deadening of my damnable conscience. One loses all sense of scruples.

One becomes a superman with not the slightest principles. And one hates magnificently."

"What would be the effect on a lover toward his or her beloved?"

"Beautiful contempt and scorn!"

PETER HAD SUSPECTED as much. But now that his suspicions were confirmed he felt sick and defeated. Susan's strange hostility was now painfully understandable. One taste of this magical stuff and she had become its slave. He could fight through an army of enemies for her, but how could he compete with a drug that turned love to poisonous hate?

Peter returned the phial to his pocket. "Yat Gow," he said, "you are the smartest man in Hong Kong. You see all, know all—"

"—And say nothing," Yat Gow finished complacently. "Yet my brain is a storehouse, a godown of riches, at your complete disposal—for five drops of the Drug of Divinity!"

Pete said firmly, "No. You have enough bad habits, with your black smoke and your whompee juice. Isn't it true that this stuff is more responsible than anything else for the downfall of the empire?"

"Who takes that drug," Yat Gow answered, in the manner of a man coining an epigram, "cares not what falls."

"What do you know about Lotus Burma?"

The beady little eyes lost their shimmer and squinted at him steadily out of their folds of fat.

"We gaze vainly at the mountain's brow," Yat Gow answered.

"Yet behind us, like wild horses, come flashing our

misdeeds," Peter said threateningly, "prepared to overtake us at the smallest misstep."

"This is more blackmail," Yat Gow sighed. "Let me think a moment. What do you wish to know about Lotus Burma?"

"Is she still a madwoman, with dreams of horrible revenge on those who slighted her in the past?"

"With advancing years," Yat Gow answered, "the capacity to love diminishes, but the capacity to hate discovers no horizons. You refer to the mysterious lady known as The Octopus."

"Tell me what you can about her."

"Hai-yah! What is there to tell? She is beautiful, fascinating—a creature of mystery. The man who has dealings with such as she does well to write a prayer to the lord Gautama Buddha on a scrap of red paper, chew it rapidly and swallow it. Otherwise, his digestive operations may cease entirely—at the source."

"You mean, a slit throat."

"You are too literal, master. I know nothing whatever of Lotus Burma. She is as mysterious as the heart of an opal, as secret as the ways of a serpent. All I can say—" Yat Gow hesitated, made a slashing, complex gesture in the air with one finger—the Chinese symbol for great danger.

"Where is the den of this octopus?"

"Will my judicious answer furnish the key to your riddle?"

"Answer the question, you fat pig," Peter answered. "You are too full of whompee juice and poetry."

Yat Gow lifted hairless brows and pudgy hands in gestures of futility. "The Octopus," he said resignedly, "lives in the great black vulture of a house spraddling the tip of the Peak. You know the house well."

"The house that Lak Chak built?"

"The same. Now," Yat Gow said covetously, "do I merit a drop of the drug—one little drop?"

"Your soul will doubtless rot in a thousand hells," Peter answered, "but you shall have the drop." And he gave Yat Gow the nearly empty phial.

"Dangerous stuff—very dangerous," a low voice said.

Peter wheeled about. A man was standing in the doorway—a tall, thin, dark-skinned man of about forty; a red-haired man who closely resembled a caricature of Satan. He had the sharp, angular features, the V-shaped smile, the cynical, dark eyes. His hair was of a dusky shade of red—it resembled the play of fire in smoke.

Moore grinned, walked over and shot out a hand to clasp the other's. "Dan de Sylva!" he cried.

THIS SATANIC INDIVIDUAL was an old friend, the companion of more than one dangerous adventure. Daniel de Sylva was a gem dealer—the brains, in fact, of the great de Sylva Corporation. He and his agents in the Far East purchased rare gems, sold them to European and American clients at fabulous profits. He lived an exciting, dangerous life. Peter Moore had not seen Dan de Sylva since the completion of a certain little episode in Bangalore, India, about a year previously.

"How long," Peter asked, "have you been standing there?"

"Long enough to realize that two dogs are barking up the tree at the same tiger. My notion is that the two dogs might be blended into one. I happen to be looking for Lotus Burma myself. That's why I came here. I knew that

Yat Gow was the one man in Hong Kong who can honestly be described as a two-legged Hong Kong directory. Well—do you want the job, Peter?"

"My plans for getting married tomorrow have been upset," Peter answered. "But I still have hope."

"This job," the Satanic individual said in his low voice, "is a dandy. Pardon us, Yat Gow. All of this will leak into your storebin eventually, anyhow. Listen and learn! Three weeks ago, Peter, one of my most trusted men was robbed of two million dollars' worth of diamonds—Malay water diamonds—in Buitenzorg, Java."

"By Lotus Burma?"

"Now, don't be vulgar, Peter. Does one arm of an octopus know what another arm is doing? You may have gleaned that Lotus Burma is mysterious and dangerous beyond ordinary reckoning. There is a possibility that she knows about the diamonds. And there is a possibility—slight—that she knows my man was murdered. I can't let my men be murdered, Peter. You know that. This matter must be thoroughly investigated by a man who knows his Far East. In brief, you have fairly walked into the job. There's a little ship pulling out at dawn for Buitenzorg. It's a dangerous job. Want it?"

"I intend," Peter answered, "to be sailing for San Francisco at noon tomorrow."

"With a bride on your arm?"

"If my night's work is successful."

"Pardon my curiosity, but is the bride-to-be involved in any way with the eight-armed mystery?"

"Yes."

"Then, knowing you, I can guess that you are paying

The Octopus a visit this evening. You might kill two birds with one stone. Bring Lotus Burma back alive! That's all. If you're the man you used to be, you'll deliver her neatly wrapped—if kicking—to my hotel room. All I want is my diamonds—or her life. But I intend to take it myself."

He stopped. Both men looked at Yat Gow. The fat Chinese was convulsed with mirth. His yellow face was pink.

"What's the joke?" Satan asked.

"You have not met The Octopus," Yat Gow explained himself.

"No, but I've seen Peter the Brazen in action," de Sylva said, almost angrily. "Will you help me, Peter?"

"I'll do my best."

"I am staying at the Colony, too. Room eight nineteen. If you don't bring The Hong Kong Octopus back alive, my offer is good all night."

PETER THANKED HIM and returned to Terry Teeple who waited with impatience on Wing Lok Street before the House with the Black Door.

"Are we on the right track?" he eagerly demanded.

"We're on the track," Peter answered, "of the most mysterious and dangerous woman in China—The Octopus. We may be trailed. We'll walk."

They took back alleys to the foot of the great black hill which rises majestically from Hong Kong. The rest of the way was up steep, tortuous mountain trails, carved along precipices by the English in the early years of their occupation of the island.

During pauses for breath, Peter told Terry Teeple what

he knew of Lotus Burma and what he knew about the house that Lak Chak built.

"Yat Gow could tell me little about her," Peter said. "She's a woman of mystery. All I know is that she's Eurasian—half white, half yellow. But I think we're rapidly learning why she's called The Octopus."

"If she's got Marcia," Terry Teeple said wrathfully, "I'll wring her damned neck!"

"You'll be lucky to save your own," Peter said. He had little faith in the successful outcome of this expedition. For many years, he had heard dark rumors concerning a woman who was known as The Octopus.

"This house in which she's living," he went on, "is known as The Palace of the Ninety and Nine Black Dragons. It was built some years ago by Lak Chak, the king of the thieves—the grand potentate of the great Thieves' Guild of China. I was Lak Chak's guest there for a month. He wanted to impress me with his superiority.

"Actually, I was his prisoner—with the freedom of the house. He wanted a house with dozens of mysterious exits. We'll reach one of them in a moment. The most amazing spectacle I ever saw in my life was a banquet he gave one night to four hundred of China's Number One Thieves. There were a thousand sing-song girls, twenty native orchestras. The food was served from great lacquered vats, and rice wine and samshu and arrack came into the banquet hall in hogsheads."

That had been long before he had met Susan. He stopped talking, fell to thinking of her again, her loveliness, her gayety, her wonderful companionship. Off to his right stretched a sea of fog. Above them the stars of China sparkled clearly. Below, nothing of the city was visible. A faint wind stirred the branches of the beefwood grove they were approaching.

In the center of it Peter stopped. In the starlight, on a great bald knoll beyond, sprawled, or crouched, a low, black structure—the Palace of the Ninety and Nine Dragons.

Peter kicked aside an accumulation of leaves and exposed a plate of blackened bronze about four feet square.

"This is our entrance," he said. "Keep your gun ready."

"What's your plan, Mr. Moore?"

"First, to find if our guess is correct."

He lifted the bronze plate. A breath of damp, moldy air floated up to the two young men. Peter's heart was beginning to thump. His senses became preternaturally alert. This was the danger line. Beyond lay trouble, danger, possible death.

A narrow stone staircase wound down into the bowels of the earth. At a depth of perhaps forty-five feet the stairs ended upon a long and narrow tunnel, damp and slippery underfoot, the walls, by matchlight, arched, rankly green with moss, flecked here and there with splotches of lichen.

At the end of the arched tunnel, at least two hundred feet from the staircase, was an iron door. Peter opened it cautiously. Beyond the door the tunnel forked. He deliberated a moment, took the left fork, advancing with all possible stealth. Behind him, gun in hand, face white and grim, tiptoed Terry Teeple.

Peter struck another match, held it high while it blazed into flame. The way ahead was clear, but he felt uneasy. Some indefinable change had been made in the arched tunnel since he had been a prisoner in this fantastic house.

The match flame expired. With renewed darkness came a sudden chill breath of air. He was conscious of the soft beat of it upon the side of his face and neck. And, before he could strike another light, powerful arms encircled his head. He was caught into a viselike grip. A knee jabbed him expertly in the solar plexus. In the same instant Terry Teeple's Colt automatic exploded twice in his ear. Then there was the thud of a falling body.

WITH THE WIND knocked out of him, Peter went to his knees. Strong hands grasped his shoulders. His hat went spilling off. He was jerked to his feet. A bag of harsh cloth was jammed down over his head. He heard Terry Teeple's cursing suddenly end on a gasp.

Hands were grasping Peter's elbows. He was being walked in a new direction. He knew that a door, cunningly concealed, had been built in the side of the tunnel since his previous visit. He was being urged, half-carried up a steep incline.

A lock rattled. A door opened, clanked shut behind them. Then came a short flight of stairs, a brief excursion over a floor that had the feel of polished marble. Another door opened, closed behind them.

The procession now halted. The captors on either side of him still gripped his elbows.

He was still short of breath, and his heart was beating in measured strokes of disgust.

His senses busied themselves. His skin felt a greater warmth, and through the coarse black cloth over his face he saw the gleam of lights and smelled the fragrance of Number One temple incense. Through this, like an insidious thread, crept the odor of the magical purple drug.

A girl's cold voice said, in English: "Remove the coverings."

The bag was snatched from Peter's head. He blinked in a sudden golden irradiation. The room itself, regally large, might have been carved from a block of purest gold. Walls and ceiling were gilded. Priceless golden Afghan rugs were strewn about the gilded floor. He had a quick impression of old Mongolian tapestries, of great gilded braziers sitting about, redly aglow with charcoal.

Then all of his awareness became concentrated on a richly carved iron-wood chair with a high back. It was like a throne.

A young woman, in the imperial red and blue brocade, with the dragon flowers of the old empire, was seated there. Her dark hair was done in fantastic swirls, oiled and doubtless scented, for it was in the old Chinese fashion. Her lashes were heavily beaded, her mouth was garishly painted. Her fingernails were lacquered a bright blue.

Her head was held imperiously. Her eyes, liquidly brilliant, stared down at him with hauteur. The pupils were dilated.

Peter Moore gasped, "Susan! Good Lord! What does this mean?"

5

CONDEMNED

THERE WAS A glassy little smile at the lips of the thrill hunter. And Peter, sickened, realized that she had found the ultimate thrill. Only one plan presented itself: To spirit her away from this place somehow, to deprive her of the devilish purple drug until she recovered her senses, her sanity.

Yet he was hopelessly outnumbered. His captors were powerful black men, naked except for sarongs, which fell straight from uniformly flat hips to naked heels. Mighty chests, shoulders and arms were discouraging.

He guessed they were Abyssinians. There were six of them, one at each of his elbows; one at each of Terry Teeple's elbows.

Terry Teeple was straining in the hands of his two black captors. He was panting through clenched teeth.

Susan was staring down at Peter with haughtiness. His heart was beating a dirge now. In that barbaric costume she was more beautiful than he had ever seen her. She was a little princess.

In a cold, regal little voice she said, "Why did you come here? I told you I never wanted to see you again. You are a fool!"

Terry Teeple burst out savagely: "Who the hell is this?"

"My fiancée," Peter said grimly.

"Where's Marcia?"

Susan was staring coldly at the wireless operator. Her eyes narrowed with displeasure. And suddenly Peter, watching her, wanted to shake her until her teeth chattered; wanted to spank her—this girl who was playing such a dangerous game of princess.

"Where is she?" Terry Teeple shouted.

"The little blond girl," Peter said.

The princess imperiously answered, "I do not know. I am not interested."

Peter uttered an outraged growl. Then a gilded door opened. A woman came in. And no possible question could exist as to the newcomer's identity.

She was tall, slender, queenly in a gown of royal purple. It was as if Peter had never seen Lotus Burma before. She was the most barbarically beautiful woman he had ever seen. Her features were as symmetrical as a porcelain Buddha's. Her eyes were large and lustrous. Her skin was like cream—not white, not yellow, but a soft and amazing shade in between. She had the slim perfection of a goddess. She was ageless. She might have been twenty or forty.

She moved with a sinuous grace that was fascinating. A slim, graceful arm moved in languid gesture as she placed a stiletto of an amethyst cigarette holder to her red lips, puffed and breathed out the smoke in an enchanted vapor.

There was something hypnotic about this woman—a dangerous, secret charm. In her was perfectly expressed the exotic lure of all Eastern lands. Peter could understand a little better how Susan might have been captivated, fascinated by this strange woman. In spite of his danger, the real possibility of his losing his precious life, and in spite of his heartbreak, he was stirred. For the beauty of Lotus Burma was of the kind that challenges the masculinity of any man.

Mysterious, beautiful, more dangerous than any hamadryad cobra, this woman known as The Octopus entered the golden room.

PETER, INSTANTLY ON guard, took in other details. Pearls. She was evidently a lover of the rarer breeds of pearls. She wore blood pearls at her ears—pearls as large as dimes, as red as blood. She wore a rope of blue pearls about her slim neck, and ropes of black pearls were wound about her wrists.

Lotus Burma only glanced at Terry Teeple. He might have been, according to the value of her gaze, an unimportant piece of furniture. Her large, dark, lustrous eyes returned to Peter Moore.

As she came nearer he became more amazed. Only in this woman's mouth was the legend of her cruelty confirmed. It was a beautiful mouth, a sensuous mouth, a mouth capable of infinite barbarity. And the lips were as vividly red as the lips of a mythological vampire.

Lotus Burma advanced to within a few feet of Peter Moore. Holding the long, thin amethyst holder to her amazing lips, she stared at him boldly, without reserve; at his eyes, his blond hair, his mouth, and so on deliberately to his slightly muddied shoes.

The astounding black veil of her lashes lifted. Her eyes glowed at him. She lowered the amethyst holder and looked into his eyes with a faint, mysterious smile.

In a sweet, husky contralto she said, drawling, "So this

is Peter Moore—Peter the Great—the Man of Bronze! I am Lotus Burma."

Peter only tightened his lips a little.

In that sweet, sensuous, remarkable voice, Lotus Burma went on. "I have heard of your exploits, your power over my people. We should have met long ago. Perhaps we should have combined forces." Her eyes narrowed. "You think not?"

A cat was toying with a mouse. Peter, the mouse, had nothing whatever to say to Lotus Burma.

"Who knows?" drawled the most dangerous woman in China. "We might have ruled the world. But I think not. We were born under warring stars. Oh, I knew that sometime we would meet—enemies!"

In spite of himself Peter was fascinated. Her languor, her very sensuousness made her as dangerous as a lazily awaking python.

"I know your life in China, your adventures," Lotus Burma went on in that seductive drawl, "in the smallest details. But what do you know of me?" Her voice had become fuller, stronger, with a promise of dynamic power. "What do you know of me?" she cried. "I, goddess of vengeance! I, instrument of Destiny!"

Her eyes had lost their soft lustre, were brilliant with waking fires. Her voice, losing none of its rich beauty, had lost its huskiness, become clear and hard. Here, in soft, alluring flesh, was a thing of steel or jade.

"You look on a woman who has been vilely wronged by your contemptible race!" she cried. "Scorned and insulted and wronged because of the yellow blood flowing in my white body! Humiliated! Treated like the dust beneath your feet! Ah! Who dares insult Lotus Burma today? No man! No woman! I am the mysterious, the ruthless! I am The Octopus! Those whom I hate, those who have wronged me, I crush!"

She was, Peter reflected, utterly insane. Beneath her amazing, beautiful eyes he saw the telltale marks of the opium addict. And from her very creamy flesh was breathed the scent, the familiar, malignant sweet spiciness of the purple drug. Yet these signs of weaknesses only enhanced the sense of her mysterious, ruthless strength.

SHE SEEMED SUDDENLY to soften. Her voice, issuing again from that cruel, lovely mouth was soft music.

"You do not know my story. I am the daughter of a princess. I do not speak of my white father. He was of the race that humiliated, wronged me. My mother was a princess of the old regime—an intimate of Her Imperial Highness Tsze Hsi—the last ruler of the greatest race ever to occupy the earth! And yet your race, your stupid race has scorned me, has called me half-caste—Eurasian!"

The rich, beautiful voice had risen again. It was like an instrument of the very devil, ingeniously calculated to sway the feelings of its hearers.

Terry Teeple, with jaw belligerently outthrust, was nevertheless staring at Lotus Burma with utter fascination.

"Your stupid, blind race," the voice went on, "refused to acknowledge that the blood of conquerors, of emperors, flowed in my veins. When I appealed to the white race for companionship I was insulted and scorned and humiliated. Did I not have the right to move in the highest circles of white or yellow? Yet was I received, was I accepted, was I treated according to the exaltation of my ancestry? No, no, no! I was a half-caste, a Eurasian!"

Lotus Burma puffed at the amethyst holder. The cigarette had come out. With pantherine grace she bent over one of the gilded braziers, thrust the end of the cigarette into the coals, inhaled deeply. Returning to Peter she blew a thin stream of hot, scented smoke into his face.

But this was not an insult. It was a gesture of mystery and despair. It was the period at the end of a sentence. She could not express herself further in words without bemeaning herself.

She continued in an altogether strange manner. The fire of resentment was gone from her eyes. A faint flush of pleasure stained her creamy cheeks.

"I have had my revenge on this one and that. I have dedicated my life to punishing those who had the effrontery to insult and humiliate me. Tonight, I am repeating a pleasure of which I never tire. I am striking the dagger of lifelong agony into the heart of Horatio Pool, who, on the night of July ninth, 1914, in Yokohama, Japan, insulted me, humiliated me—had me ejected by servants from his house!"

"Where is she?" Terry Teeple snarled.

Lotus Burma as if for the first time, seemed to become aware of the wireless operator's presence. She regarded him with an air faintly repugnant, faintly amused.

"Ah," she breathed. "You. You are her lover, are you not? Perhaps, if it pleases me, I shall let you see her die."

"You slimy rat!" Terry Teeple roared. The black men held him firmly. His complexion was almost blue with fury.

Delicately, contemptuously the woman known as The Octopus contemplated him.

"Yes," she purred. "I have decided I shall let you see how horribly the sons and daughters of the men and women who have affronted me can die. I shall let you carry back to Horatio Pool a vivid word picture of her agonies, her tortured screams—the sight of her bloody little carcass palpitating its last!"

Terry Teeple uttered an inarticulate snarl. He tried frantically to free himself; relapsed to ripe shipboard profanity, and fell to futile panting.

Lotus Burma had turned to Susan.

"You—Tsi Lo Lan—what is your opinion?"

Susan had been staring at Peter. A change had come over her. Her pupils had lost most of their dilation. She seemed sobered. The beginnings of terror were in her lovely violet eyes. Her small hands were clenching the arms of the great ironwood chair, as if she were preparing to spring out of it. **THE OCTOPUS SAID** sharply, "Tsi Lo Lan!" It was Chinese for "violet," a name by which Susan had come to be known in China because of the rare, beautiful coloring of her eyes.

Susan said feebly, "Peter! Peter! What am I doing—"

"Tsi Lo Lan!" Lotus Burma cried harshly. From the fold of her dress she had whipped a little phial. She took out the stopper. She stood threateningly over Susan. "Open your mouth!"

"Don't do it!" Peter shouted. "Don't take it!"

But Susan had, like a girl in a trance, opened her mouth. Peter, struggling against the powerful black hands, saw the purple drop fall on her small pink tongue. Lotus Burma was holding Susan's hands. Seconds passed. Watching Susan's eyes, Peter saw the pupils begin to dilate again.

It was horrible. On the very verge of normality, she had been snatched back, driven back into the vile mists of the purple drug.

Satisfied, Lotus Burma stepped back. Insidiously came her rich, beautiful contralto: "What is your opinion, Tsi Lo Lan?"

Susan straightened in the ironwood, thronelike chair.

"Let the two of them see the little blond girl's agonies?" The Octopus insinuated.

Susan made an imperious little gesture. The haughty smile was back.

"Kill them, too?" Lotus Burma purred.

"Banish them. Make slaves of them," Susan regally answered.

The Octopus sent a thin smile of contempt at Peter.

"How splendid that I have delivered this charming, beautiful young woman from your clutches!" she said.

"I want them out of my sight," Susan cried.

"But to witness the delicious murder of the sweet little blond one?" Lotus Burma suggested.

"No. I don't want to see either of them again—ever."

"Very well."

The Octopus made a gesture of dismissal with the amethyst cigarette holder. In Chinese she said to the black men, "Lock these swine in a strong room. Guard them well."

Peter sent a final glance at Susan. She was still regarding him with that air of princely scorn. The black men pushed Peter and Terry Teeple out of the room. Peter recognized the great black marble hall into which they were inducted, and the Alley of Jade down which they were taken. This was one of Lak Chak's many incredible extravagances—a long corridor panelled from floor to ceiling with slabs of green jade.

Fine Ming tapestries partly covered the walls. Below the tapestries were Chinese war chests of red and blue lacquer—each one a museum piece.

Conducted briskly down the Alley of Jade, Peter's mind was working as briskly. Somehow, he and Terry Teeple must contrive not to be locked in a room.

Under his breath, very softly, very tunelessly, Peter began to whistle. Terry Teeple stopped his cursing and gave Peter his closest attention. When Peter had whistled a tuneless measure, Terry Teeple began whistling, too, softly, without melody.

What Peter had said, in a short whistle for a dot, a longer stream of tunelessness for a dash, was, in terms of the International radio code: "Get ready for action. I will make them release us in a moment. Fight hard."

And what Terry Teeple had whistled tunelessly in answer was, "O.K. All set. Make it soon."

To the black man on his left Peter said loudly, in gutter Chinese: "What price a bottle of the Divine Drug?"

The black man on his right answered in pidgin: "Pay my look see!"

"Can do," Peter said. "But how can do with arms alla-time tight?"

His arms were released, but Terry Teeple's were not. However, the six black men managed to crowd close about Peter.

He removed the white jade phial from his pocket. He

held it up, gripping it firmly. Next instant, six pairs of black hands were snatching, clawing for that precious phial.

Peter doubled the phial into his fist and struck mightily at a black jaw. He heard a skull behind him crack against a jade panel, the war-growl of Terry Teeple as his two hamlike fists sought more jaws. Peter occupied himself with a yelling black man, knocked him senseless and assaulted another.

In perhaps forty seconds the two belligerent young Americans had vanquished six surprised black enemies.

Peter yanked at a tapestry, but only the white silk lining came away. He made strips of it.

He panted, "Work fast. Bind hands and feet and gag each one." He knew that the great war chests were empty.

The two young men tied the hands and feet of the six blacks, gagged them, lifted them one by one into six chests.

There was a sudden shout at the far end of the Alley of Jade. Peter and Terry Teeple slid behind one of the fabulous Ming tapestries.

The jade panel behind them gave way with sickening suddenness. Magically it swung wide, a gleaming green hinge. And both young men fell backward into a room dimly lighted by a single lamp suspended by fine brass chains from a dark ceiling.

A voice sadly intoned: "Ah! Though a man never trips over a mountain, he may trip over a clod!"

6

THE PIT

A WIZENED OLD Chinese in the black of lounging was kneeling on cushions at one end of the small dark room. Before him on a little teakwood taboret were a tray, a spirit lamp and implements with which years in China had made Peter Moore familiar.

Chay Quon did not seem surprised or at all agitated by Peter's and Terry Teeple's startling entrance. Peter removed the phial of purple drug from the pocket to which he had restored it at the conclusion of the shambles; held it into the feeble rays from the lamp, and said, "Chay Quon, I am indebted to you for still another chance at trouble."

The old Chinese who had accosted him in the fog and later come to his hotel room with a dire warning, nodded his gray head with indifference.

"The friendships of the day," he said sadly, "are those of self-interest alone. Yet I am indebted to you."

Calmly, he proceeded with his ritual. He selected a pipe from the collection on the taboret—a satinwood pipe with a brown tortoise-shell tip. He plied needle, blew on flame, kneaded amber-colored chandoo cube and inhaled the biting smoke deeply. The opium sizzled, melted, evaporated in dense fumes.

Chay Quon laid the pipe aside, brushed his hands with the gesture of a man satisfied, and took on generally the air of a man refreshed and stimulated. Having finished what is, to a Chinese, the equivalent of a cup of bracing tea, he was now prepared to discuss matters.

"A man burning with passion," he stated serenely, "follows the undulations of a thought. Master, I am indebted to you for my life. But I must warn you that I am this woman's slave. If I am detected in the act of betraying her trust, not only I but my sons, my little grandsons will rot in the death tower of Macao. As a man of great honor, I shall do your bidding. Perhaps a man can ride two tigers, despite the warnings of the Wisest One of all."

Terry Teeple interrupted impatiently: "What's he saying? Is he a friend?"

"Yes. He'll help."

"Ask him where Marcia is."

Peter put the question to Chay Quon, who answered: "The little blond one is locked in a room. She is to die tonight. She is the nineteenth."

"We have come to take her away," Peter said.

"Master, it is impossible."

"To a man of merit and honor," Peter said swiftly, "the word impossible is nothing but a challenge. What is your purpose in this shameful place?"

"I am in charge of the ceremony—the death ceremony. It is to begin in twenty minutes."

"Then there is no time to lose," Peter said briskly.

Chay Quon shook his head. "At risk of my own life, I will escort you and your friend to safety."

"No, Chay Quon. We have come for the little blond girl."

The eyes of the old man narrowed again.

He made a hissing sound through his teeth.

"There is little hope, but I am a man of honor, I am indebted to you for my life. I will think." He meditated a moment, staring intently at Terry Teeple, then at Peter.

"The little blond one is to be given to the octopus in twenty minutes," he said.

"Then there is truth in that fable?"

"Yes, master. She lets her victims be crushed and sucked to death by a giant octopus. I can think of no way to save this girl, master. She is doomed."

Terry Teeple impatiently broke in: "What's he say?"

"He says," Peter answered, "it's a pretty tough assign-ment."

"Is there any hope?"

"Sure, there's hope."

CHAY QUON HAD risen, was pacing to and fro, his eyes dark, his brows knit.

He said finally, "Master, there is but one way. You will wear my ceremonial costume. I will give you a Malay dagger and a revolver. I will give your friend a revolver. The young man may wish to use it on himself before this night is done."

Chay Quon had produced from a rosewood cabinet the three weapons, two revolvers and a long, curved dagger.

"What does he say?" Terry Teeple asked.

"We may be able to shoot our way out of here with these guns."

"What's the dagger for?"

"Emergency."

"Come with me," Chay Quon said. "There is little time."

The old Chinese touched the surface of the near-by wall. A square aperture appeared in the floor at Peter's feet. Below this opening, stairs of stone led down into darkness.

Chay Quon started down the stairs. Peter and Terry Teeple followed. Peter was familiar with this secret stairway. It led directly into Lak Chak's famous banquet hall.

But the door at the end of the stairs opened upon a surprise. The great room, once paneled in varicolored nara-wood, had been converted into a hideous enormity of purple. More than two hundred feet in length, by a hundred in width, the one-time scene of gargantuan revels had been done over according to Lotus Burma's strange preferences.

She was evidently infatuated with that color of the old royalty. It was as if her very soul had been tainted with the purple of the malignant drug.

The color, laid on boldly, seemed to writhe and squirm in the blood of brilliant electric illumination. Peter gazed about him with startled amazement. Here, he had been privileged to gaze on that astounding scene—the Number One thieves of China gathered together, stuffing their bellies with bird nest soup, pickled rotten eggs, broiled rats, toasted octopus tips; swilling these delicacies down with rice wine and whisky and arrack.

But the massive furniture had been removed. The great purple hall was bare save for a half dozen huge jars of the Kiang S'u period—great porcelain containers in which the bodies of emperors had once been preserved in honey and mercury. Some of these were eight feet in height.

A dais had been erected against one wall. On this, in a row, stood six heavily carved teakwood chairs.

Peter's eyes wandered quickly to another object of greater interest. This was a length of slender ladder made of some translucent pink stuff, which hung from the ceiling by bronze chains. The upper end of the ladder vanished into a round hole in the ceiling. The purpose of the chains was apparently to lower the ladder from this hole.

The lower end of the ladder came within about thirty feet of the purple-lacquered floor. And just below it, suddenly, Peter saw the white lip of the tank.

He walked quickly over. The tank was set in the floor, like a kind of cistern, and it gave off a pearly glow. Going close, he looked down shining white walls of a substance which appeared to be alabaster, and into crystal clear water. Fastened to one side of this round alabaster cistern, or tank, was another ladder of rose quartz. The top of the ladder came to within about six feet of the top of the alabaster cylinder.

And in the clear water at the bottom of the tank was sprawled a shapeless black mass.

Peter, staring with horrified fascination, could not repress a shudder. He could see the little ice-green eyes of the octopus, the tangled mass of its arms, the beak with which it disemboweled its victims.

TERRY TEEPLE, STANDING beside him, suddenly seized his arm.

"Good Lord, man! Is—is that how Marcia is supposed to die?"

Chay Quon was rapidly explaining to Pater, who translated.

"The victim is sent down that ladder from the hole in the ceiling. The ladder is lowered until it connects with the ladder fastened to the wall of the tank. The victim climbs down into the tank. When she is on the lower ladder, the upper one is raised. She cannot possibly escape. Then the water is slowly, very slowly raised in the tank until—"

Peter stopped. Terry Teeple was cursing. Peter explained the rest of it. Then:

"Chay Quon says the victim is given a so-called chance. Immediately below the ladder, do you see the square of alabaster fitted in? It's a door. A push opens it. If the victim can dive under water, escape the octopus and open that door—she is free. A tunnel leads to safety outside. But no victim has lived to reach that opening. This octopus, Chay Quon says, has never tasted anything but human flesh since Lotus Burma secured it. If we can't prevent it, your fiancée will be the nineteenth human being who has been fed to that horrible monster."

"It is nearly time, master," Chay Quon finished.

Peter said: "Frankly, I can't see much hope, fellow. But we'll do our best. I will wear Chay Quon's costume and take charge of the ceremony. From now until the time is ripe to strike, you will hide yourself in one of these jars. Don't be impetuous. Control yourself. A false move means you'll lose Marcia—and we'll lose our heads! We're hoping that Lotus Burma will forget our existence—believe we're safely locked up—until after this matter is attended to. Climb into that jar. At the right moment I'll shoot the guards, you'll jump out of the jar, we'll grab Marcia—and make our getaway through that window. Be ready to shoot, be ready to fight—but don't lose your head."

"How many guards will there be?"

"Chay Quon says only three."

Terry Teeple grimly climbed into the great vase, and Peter and Chay Quon returned to the latter's quarters, where the ritual of the death-by-octopus was explained to Peter while he donned the strange, fantastic garment devised by Lotus Burma for the occasion.

It consisted of a purple satin robe with a sash of gold brocade. The headdress was a miniature octopus, carved beautifully of black onyx. Fortunately, it came down over the face, as a mask, with slits for eyes and mouth. And even more fortunately, Peter Moore and Chay Quon were sufficiently of a size so that both robe and headdress fitted well or well enough.

"Now, master," Chay Quon said, "there is time only to bind and gag and mutilate me. Do not hesitate. The knife is sharp. Do not forget: Lotus Burma is diabolically shrewd. If I am found here, only bound and gagged, how can you have come into the possession of the ceremony? I must have the appearance of torture. I am a man of honor and great merit. I have no fear. Proceed, master!"

Peter swiftly bound Chay Quon's hands and feet, gagged him, and then picked up the knife. He shuddered at the prospect of deliberately inflicting hurt and injury, yet, as Chay Quon had said, there was no alternative.

Chay Quon closed his eyes. Peter made a series of shallow cuts in the old man's muscular forearm, others, as Chay Quon had directed, on the calves of his legs. None of these slashes was deep enough to cause serious bleeding, but they gave Chay Quon a gory appearance.

IN THE DISTANCE a bell clanged softly. It was, Peter knew, a command for his appearance as master of the death-by-octopus ceremonies in the hideous purple hall.

He threw a light cloak of yellow silk over Chay Quon, as a safeguard against his premature discovery by guards or Lotus Burma, and descended the narrow stairway into the purple chamber of horrors.

Peter's heart seemed to have climbed; was banging furiously somewhere in the region of his ears. His mouth was dry. He was shaking with apprehension, with expectancy. He went into the purple hall knowing that a single wrong gesture would result not only in the ordained death of Marcia Pool, but in his and Terry Teeple's.

He steadied himself; told himself to stop this damned shaking—and boldly walked into the hall. He was thankful for the mask, thankful that the ceremony called for no speeches on his part. Throughout, it was to be conducted in silence.

He advanced slowly, with measured strides, to the edge of the alabaster pool. There, with arms folded on chest, he sharply executed an about-face. This brought him face to face with the occupants of the dais.

Only three of the chairs were occupied. In the center sat Lotus Burma. On her right sat Susan. On her left sat a fat, middle-aged Chinese with black wisps of mustache, worn in the mandarin style.

A door on the side opened. Black men filed in. Peter, counting them, felt his heart give a sickening thump, a chill dance along his backbone.

Five—six—seven!

Chay Quon had said there would be only three! One at the valve which caused the water in the alabaster cylinder to rise, and two at the tank with the master of ceremonies, to seize the victim in case she attempted to leap from the ladder to the floor in an attempt to escape her exquisitely horrible fate.

Eight—nine—ten!

Ten black giants! With the sickness of despair, Peter wondered if Chay Quon had betrayed him, if Lotus Burma were suspicious—if she had discovered that he and Terry Teeple had escaped their guards and were dangerously at large in this black palace!

He watched her face. It showed no suspicion. It was tranquil. She was gazing expectantly at the aperture in the ceiling from which hung the rose-quartz ladder.

Her eyes darted here and there. She was wearing her secret smile—a smile of anticipation. A greedy, pleased little smile. You might almost see her lick her lips with relish.

Peter waited, watching her. The black men filed about the room. One took his place at the valve. The remaining nine formed a semicircle on the side of the tank farthest from the dais, in order not to obstruct Lotus Burma's view.

THE PREPARATIONS WERE complete. Lotus Burma raised her right hand to a level with her slim, beautiful, creamy shoulders. Peter unfolded his arms, commanded them not to tremble, and made a sweeping salaam. He wondered again if this whole ceremony, in its hideous entirety, were not based on some old and secret ceremony practiced by the Chinese emperors—a secret of Lotus Burma's royal mother.

He made a curt gesture to one of the black men, who promptly knelt and pursed his lips and blew upon a potbellied brass incense pot which stood beside the tank like a metallic pig. A cloud of dense blue smoke rose into the air. It was, of course, the finest of sacrificial incense.

Then Peter made a circuit of the tank, lifting his feet slowly, bobbing his head each time a foot went down. This was presumably for the purpose of driving certain unfavorable devils from the scene, to give the octopus every fair chance at enjoying his human meal.

Completing a circuit of the tank, he stretched his arms high over his head, a gesture made difficult and hazardous by the eight glassy black arms of the octopus headpiece which projected in as many directions.

This was a signal to eyes at peepholes in the ceiling that the victim was to be sent down the ladder, Peter sent a glance at Susan. In spite of drugs, he could not believe that she could stomach this proceeding. She was gazing with fascination at the hole in the ceiling.

A girl's whimpering voice came floating down; a protest. There were sharp interjections in Chinese, then a little wail came down, "But why?"

Peter steeled himself; hoped that Terry Teeple was doing the same, would not lose his control and run amuck.

A small pink foot appeared at the ceiling aperture, then another. Then the small blond girl started down the ladder. She came slowly but with apparent certainty. Not until she was a dozen feet down from the ceiling did she look down.

She seemed to look square into Peter's face—that black glossy mask. Her blue eyes were large with horror. Her golden hair was disheveled. Her face was white, her lips gray.

Peter's heart was thudding. Marcia Pool was going to her death as a slave girl of the old summer place in Peking.

She wore white silk crepe pajamas—the tight jacket and skimpy trousers of all Chinese girls. She was so small, so innocent, so childlike that Peter ground his teeth to control himself.

For a long moment she stared down at him, down into the tank. For the first time, she realized what her fate must be. Suddenly she screamed—a shrill, heartbreaking sound. And Peter, with sickly thumping heart, hoped she would not fall. The victim who fell went to a swifter doom—plunging into the very center of the tank, within easy reach of those eight horrible arms.

But Marcia Pool did not faint. For a moment she stared, then she started down the ladder. Looking up, Peter saw why she did not try to go back up. The ladder had been slowly lowered until the top of it was now about five feet from the ceiling. And the round aperture was closed.

She came down a few steps, hesitated, stopped.

Clinging midway down the ladder, she clutched at the rungs, stared down and trembled. She did not cry out again. Slowly, the ladder came down until the lower end was level with the floor. It continued to go down until the lower end touched the top of the ladder that was fastened to the wall of the tank.

MARCIA POOL DID not attempt to leap off the ladder to the floor, to escape her hideous fate. Black guards had been stationed there to prevent that. If she had leaped, they would have caught her—thrown her into the tank without ceremony.

But the small blond girl did not attempt to escape. And Peter could guess why. She was paralyzed with terror. Her little hands were fairly frozen to the rose-quartz rungs. The sight of that deep-sea monster in the tank, the knowledge that she was to be its victim, had stupefied Marcia Pool.

Watching her, Peter tried to keep his thoughts in order. The attempt to rescue her must be made soon. He darted a glance at Lotus Burma. The smile at her vampire lips had brightened. Her eyes were avid with expectancy. Clearly, Peter could see into her twisted mind—could see there the gloating hideous soul of this woman, could glimpse her insane joy in seeing this innocent, delicate girl clasped and devoured by the hungry sea monster.

He glanced sharply at Susan. She seemed to be coming awake again. Her lovely mouth hung ajar, her eyes were round and large and dark with a quickening terror.

A Negro with a long black whip in his hand had stepped forward. Peter made the gesture for the blond girl to climb down. She must go part way down before he could act. In another moment bullets would begin to fly, and she would be directly in their path.

The blond girl looked at him piteously, too dazed to understand, too frightened to move. Yet she must climb down onto the lower ladder.

The black man with the whip advanced. She saw him and recoiled. She was shaking so violently that Peter wondered how she had strength enough to climb to the rungs.

The Abyssinian lifted the whip. He flicked it at her. The tip struck the flimsy silk stuff at her shoulder. The girl uttered a little cry. The black man pointed down. She looked down. Her breast was rising and falling with little gasps.

The black man lifted the whip again. Peter heard a low, soft burst of laughter. He looked toward the dais. Lotus

Burma was laughing. And for the first time in his life, Peter wanted to shoot a woman.

Marcia Pool was going down the ladder. She reached the lower one. Her great blue eyes stared at the monstrous mass at the bottom of the tank. She clunk to the lower ladder, her slim body, so slightly clad, silhouetted against the glowing alabaster.

The upper ladder went up.

Peter backed away from the tank, reached inside the purple robe and grasped the handle of the revolver Chay Quon had given him.

Before he could fire the shot which would apprise Terry Teeple that the time to act had finally come, Susan uttered a shriek.

She screamed, "No! No! This can't go on! Stop it! Get that girl out of there!"

And out of the tail of his eye, as he flashed out the revolver, Peter saw the black man give the valve a twist, and he heard the sudden gushing of water into the alabaster cylinder.

Near by occurred a sharp, ponderous crash. One of the massive Kiang S'u vases had toppled over. The priceless blue neck of it cracked. Out of it crawled Terry Teeple, snarling robust curses, shooting as he came.

7

HYPNOTISM?

PETER THREW OFF the grotesque black headgear and stepped backwards out of the purple robe.

He heard Susan shriek, "Peter!" as he fired at the first black man who started toward him. This one collapsed and slid face down along the purple-lacquered floor and Peter pulled the trigger a second time, aiming squarely between the eyes of the man at the great bronze valve.

Long knives had appeared as if by magic from the black men's *sarongs*. One of these knives whistled past Peter's ear. He shot down the man who had thrown it.

Terry Teeple had shouted, "Hang on, Marcia! We'll get you out!" His revolver had disappeared. He had evidently gone too primitive for firearms. Peter saw him seize two ebony necks; saw him send two gleaming black skulls cracking together; saw him pick up, in the following split second, a third Abyssinian and, lifting him over his head, kicking and shouting, hurl him down into the tank.

Peter saw, to his horror, that the water had risen; that the blond girl had climbed as far up the ladder as she could, and that one of the eight black arms had reached up to coil about one slim pink ankle.

The octopus had so far ignored the black man, who

kicked and blubbered, who could not swim, who threshed the crystal clear water into foam.

The enemy had been reduced to two. Terry Teeple was taking them both single-handed, unarmed, dodging their knives, trying to reach them with his tremendous fists.

Peter, running to his assistance, stopped at the bronze valve, to twist it in the opposite direction.

A woman was screaming. It was Susan.

One of the two remaining black men slipped. Terry Teeple sent a fist crashing into his face. The remaining enemy sprang at him with knife uplifted—and Peter shot him accurately in the forehead!

Terry Teeple picked up the man he had just floored and threw him into the alabaster tank as Peter started toward the dais. In another moment, he was certain, this great hall would swarm with reinforcements. This was his last chance to get Susan away. It was his only chance to seize Lotus Burma—to deliver her to Dan de Sylva.

Lotus Burma, the fat Chinese and Susan were standing at their chairs, in petrified attitudes, when Peter started toward them. The plump Chinese decided on instant departure. He vanished through the arched doorway behind the dais.

Lotus Burma also vanished, but more swiftly, and with all possible mystery. She dropped through the floor. When Peter reached the dais she was gone—had vanished, leaving behind no clue as to the manner of her escape. An ingenious trap-door had, of course, accomplished it.

He had lost his chance to help Dan de Sylva. He said grimly, "Come on, Susan," and seized her hand.

She wailed, "I can't go—not yet!"

He bent down, swept an arm about her knees, swung her to his shoulder and strode toward the alabaster tank.

WHEN PETER REACHED the tank, an octopus and five black men were actively engaged in the water. Five black snakelike arms were busy, each with the largest morsel of food the monster had perhaps ever contemplated. But the sixth arm still clung, with its sucking disks, to the slim, pink ankle of the intended victim.

Terry Teeple, on his knees, was shouting advice and encouragement. "Hang on, honey! It won't be long now!"

And the little blond girl cried, "I can't! I'm fainting!"

Peter picked up the other gun from the floor where Terry Teeple had dropped it. He saw there were three unexploded shells in the cylinder. He fired them in the octopus's head, aiming at the eyes. This had the effect only of aggravating its threshings. Such monsters die hard.

Peter said, "We've got to go out that way. No other is safe." He had taken the long, curved dagger from his belt. "Don't let Miss O'Gilvie get away."

"What are you going to do?"

"Going down there. The water's below that door now. That's how we get out of here—with luck!" He picked up the golden sash of the ceremonial costume he had worn. Terry Teeple held fast to one end while Peter slipped down to the ladder. He said to the blond girl, "Hang on a little longer. We'll all be out in a minute."

She whimpered, "I—I could die! Can you get this horrible thing loose?"

Peter slid down past her. He bent down, slashed at the tentacle. It held fast. He could hear, above the splashings and shouts below him, the sucking sound of the black disks against the girl's ankle.

He hacked at the black arm, finally hacked it almost through before it uncoiled and fell writhing into the water.

There were two bullets left in his own revolver. At closer range he aimed again at the icy-green eyes of the monster, fired with deliberation, saw both eyes, in turn, vanish.

Blind, if not dying, the octopus was no longer so dangerous.

Peter called: "Send down Miss O'Gilvie. Don't let her get away from you!"

He heard Susan's shriek of fury. He reached down and pushed at the oblong of alabaster. As Chay Quon had promised, the alabaster block swung away from his touch. He bent down and looked into a tunnel of gray stone, round, no greater in diameter than four feet.

Peter said, "Okay, Miss Pool. This way!" He gave her his hand, helped her down the ladder, through the oblong opening, and into the tunnel. Susan, angrily protesting, came down the ladder and followed the blond girl. Then Terry Teeple let himself drop. His feet struck the upper rung of the ladder, fractured it, found safety on the second. And Peter, reaching out, prevented him from swaying and falling into the water.

The two young men followed the girls into the tunnel. On hands and knees they followed it until it opened into another, larger corridor, which they followed, always in the same direction, for perhaps an eighth of a mile.

Peter did not recognize this exit as one of Lak Chak's until it ended in a clump of bushes.

They were on a knoll. Below them, at the foot of the

Peak, the lights of Hong Kong sparkled with the brightness of diamonds. The fog had gone.

Peter said uneasily, "We'd better keep moving. We may have outwitted her, but she's still the most dangerous woman in China."

Yet he could not have guessed, as he said it, in just what shocking way his semi-prediction was to be fulfilled.

MARCIA POOL WAS giving way normally to hysterics. Laughing and crying, she was reliving an experience that would no doubt haunt her as long as she lived. Terry Teeple, with an arm about her, was trying to comfort her. They started down the trail.

Peter, firmly holding Susan by the elbow, waited for her to speak. She had, so far, said nothing.

Now, she said, "Darling, you'll never forgive me. You'll never understand."

But she made no gesture, no move, to go into his arms.

He said quietly, "Are we sailing tomorrow?"

"Of course!"

"Do you still feel you want to marry me?"

"Of course, darling!"

Peter said nothing. New doubts were rising. He was certain that Susan was no longer under the influence of that baleful purple drug. Its effects were apparently short-lived, despite their drastic power while they lasted. Yet something was wrong. He held her arm firmly.

She said impulsively, "I'll always love you. There never will be any one else. But—"

His heart was beating a dirge again.

"If I could only make you understand!" Susan cried.

"That you don't actually mean what you've been saying,"

Peter said. "That you don't love me, that you don't want to marry me."

She panted: "I can't! I can't marry you. I can't leave China!"

"That woman has you hypnotized."

"Ah, darling, you don't understand."

"I know she's had you doped with that damned drug for days!"

"It isn't that!"

"Then, good Lord, Susan, tell me what it is!"

He could feel the soft sobs shaking her.

She whispered, "If—if I only knew!"

Peter knew that she wanted to put her face into her hands. He reasoned that hysterics would clear the air. But she didn't have hysterics. She cried only a moment, and she quickly freed herself of his arms.

"We'd better go back to the hotel," she said.

They took sedan chairs down the hill; rickshaws from the base of the hill to the Colony.

The night clerk said, "Miss O'Gilvie, all of your baggage came a moment ago. We sent it up to your old room."

Susan thanked him. She and Peter entered the elevator and went up to her suite.

At the door, she said, "I don't want you to come in. I want to be alone—I want to think."

"We're going to be married in the morning," he said grimly. "We're sailing for America at noon."

"You'd better come in," Susan said.

They went in and she closed the door. Peter thought she had relented. He took her hungrily into his arms, but when he tried to kiss her, she averted her head and pushed him away.

"I can't make you understand," she said wearily.

"Then we'll talk it over until one or the other of us does understand." He pulled her down beside him on a settee. He picked up one of her hands and held it. "You know China as well as I do," he said. "You know there are people here like Lotus Burma—dangerous people. We've always managed to avoid these traps. Let's try to reason this out."

"You can't reason a thing like this out," Susan said. She pulled her hand away and jumped up.

"You saw her try to kill that poor girl by means of that octopus."

"It's like a nightmare," Susan said. "Oh, how horrible!"

"Then why do you want to go back to her?"

"Do I want to go back to her?" Susan cried. "Did I say I wanted to go back to her? I have no intentions of going back to her!"

"Are you contradicting yourself? Do you want to marry me—go back to the States?"

"No!" Susan cried. "Never!"

Peter got up and went to the door. She was staring at him almost pityingly.

As he went out, she wailed, "You don't understand, Peter!"

Peter said nothing more. He had recalled seeing on the streets of Hong Kong a liberty party of sailors from an American battleship in port.

A LITTLE MORE than an hour later, Peter Moore, Terry Teeple and a small mob of American sailors, thirsting for a fight, went up the Peak, surrounded that black vulture of a house, battered down the doors and rushed inside.

Emptiness met them. Lotus Burma had evidently decided on immediate flight. The great, bizarre structure was empty. Even the furniture and furnishings were gone!

Peter returned to the hotel. It was now a little after four o'clock. He proceeded directly to Room 819. He banged on the door.

It was promptly opened by a man with a gun in his hand. The Satanic de Sylva stared at him a moment, then smiled his V-shaped smile. He lowered the revolver, opened the door, and drawled: "You didn't bring her back alive."

"No."

"I have just learned, from one of my most trusted observers," Satan said, "that The Octopus and her entourage are aboard a small steamship that is sailing at dawn for Java. That's less than an hour away."

Peter said nothing.

"This agent of mine who was rolled for two million dollars' worth of diamonds," de Sylva said, "was murdered in a peculiarly cruel way. He was hung up by his toes and stabbed to death by infinitesimal degrees with a sharp hairpin. In case this job still appeals to you, it seemed only fair to warn you—"

"I'm taking the job," Peter said.

www.ingramcontent.com/pod-product-compliance
Lightning Source LLC
Chambersburg PA
CBHW031152020726
47499CB00002B/341